I0825929

Published in the USA by Savant Books and Publications LLC
2630 Kapiolani Blvd #1601
Honolulu, HI 96826 USA
http://www.savantbooksandpublications.com

Printed in the USA

Cover design by Daishi and Mari
Cover photos by Daisuke Idehara
http://homepage3.nifty.com/iddi/

Edited by Daniel S. Janik

ISBN-10: 0-9841175-3-9
ISBN-13 (EAN13): 978-0-9841175-3-6

All names, characters, places and incidents are fictitious or used fictitiously. Any resemblance to actual persons, living or dead, and any places or events is purely coincidental.

The Interzone

A Man of the Dark Grey

Tatsuyuki Kobayashi

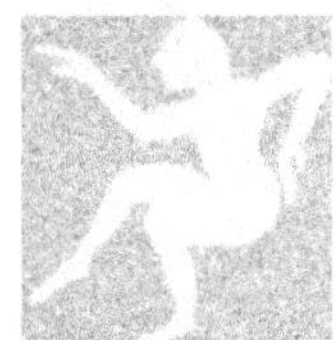

Savant Books
Honolulu, HI 96826

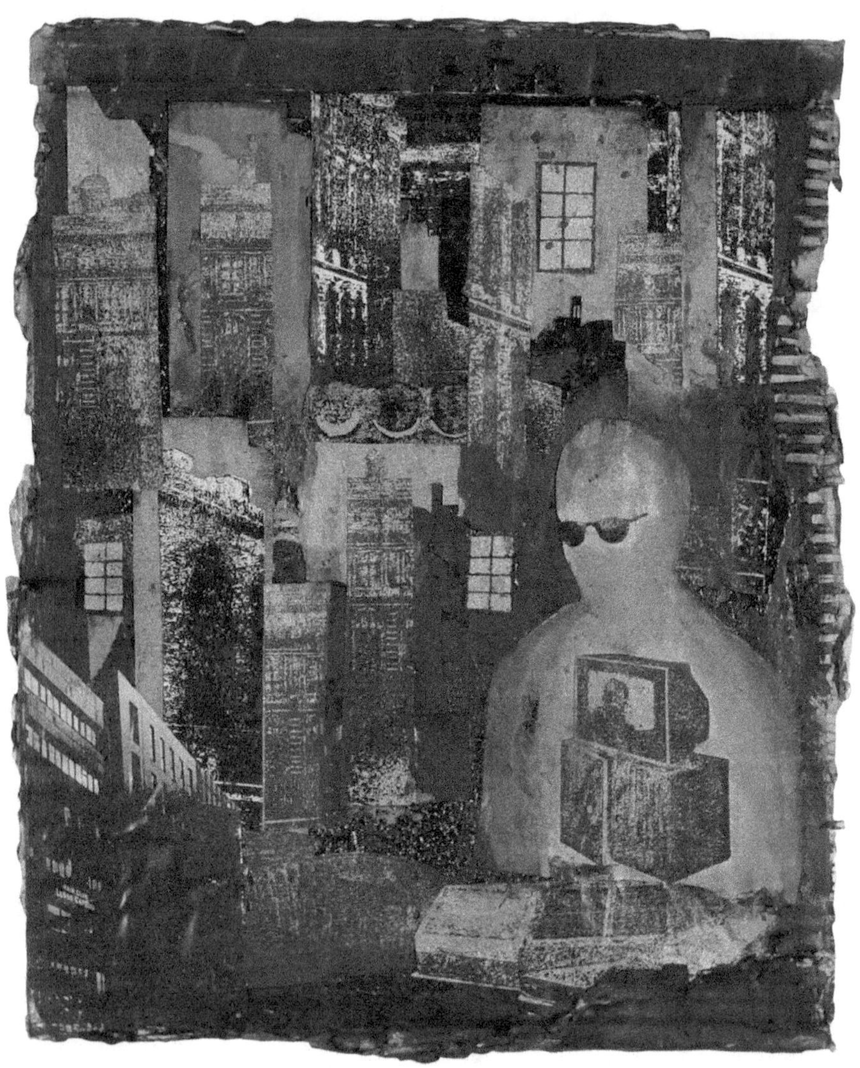

1. City Life

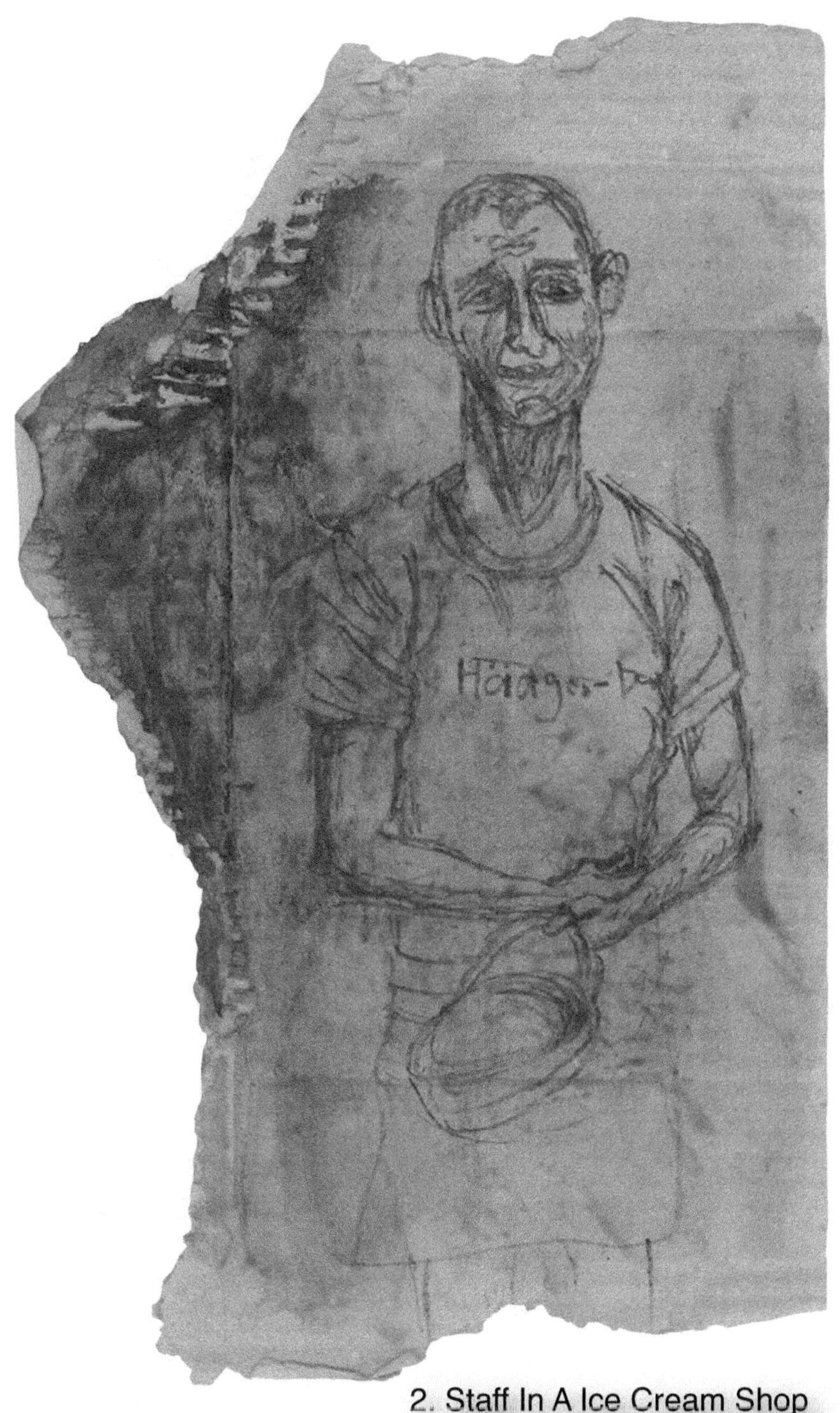

2. Staff In A Ice Cream Shop

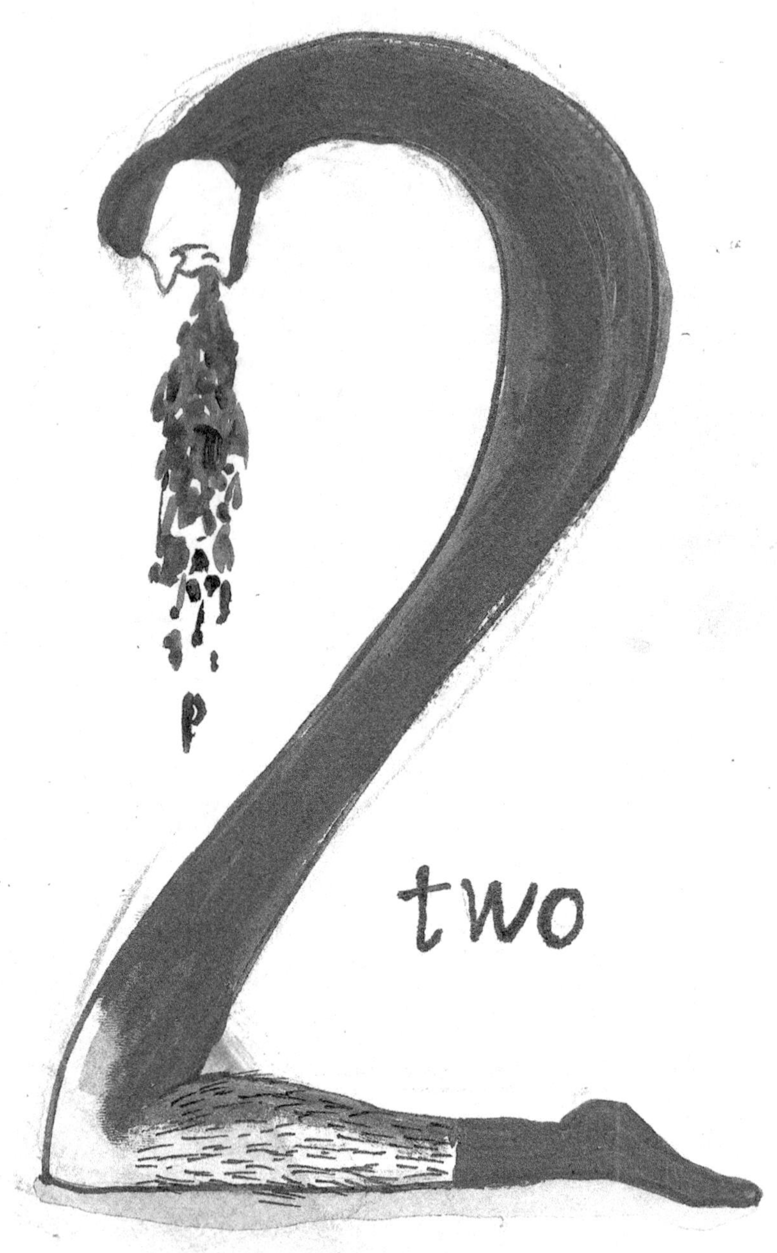

3. Two

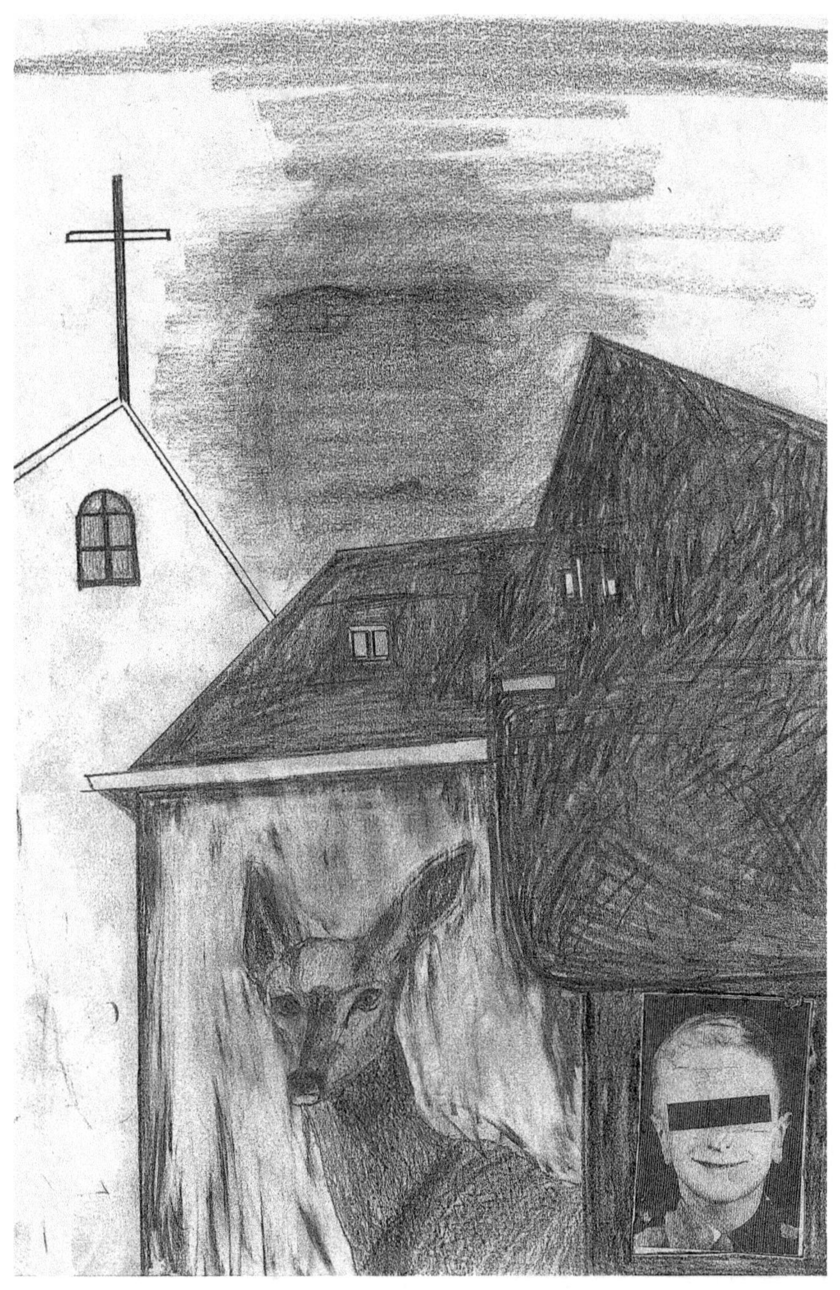

4. Not Church

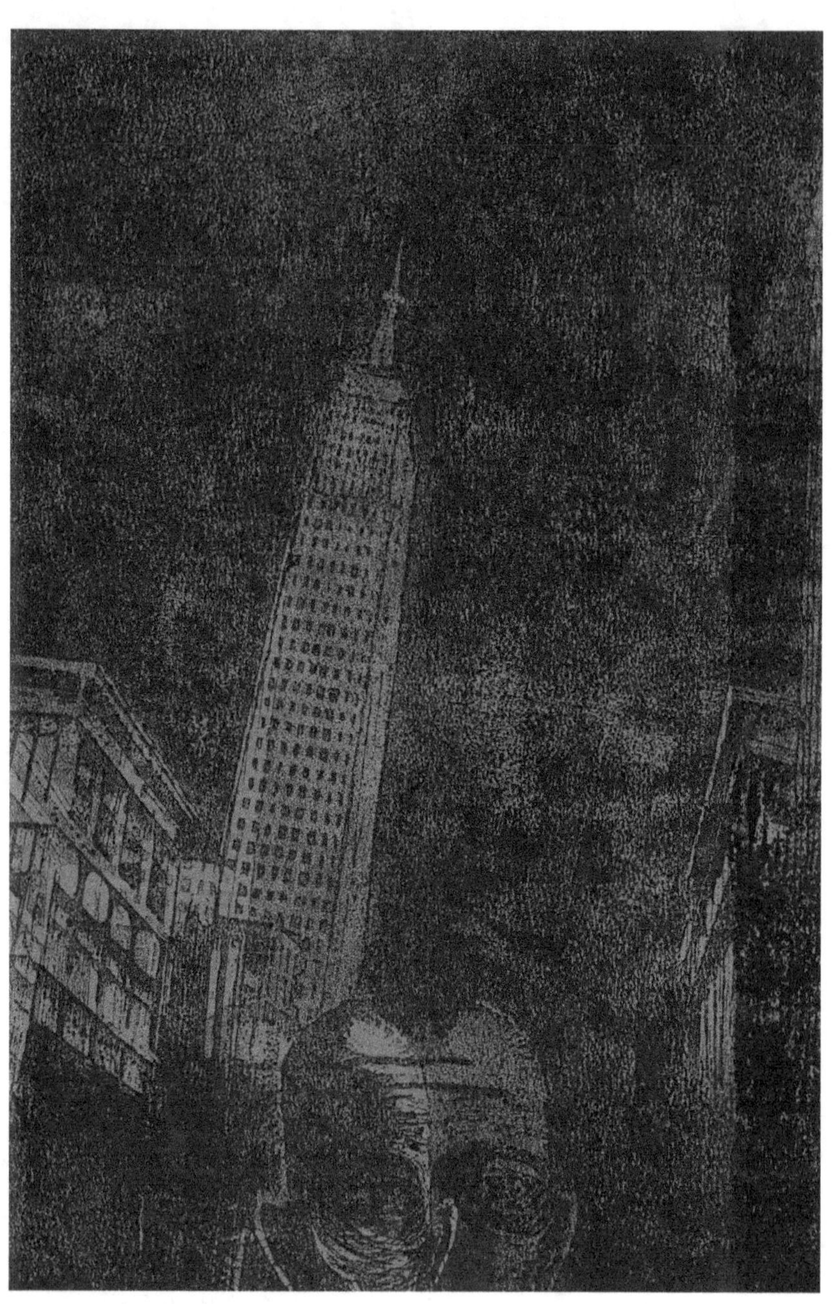

5. Astigmatism

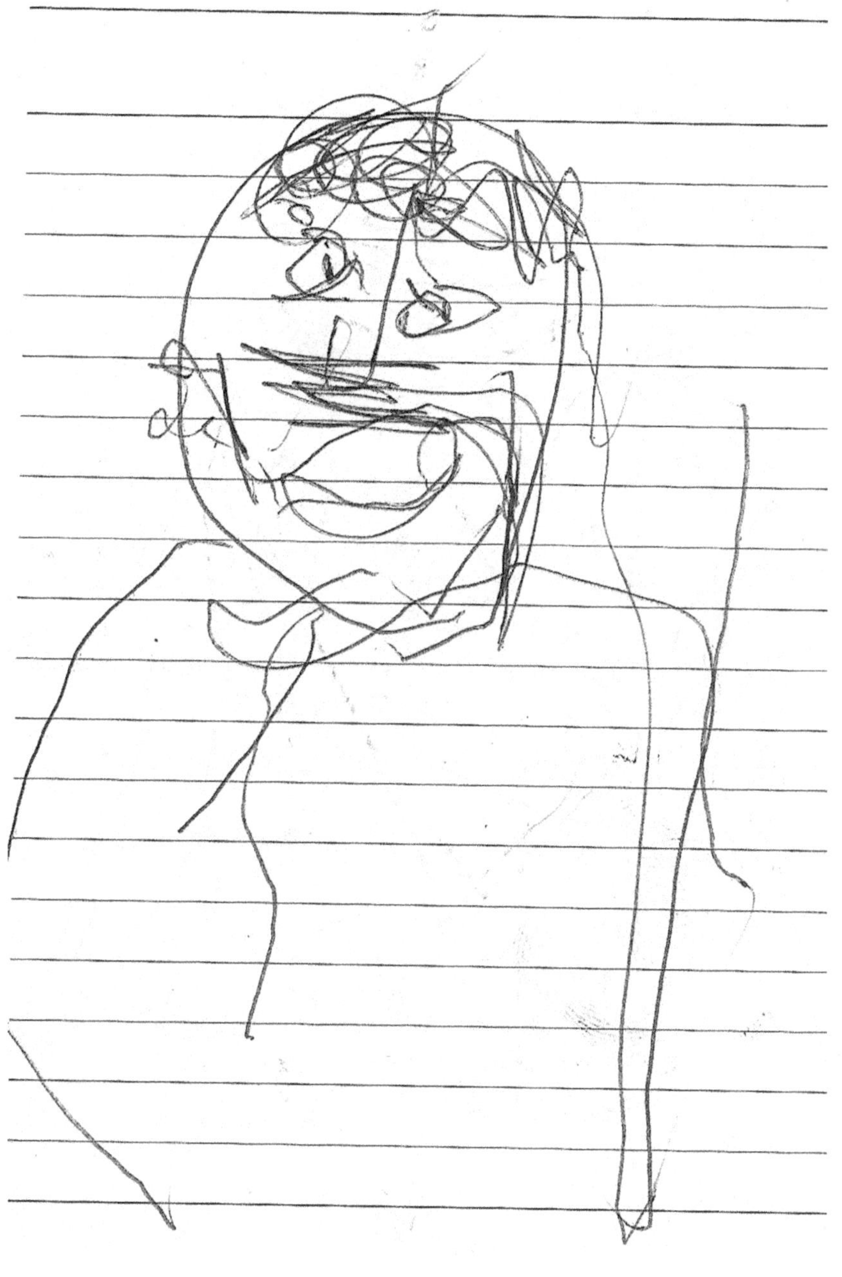

6. Junkie man

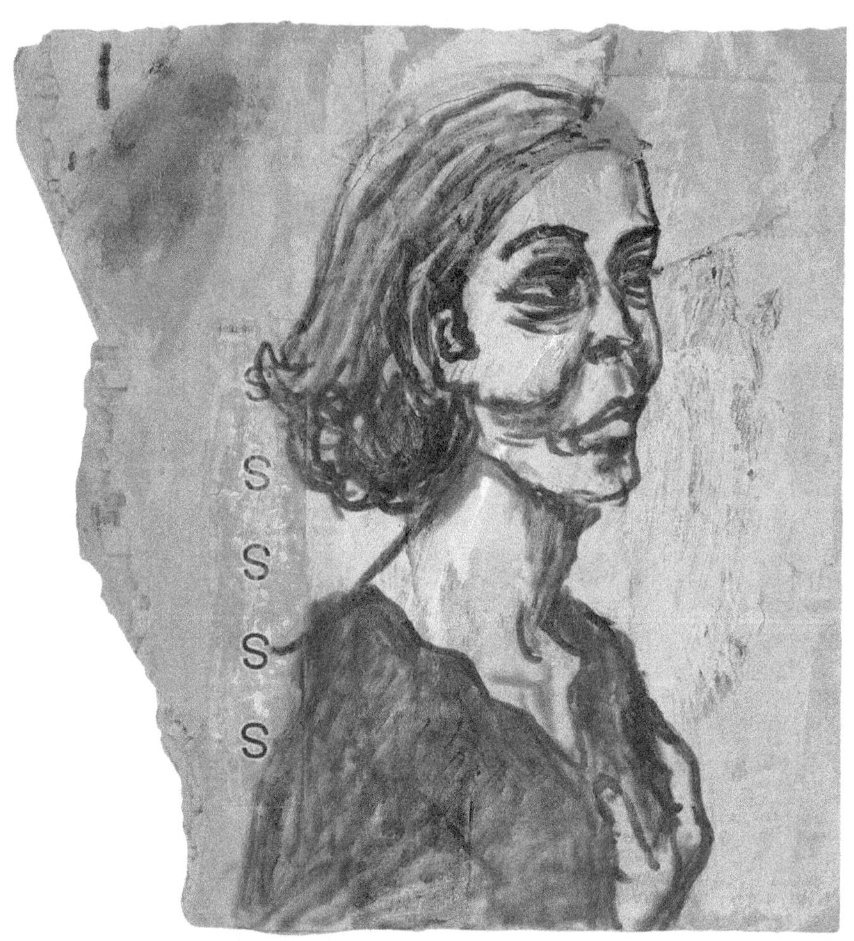

7. Doubt

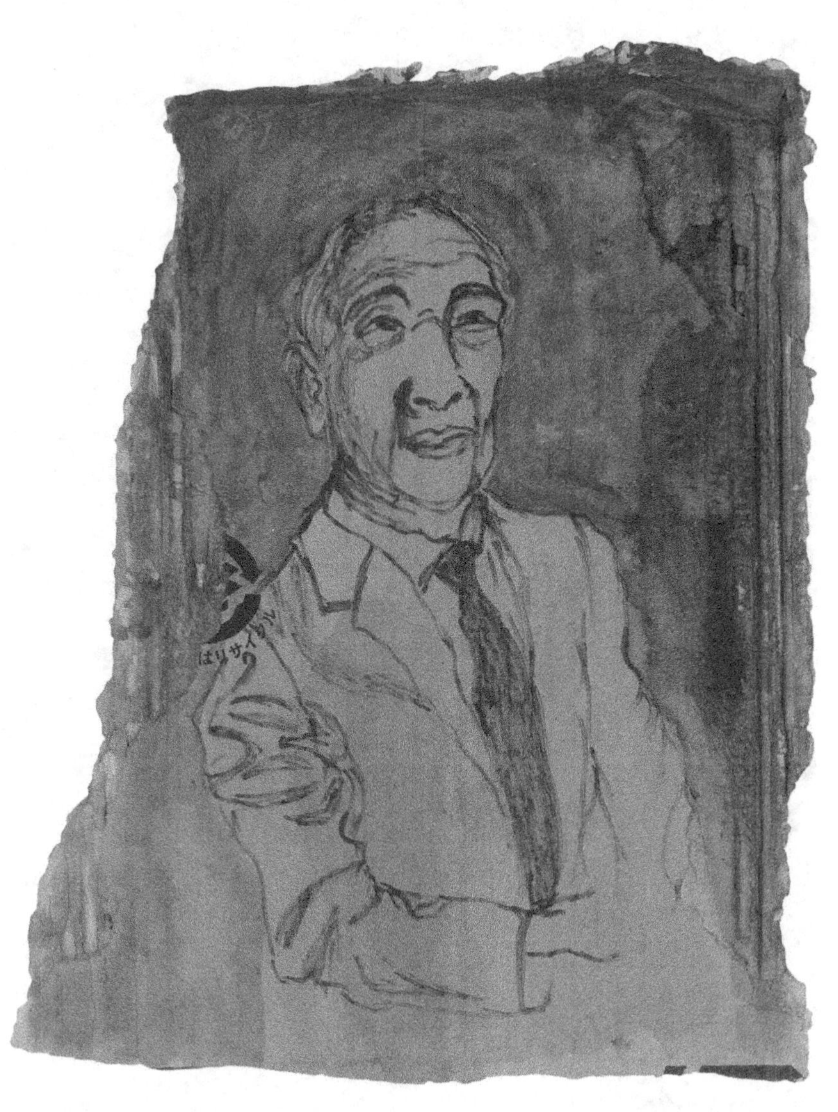

8. Mr. Kurosawa

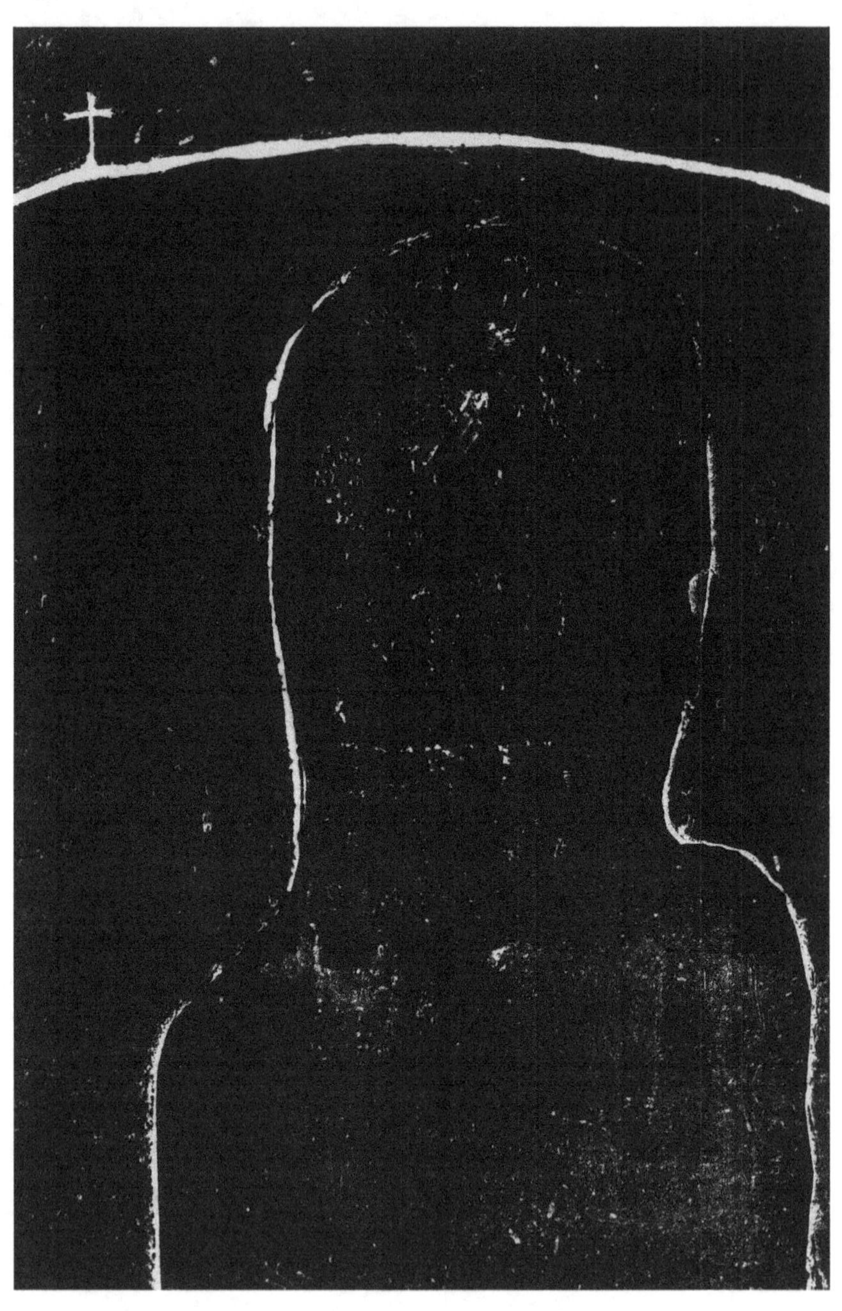

9. Self Portrait

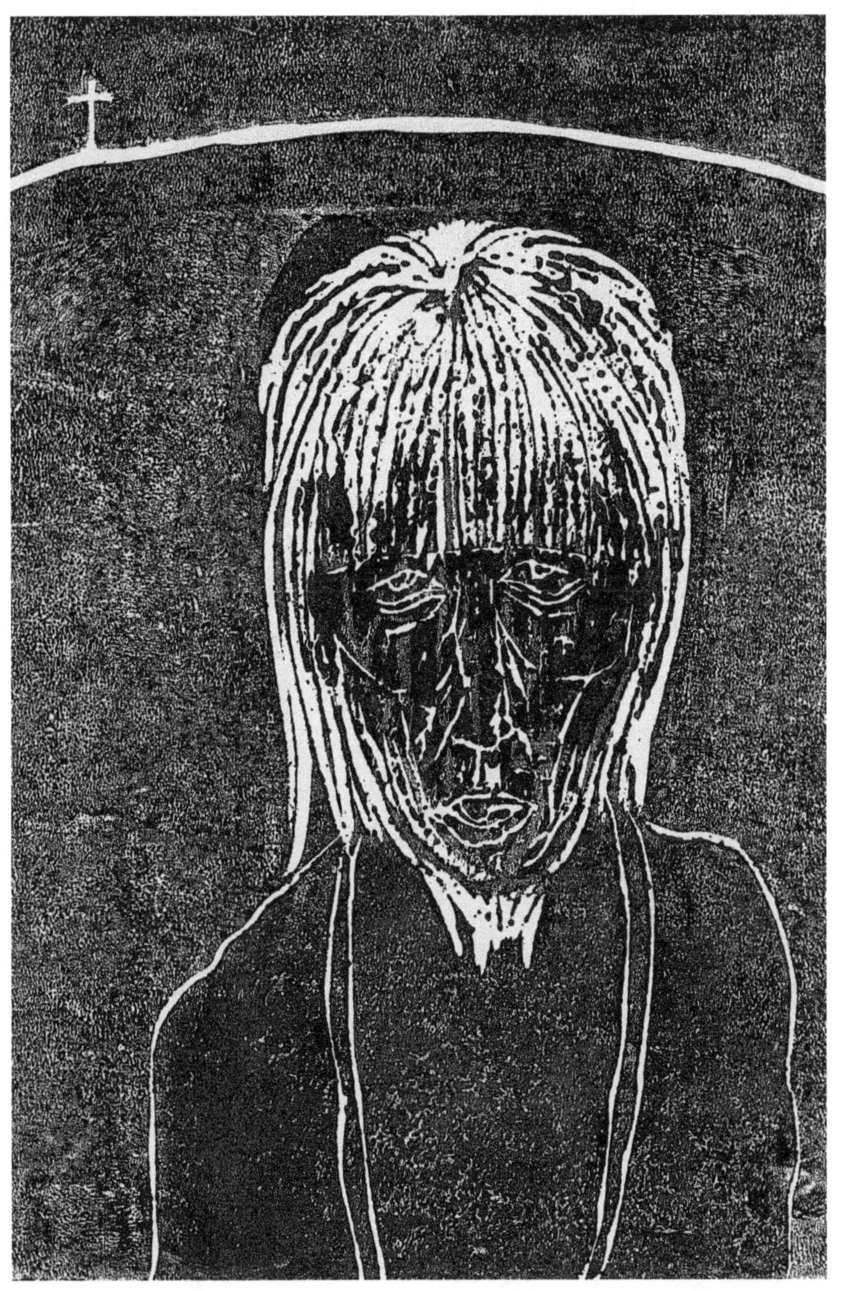

10. Self Portrait

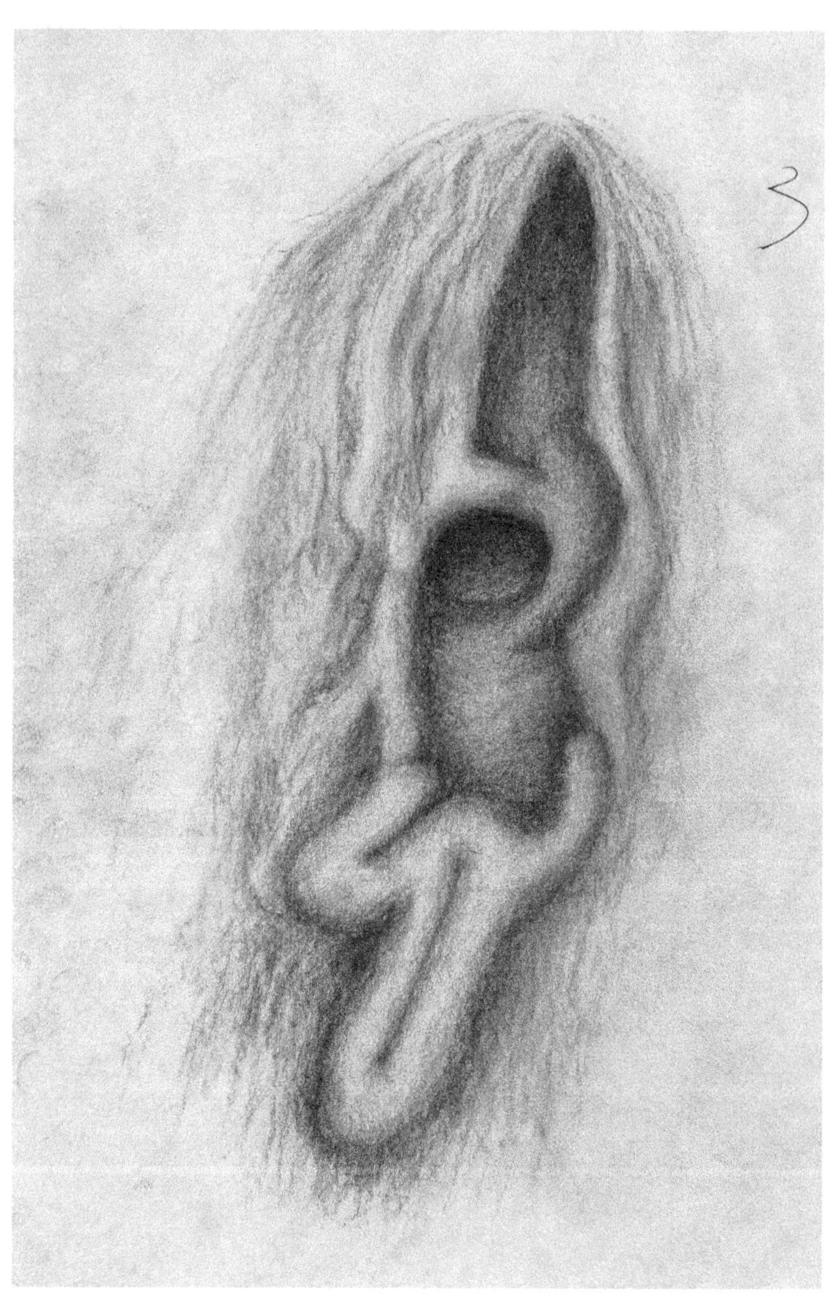

11. Indy

Sometimes I'm scared by my completed paintings because I usually draw with my feelings.

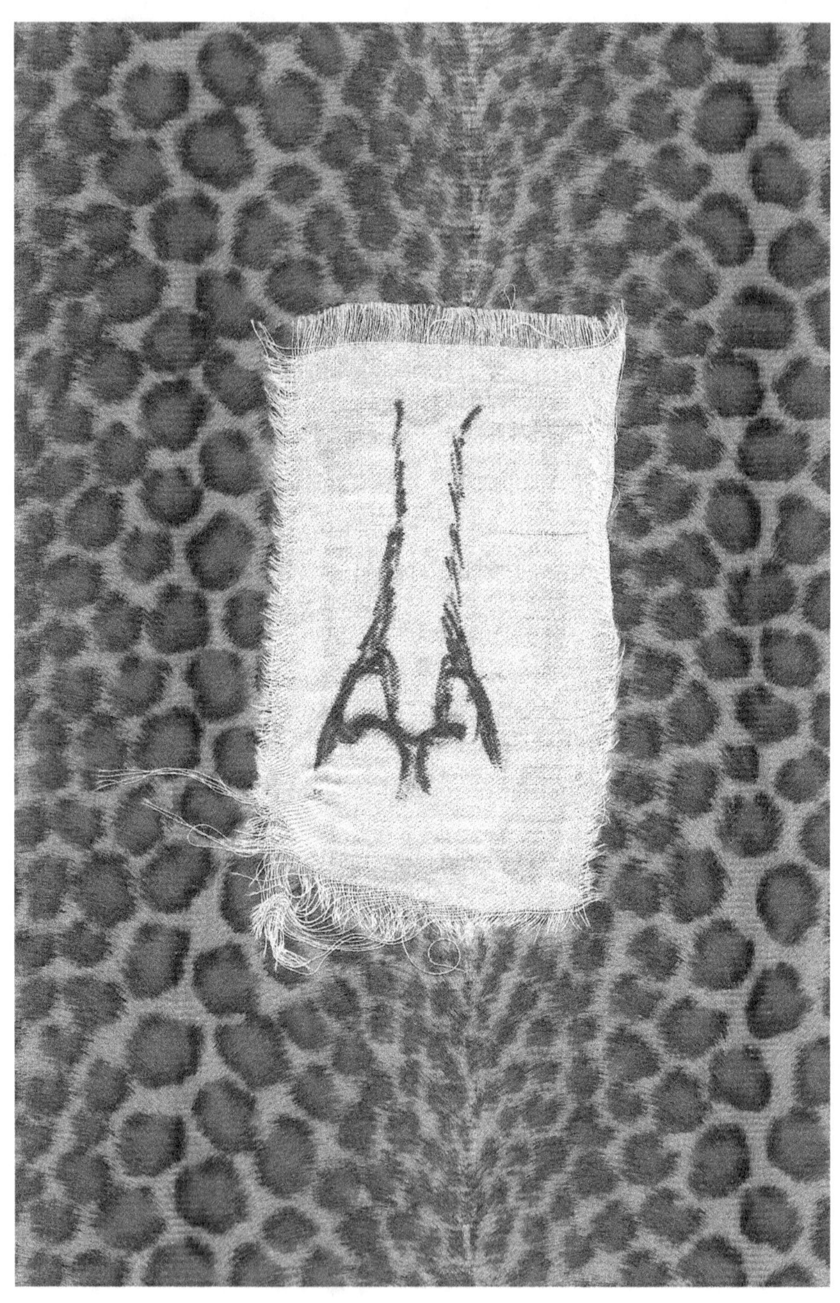

12. Mr. Osada: Nose On The Fur

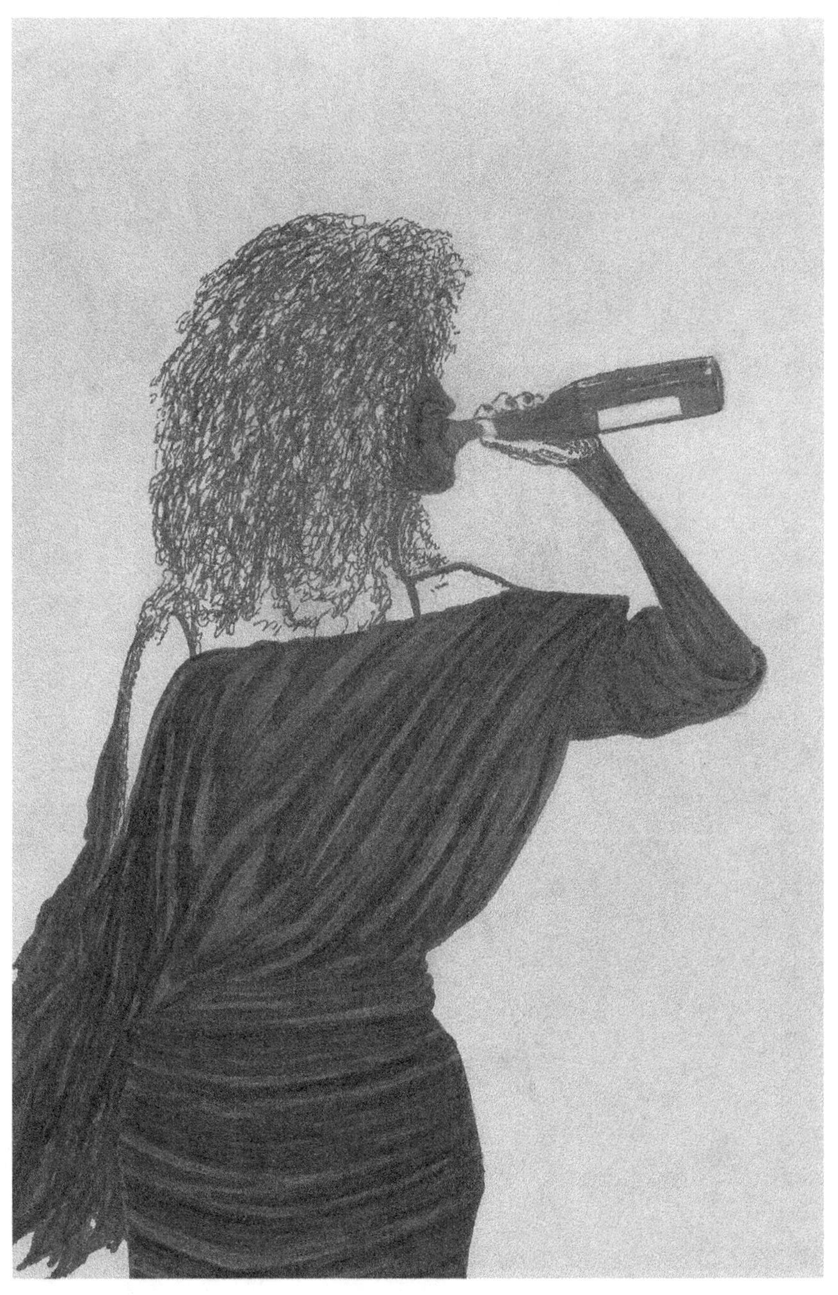

13. Night Club

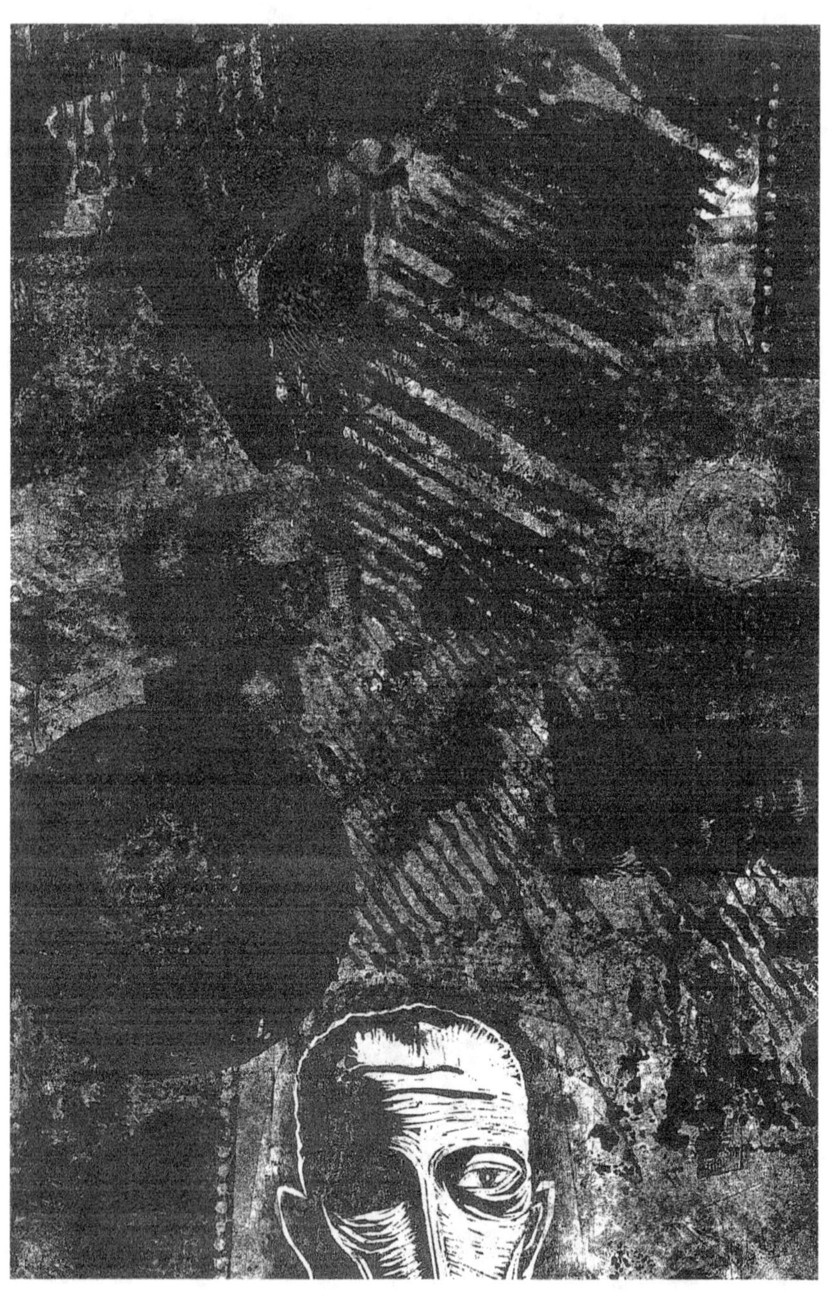

14. No One Knows What I Am Thinking

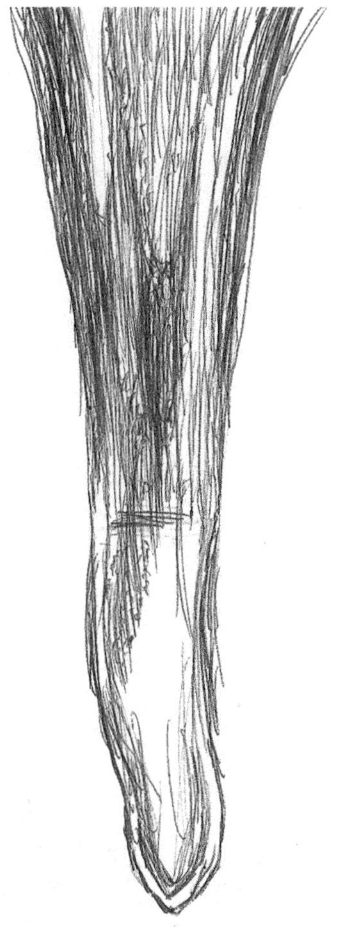

15. An Unidentified Object

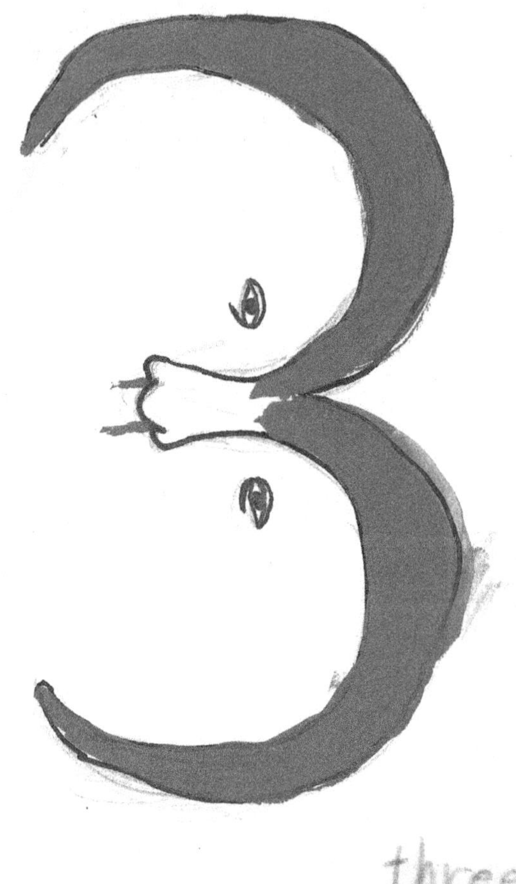

16. Three

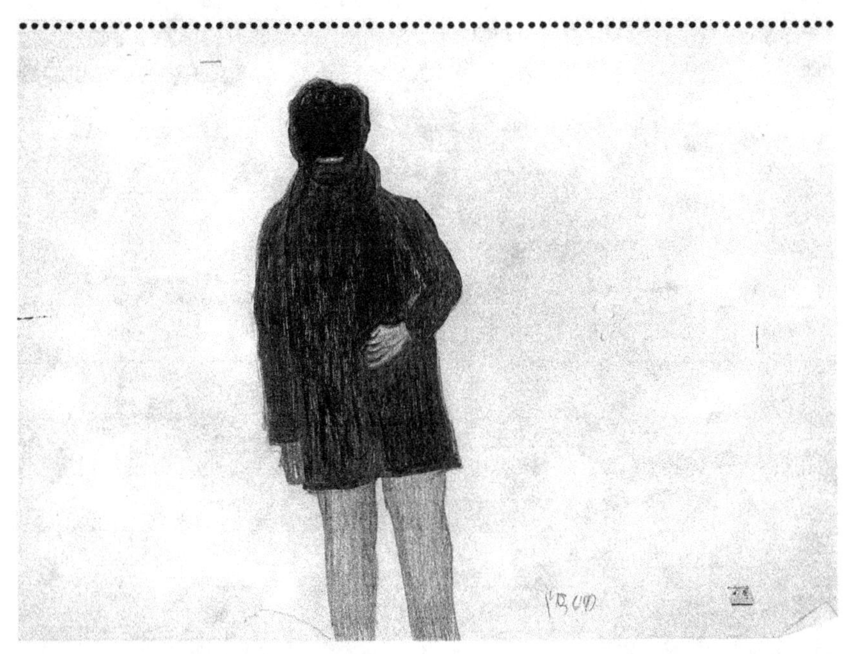

17. Unknown Partner

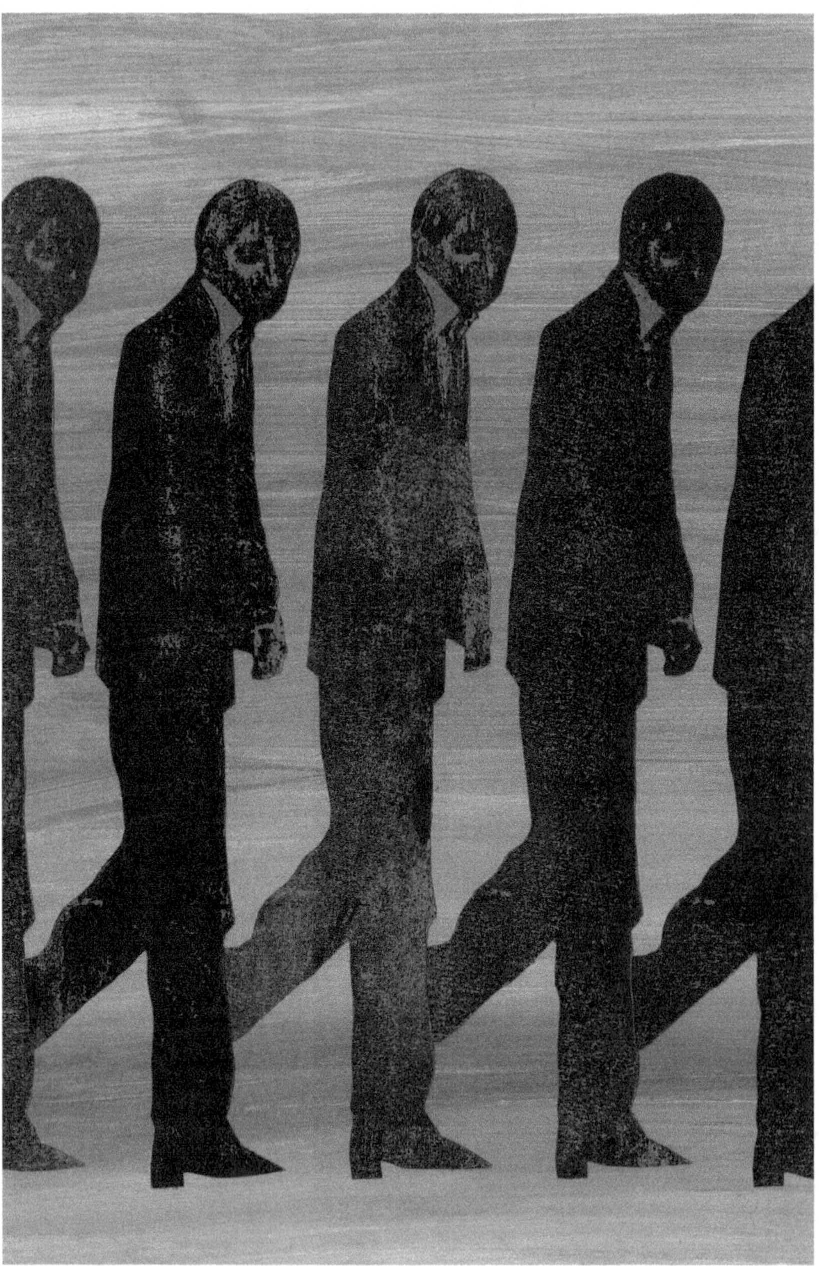

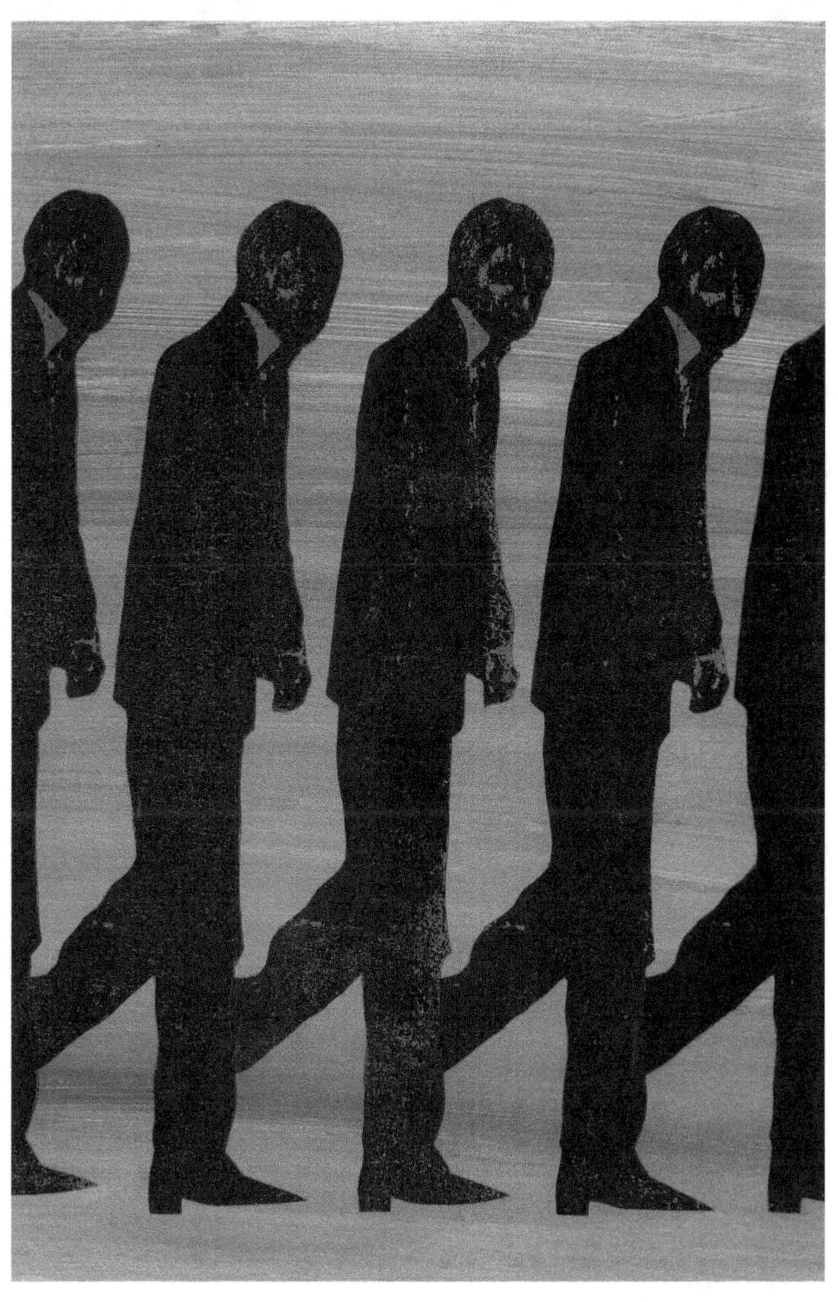

18. Walking Distance

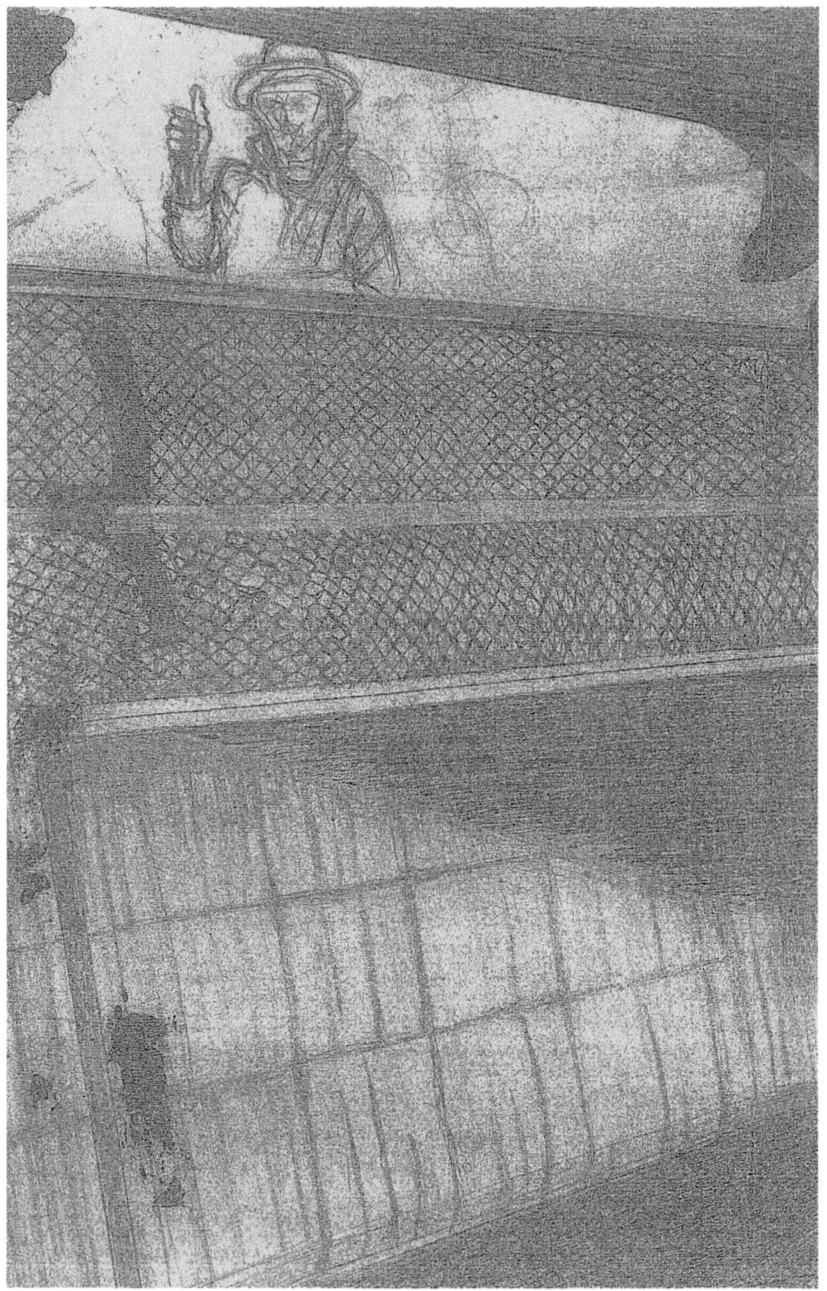

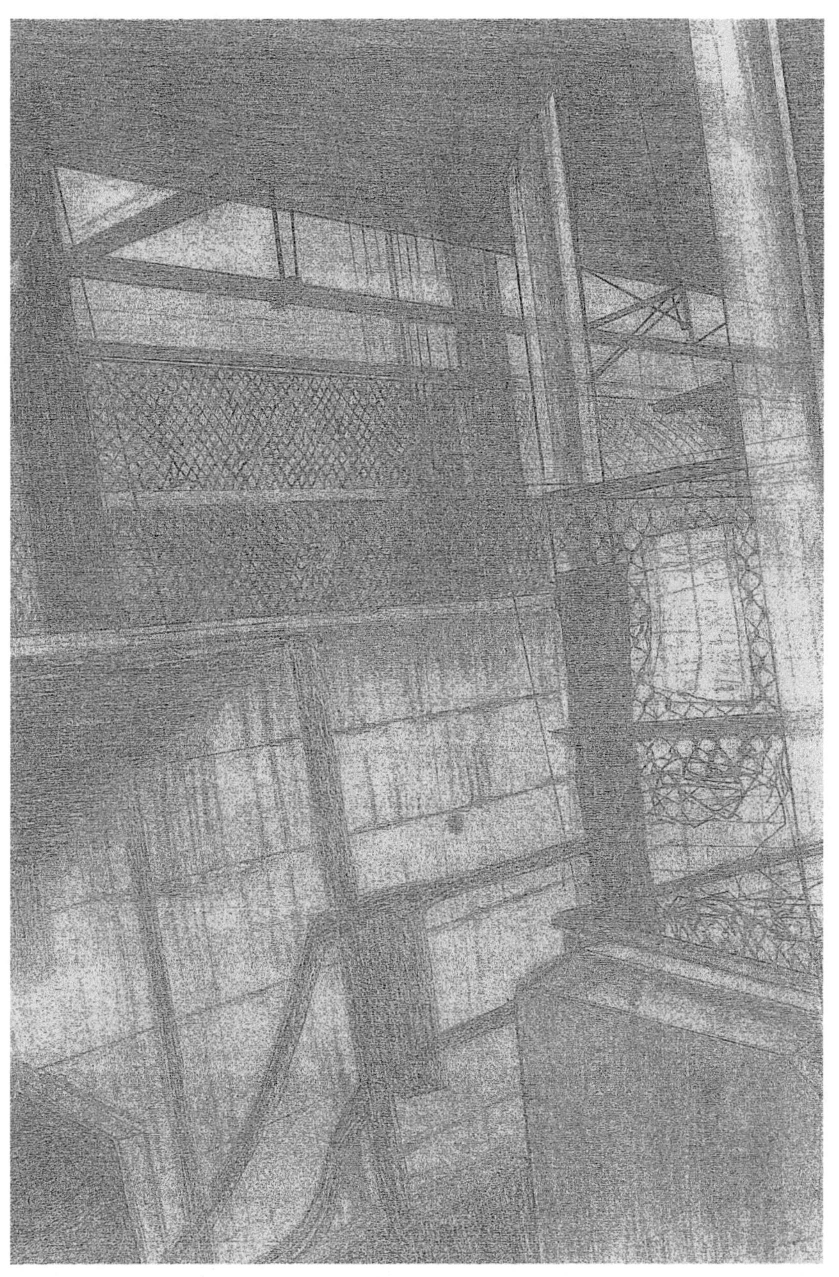

19. Time To Leave School

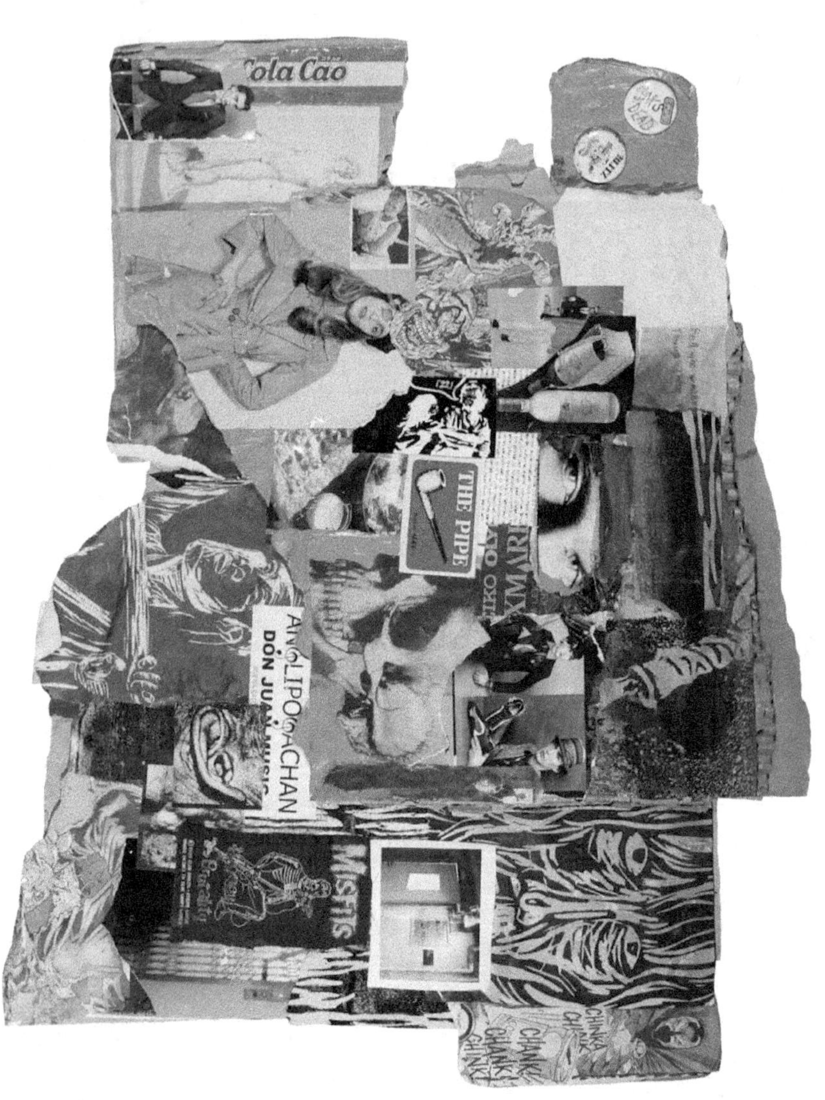

20. Pop Fear

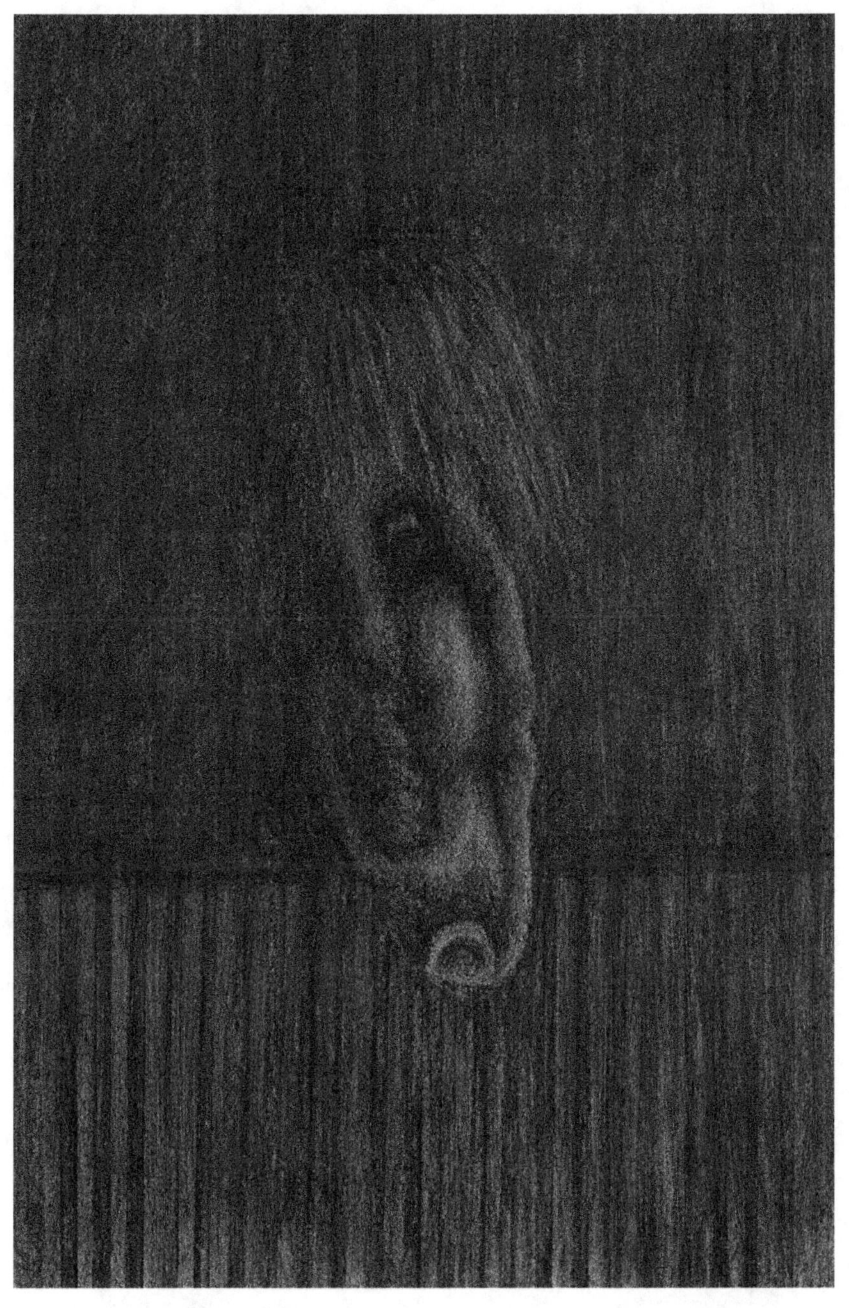

21. Young Horse

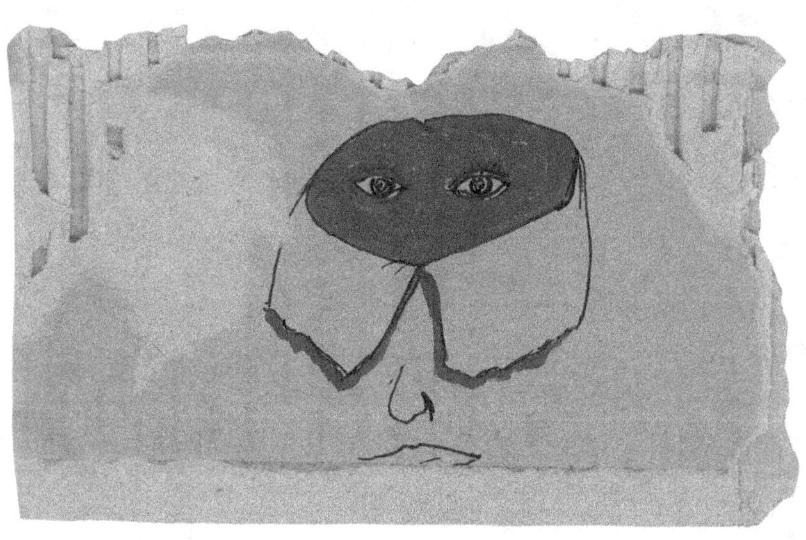

22. Sadaharu

When I was a student I showed a painting of a portrait to my teacher. I worked very hard to draw it as a real person. However my teacher said "draw it in a mess!" I didn't understand what he meant but I drew in a mess and showed him again. He said "It's not enough. More!" Then I drew this painting because I wanted to make him angry. When he saw this he said "Great!" I thought he was crazy.

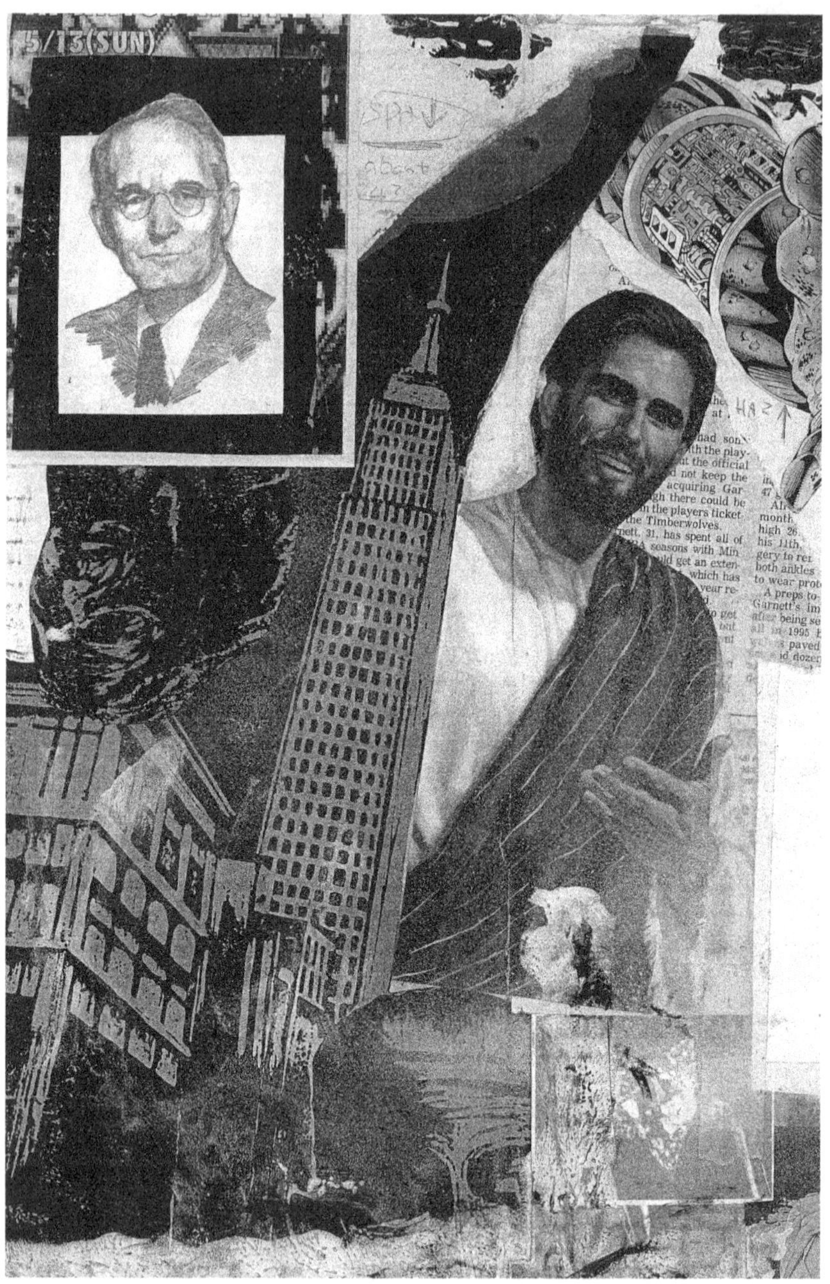

23. N.Y.C

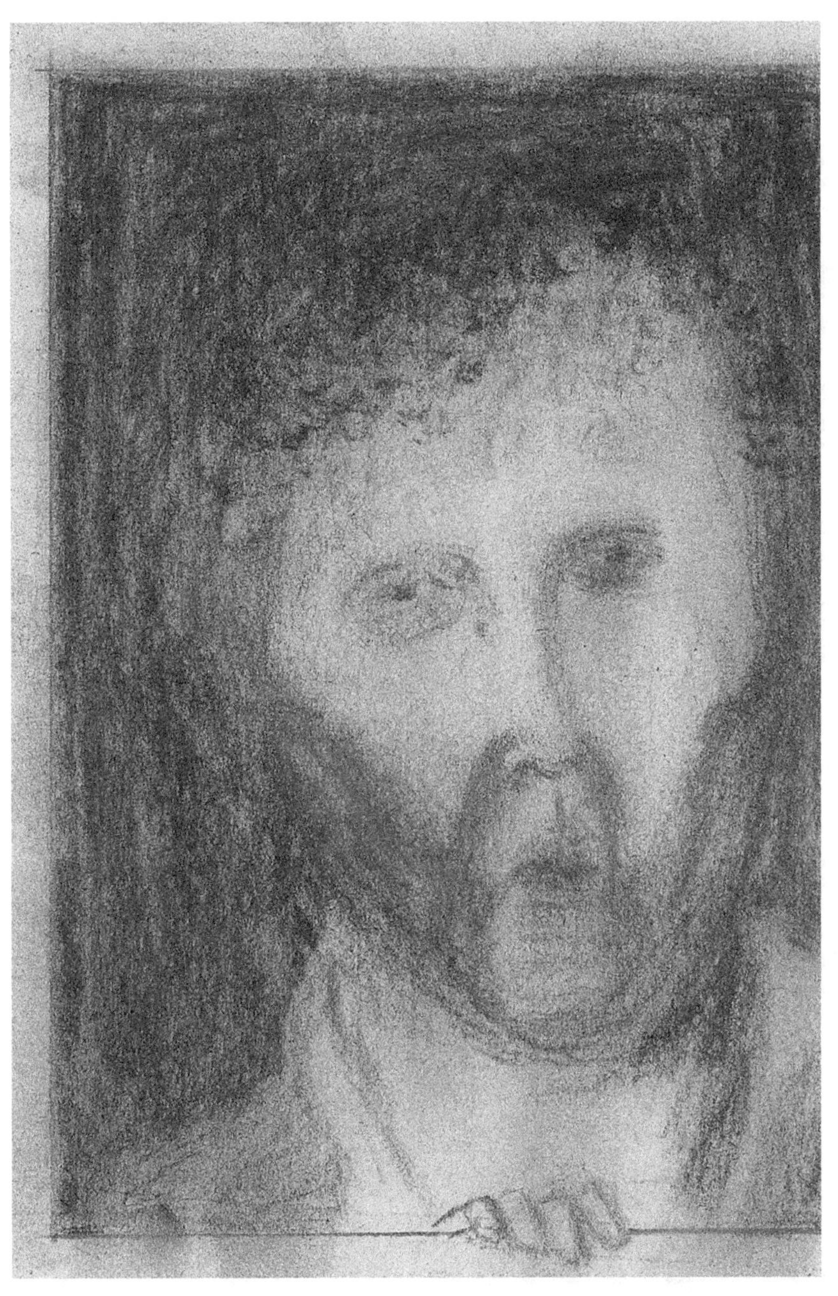

24. Comedian On The Downward

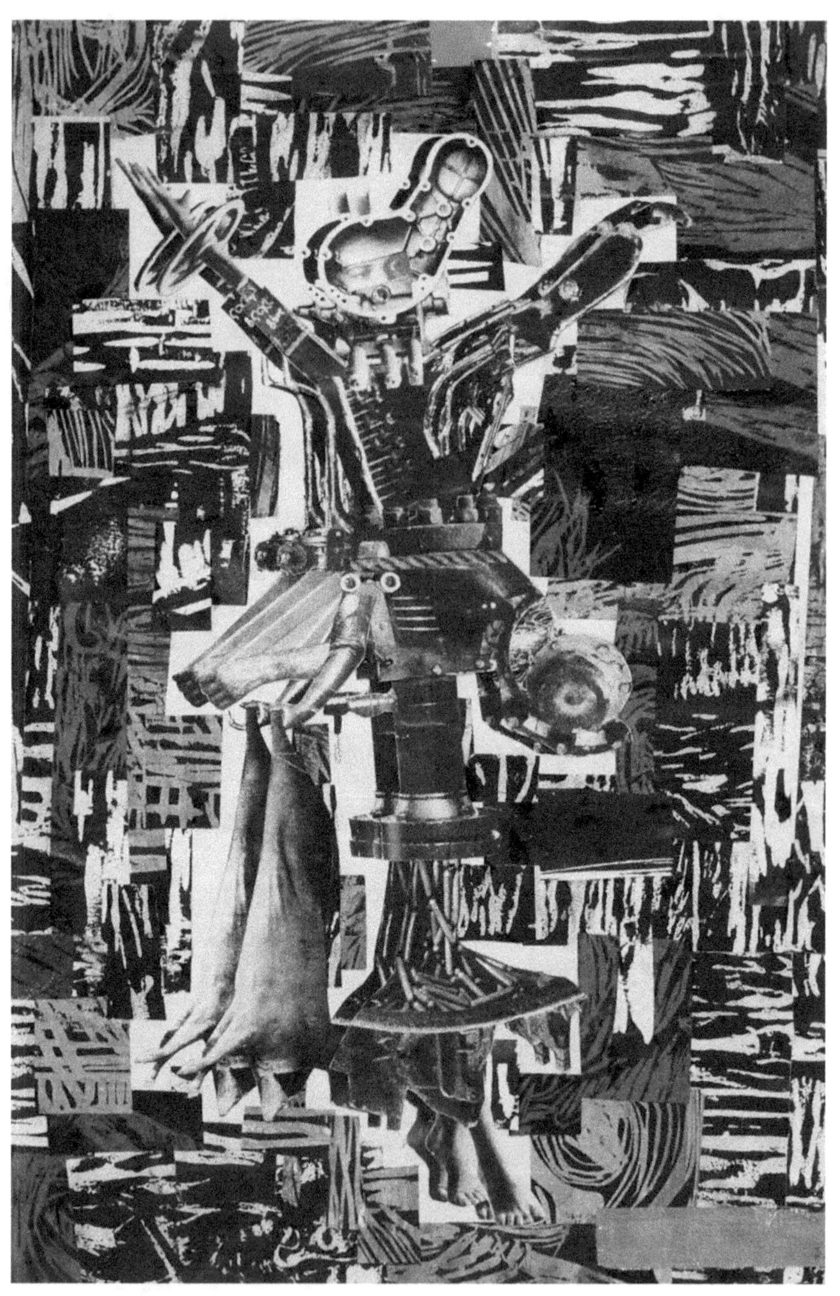

25. Sausage Machine

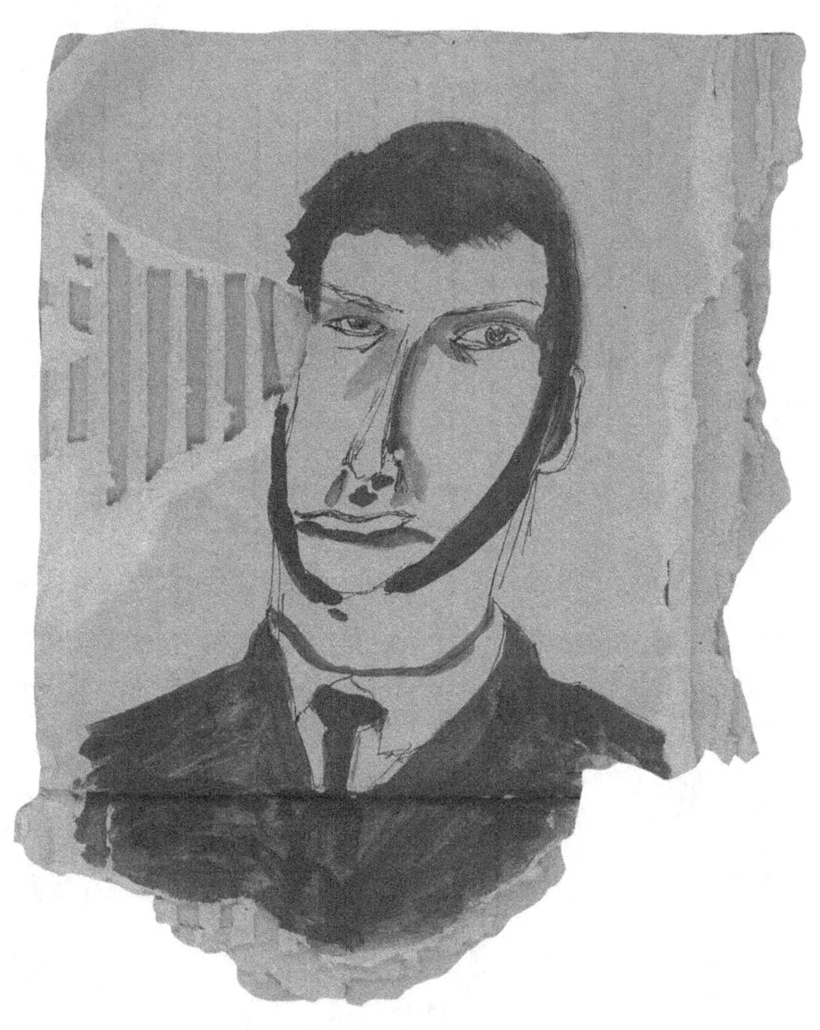

26. Blue Man

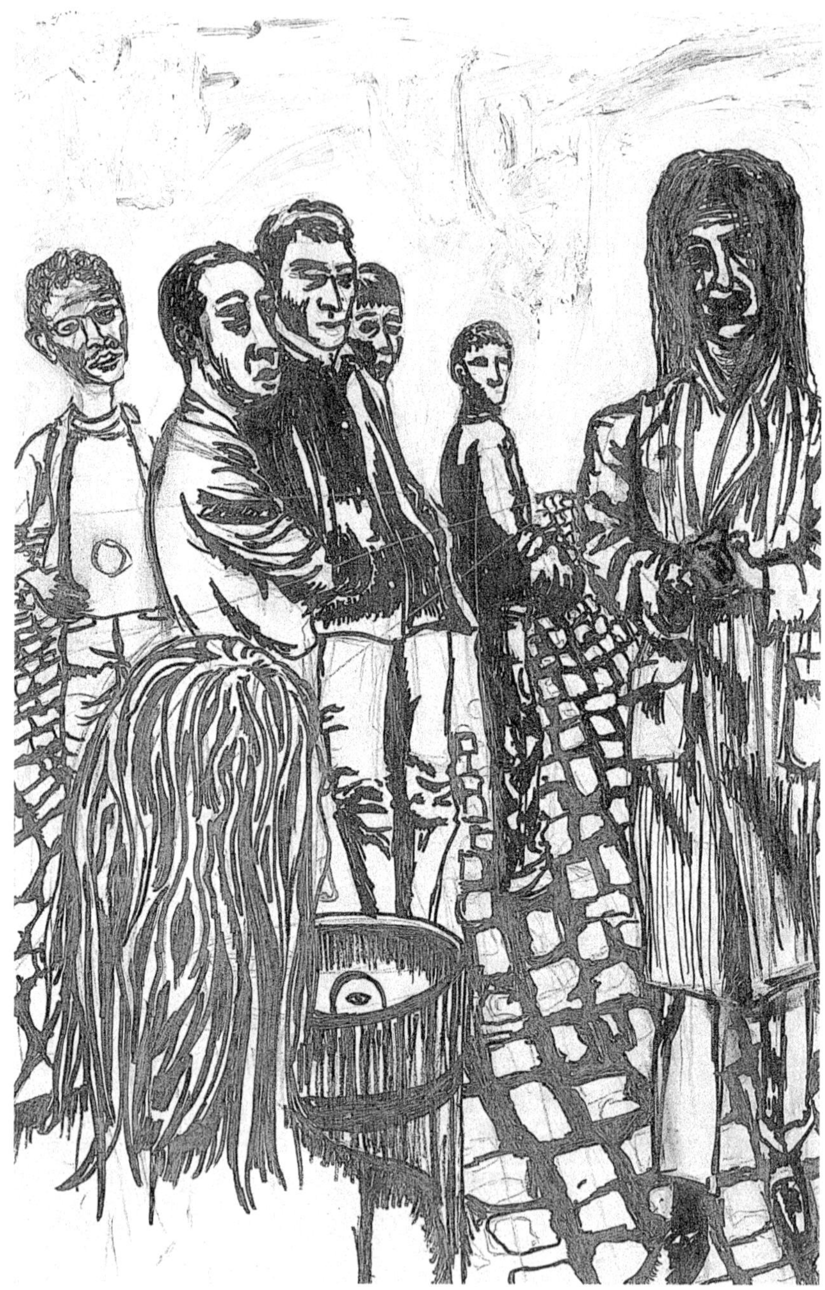

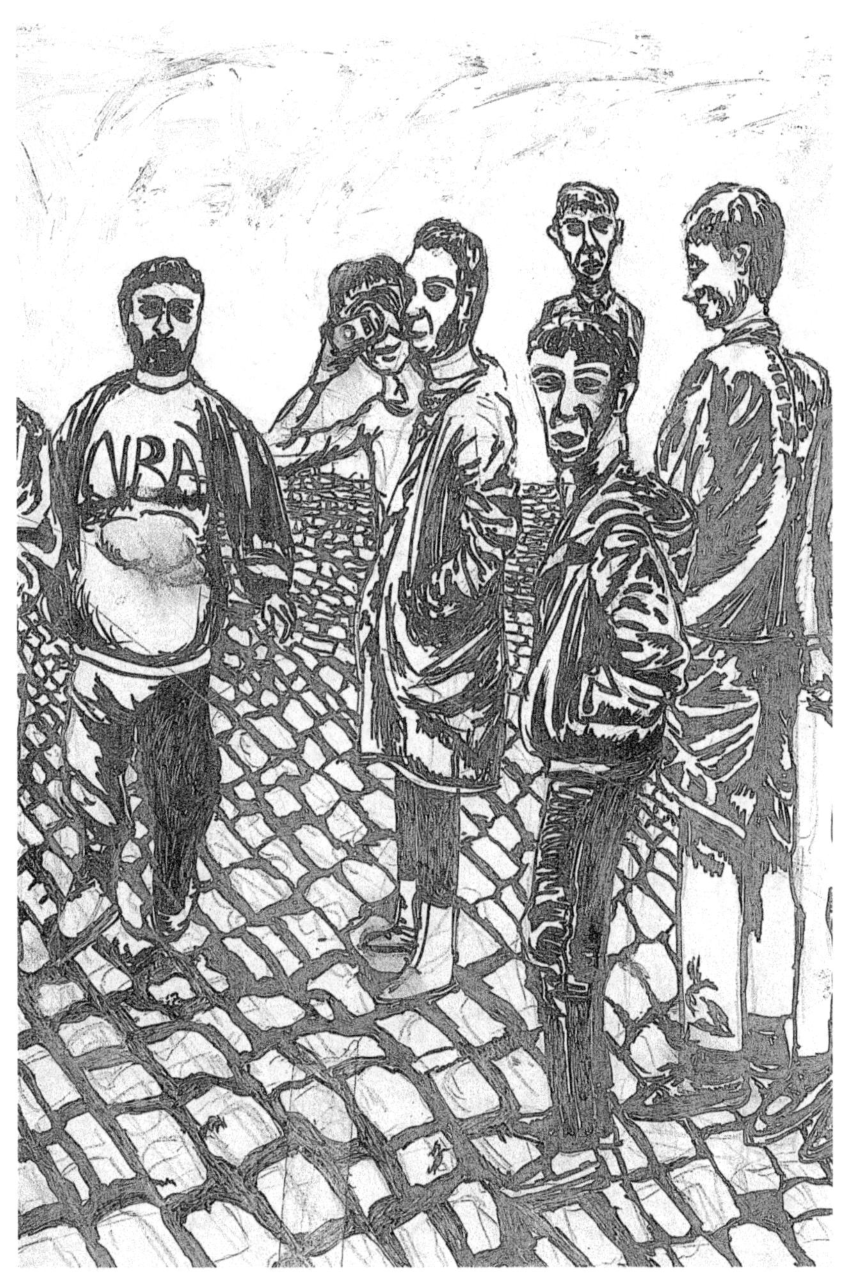

27. A Rock Star

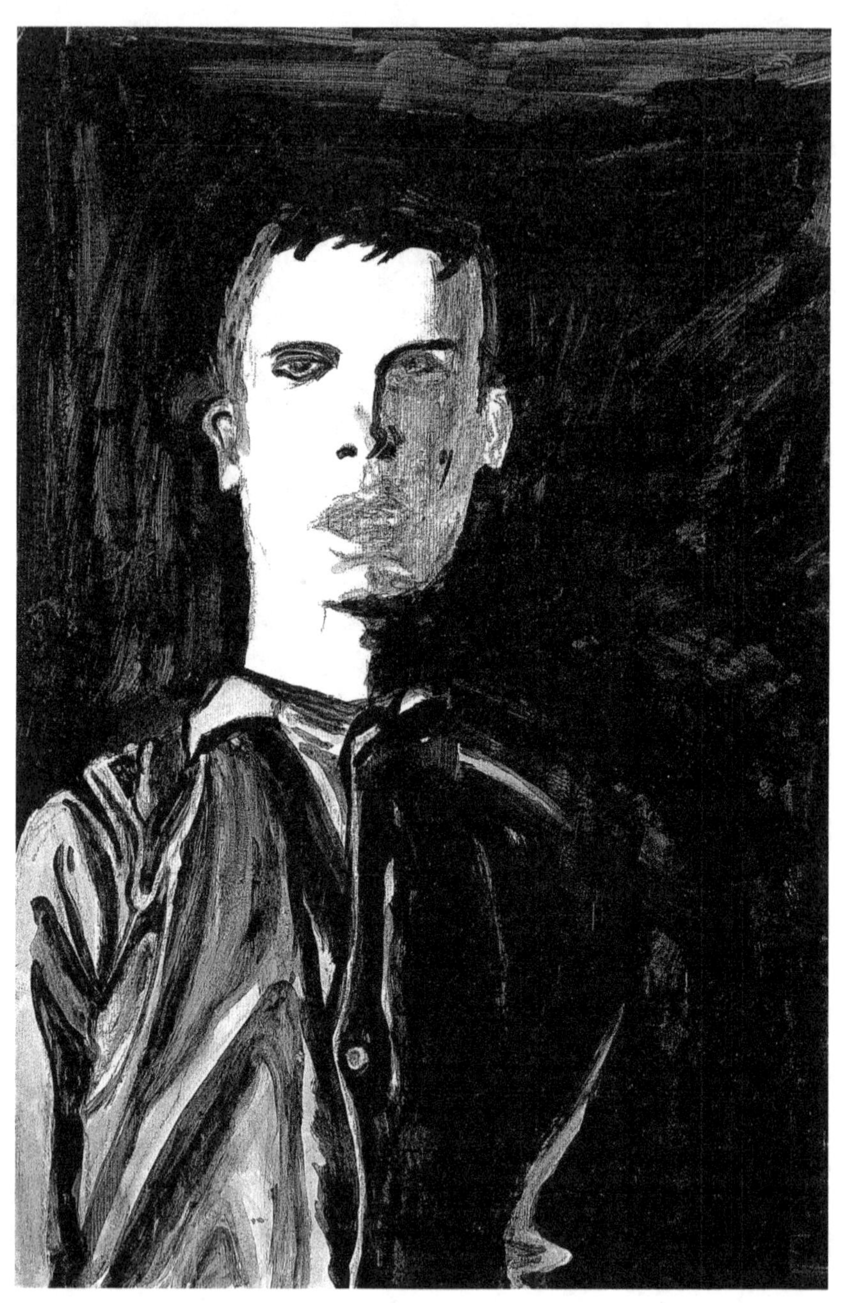

28. Killed By Himself

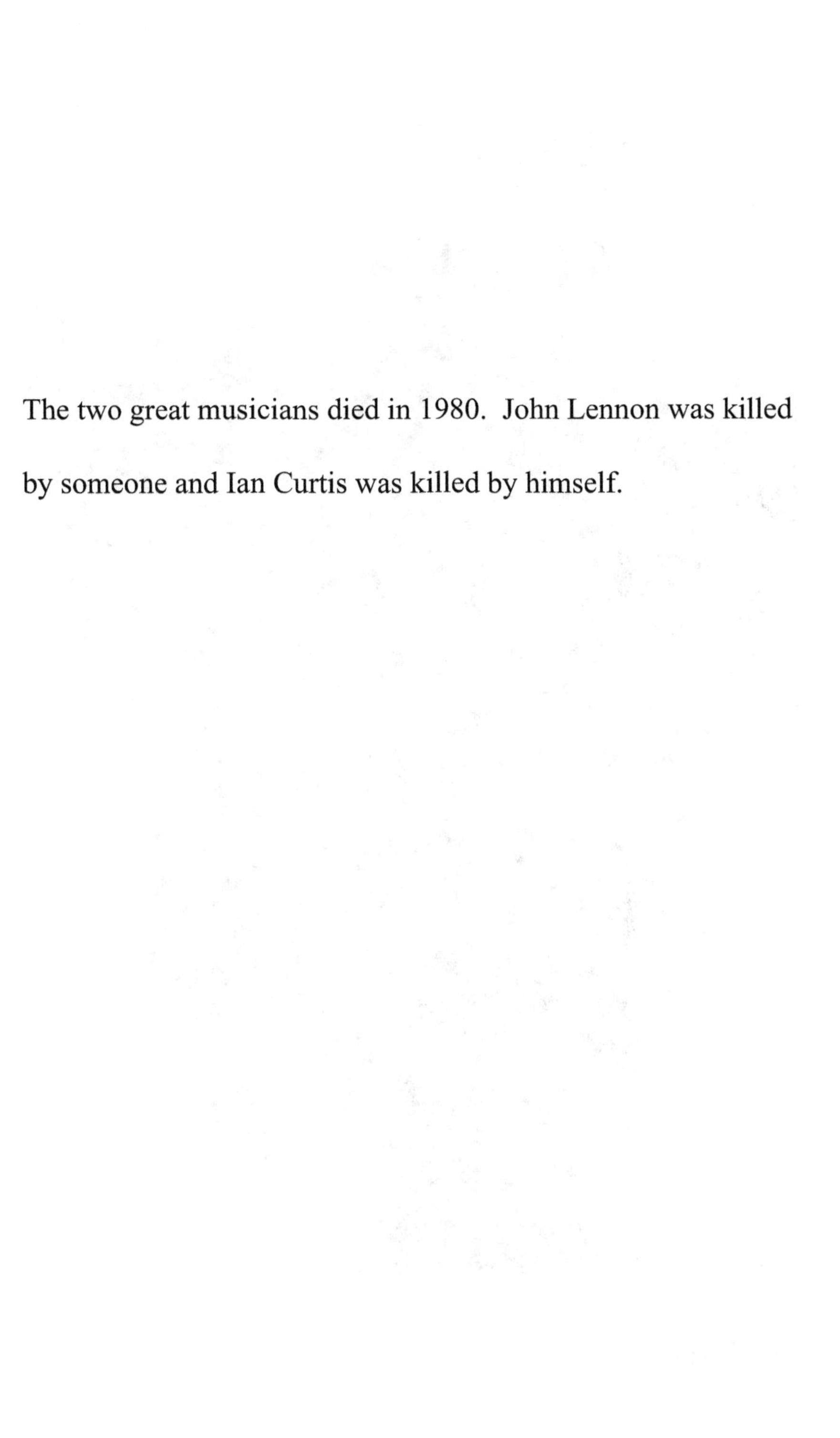

The two great musicians died in 1980. John Lennon was killed by someone and Ian Curtis was killed by himself.

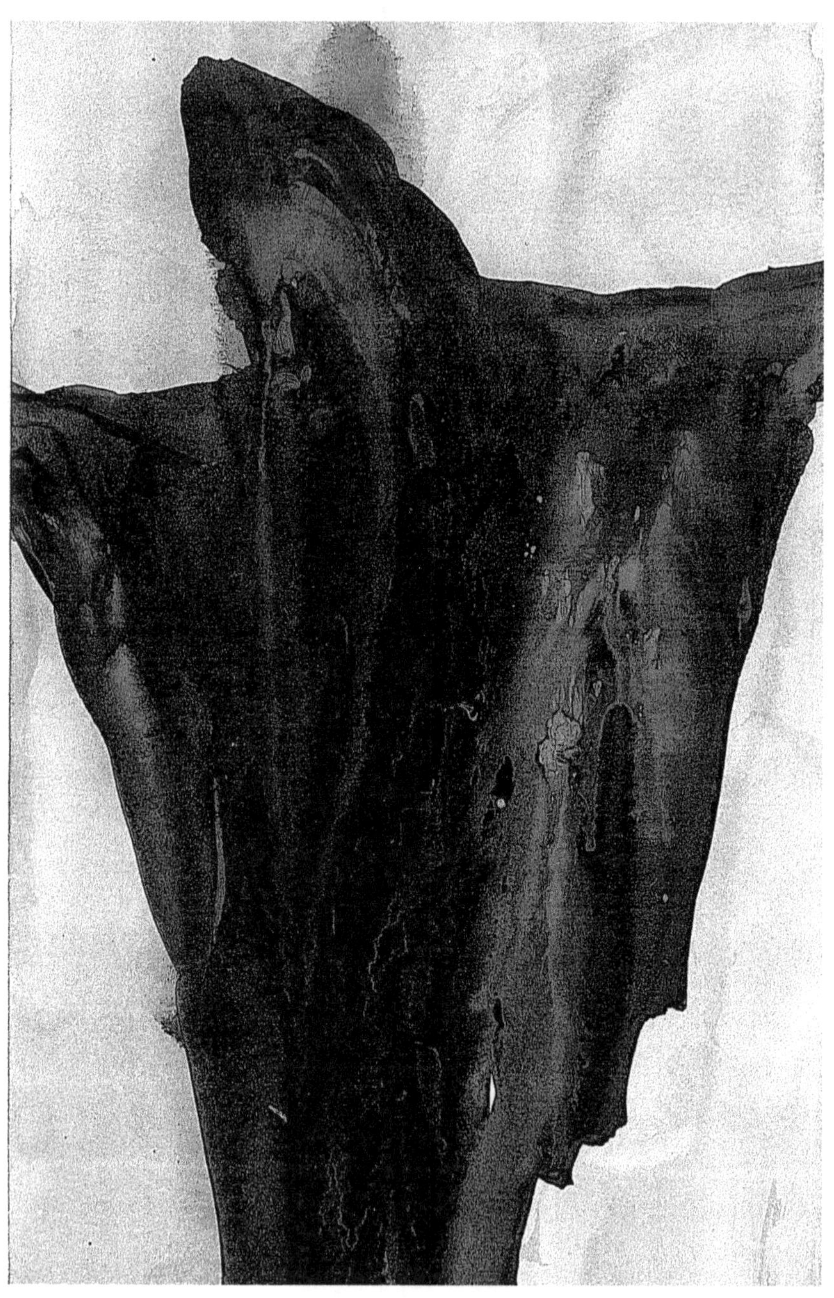

29. Fairy

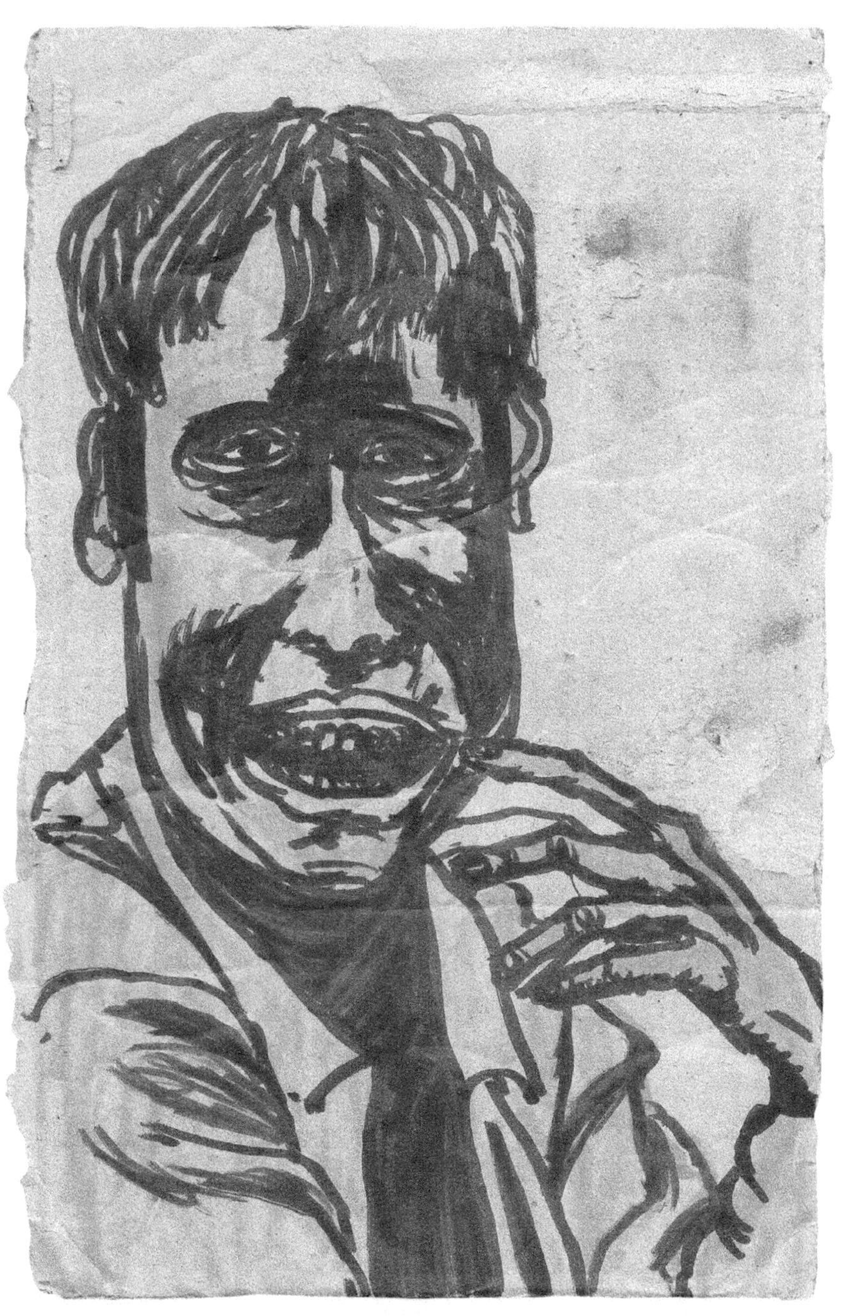

30. Telephone Shopping Show

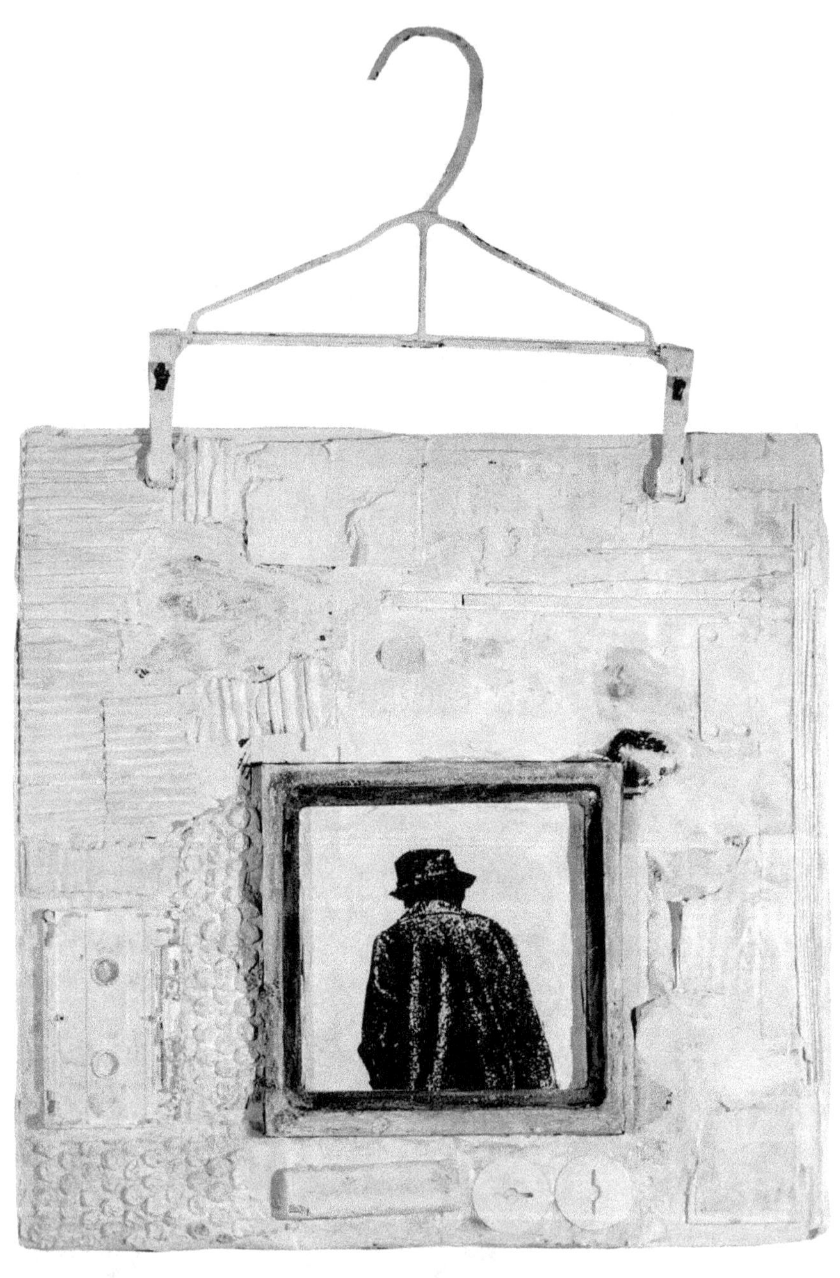

31. White Dust

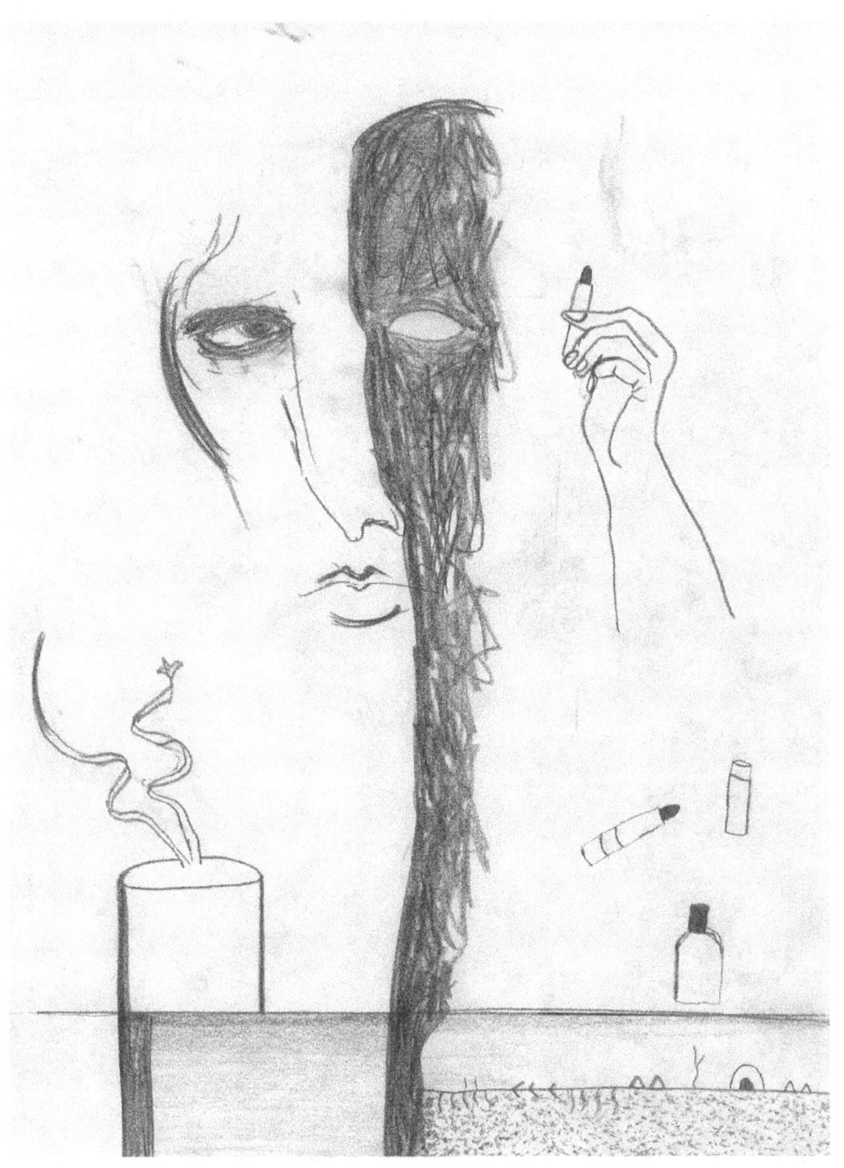

32. Make Up

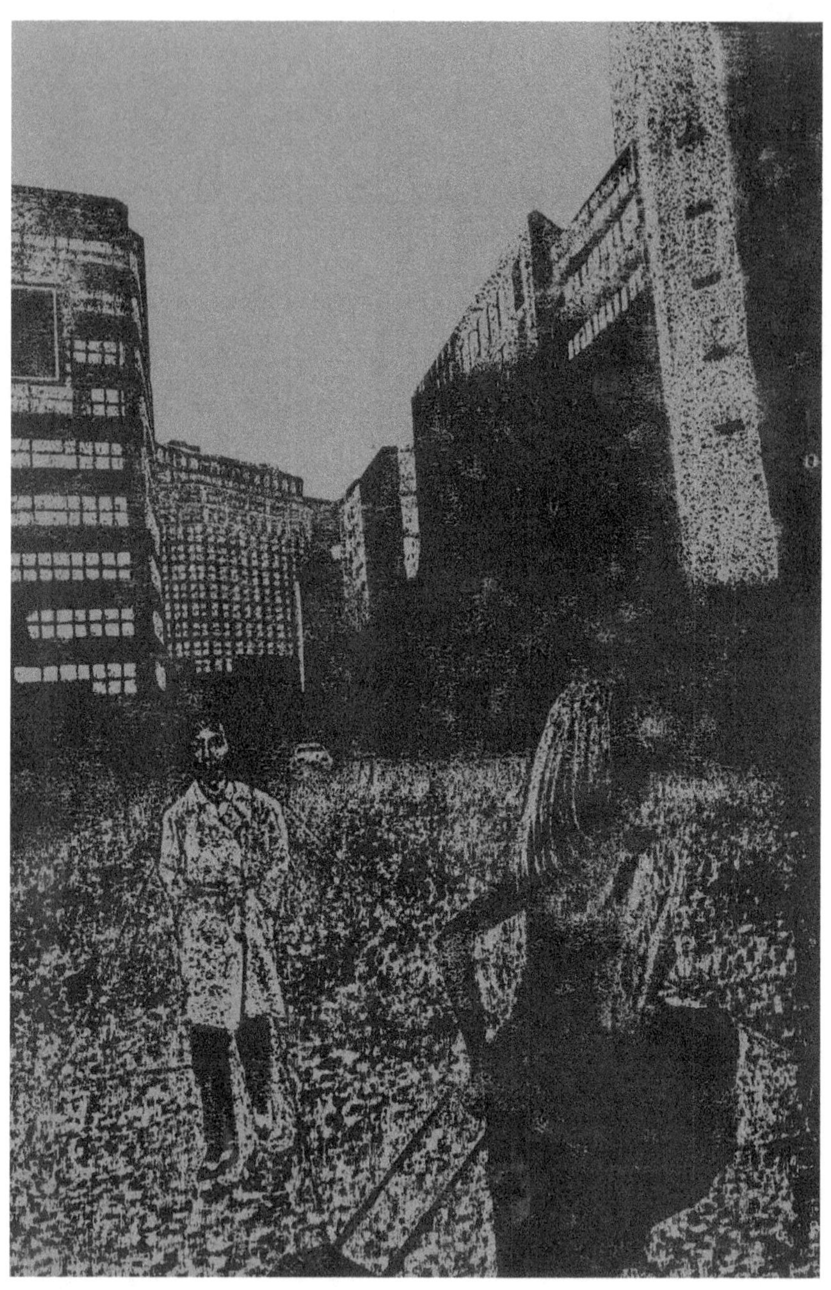

33. Shinjyuku

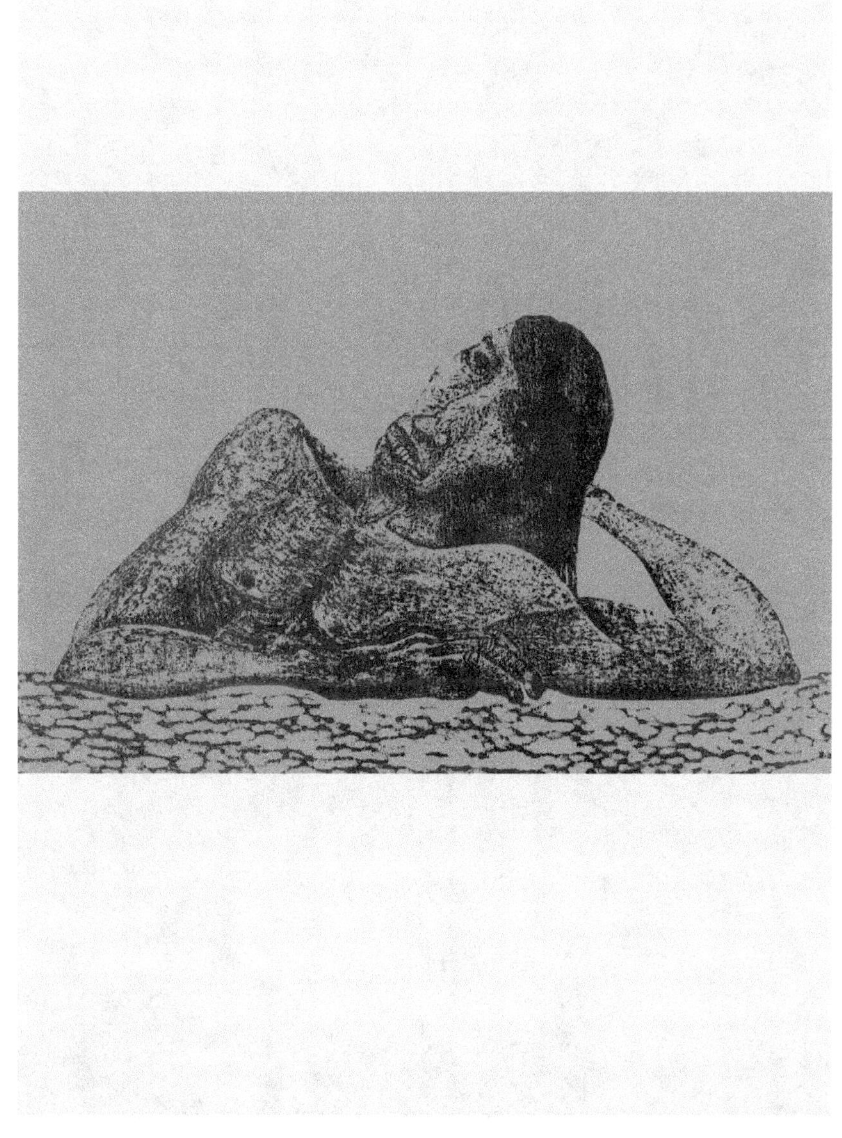

34. Self Portrait

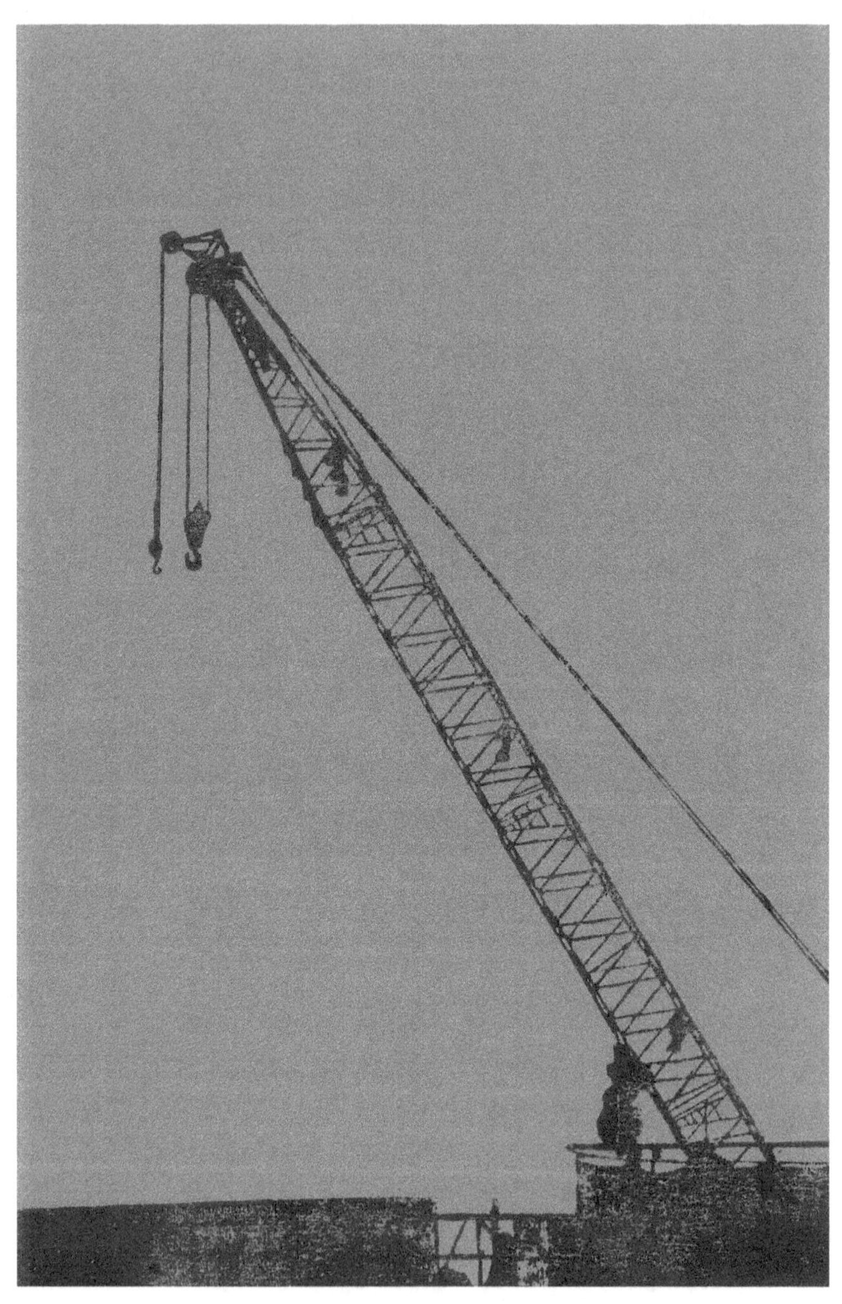

35. Construction Work

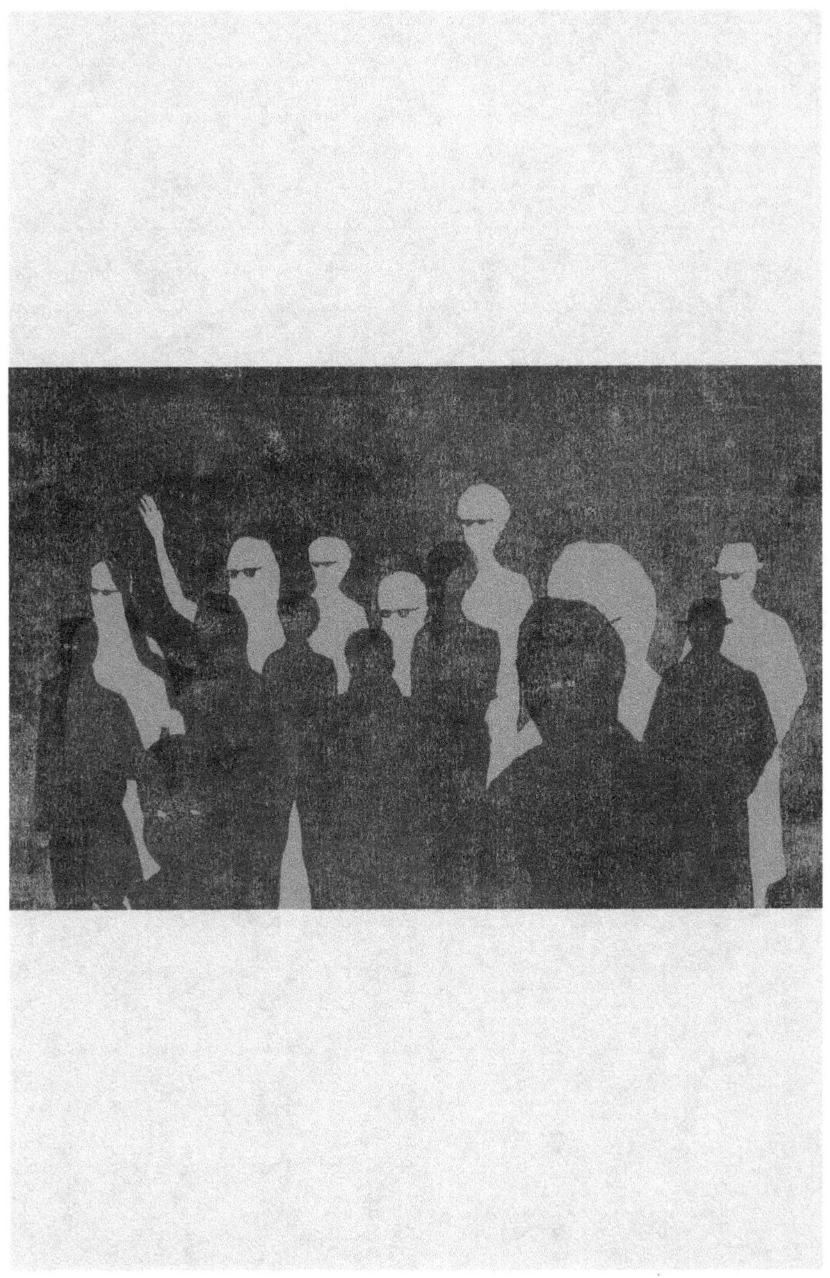

36. Fiction

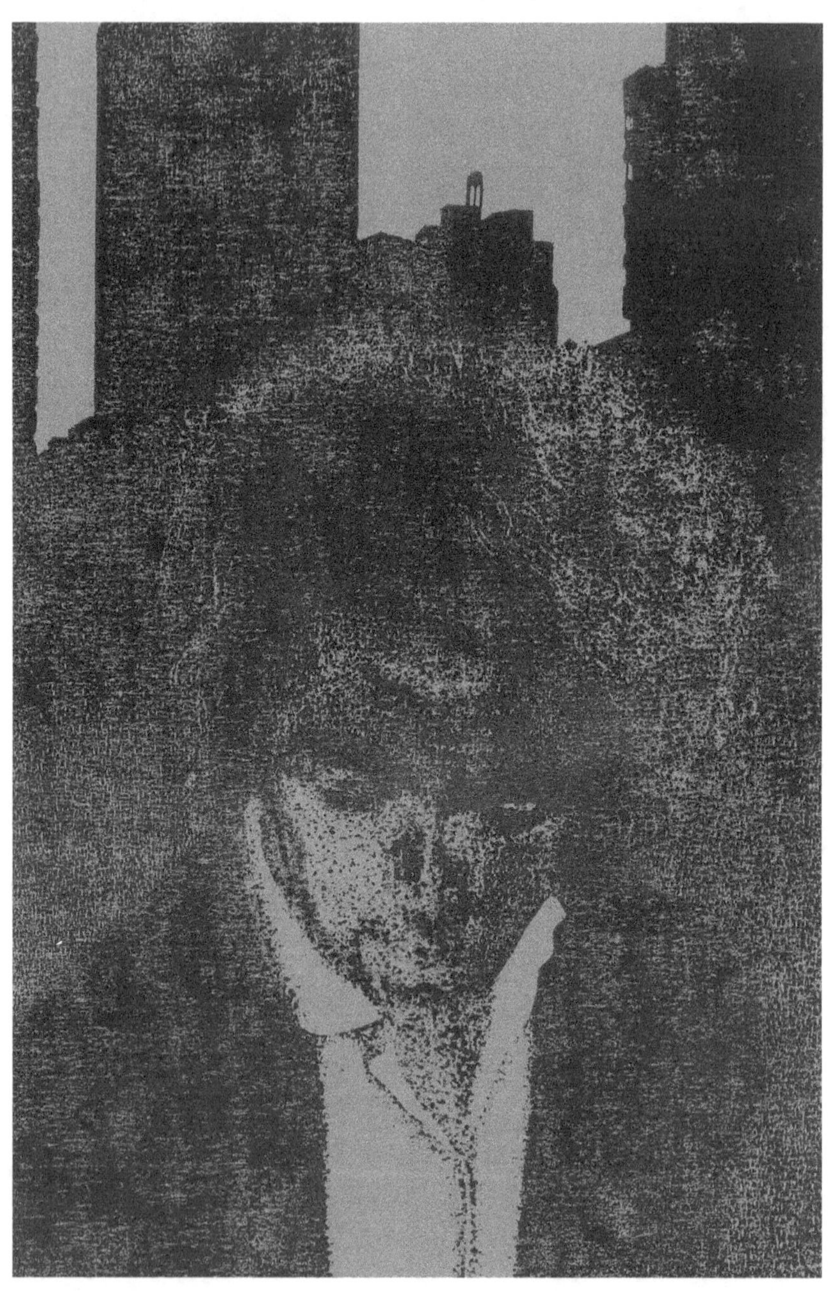

37. This Is Not A Dream

I dream every night and sometimes during daytime. I forget what I saw in my dreams, but it's no problem. If I remembered all of my dreams, it would be a bit confusing because I couldn't tell which was a dream and which was a reality from my past.

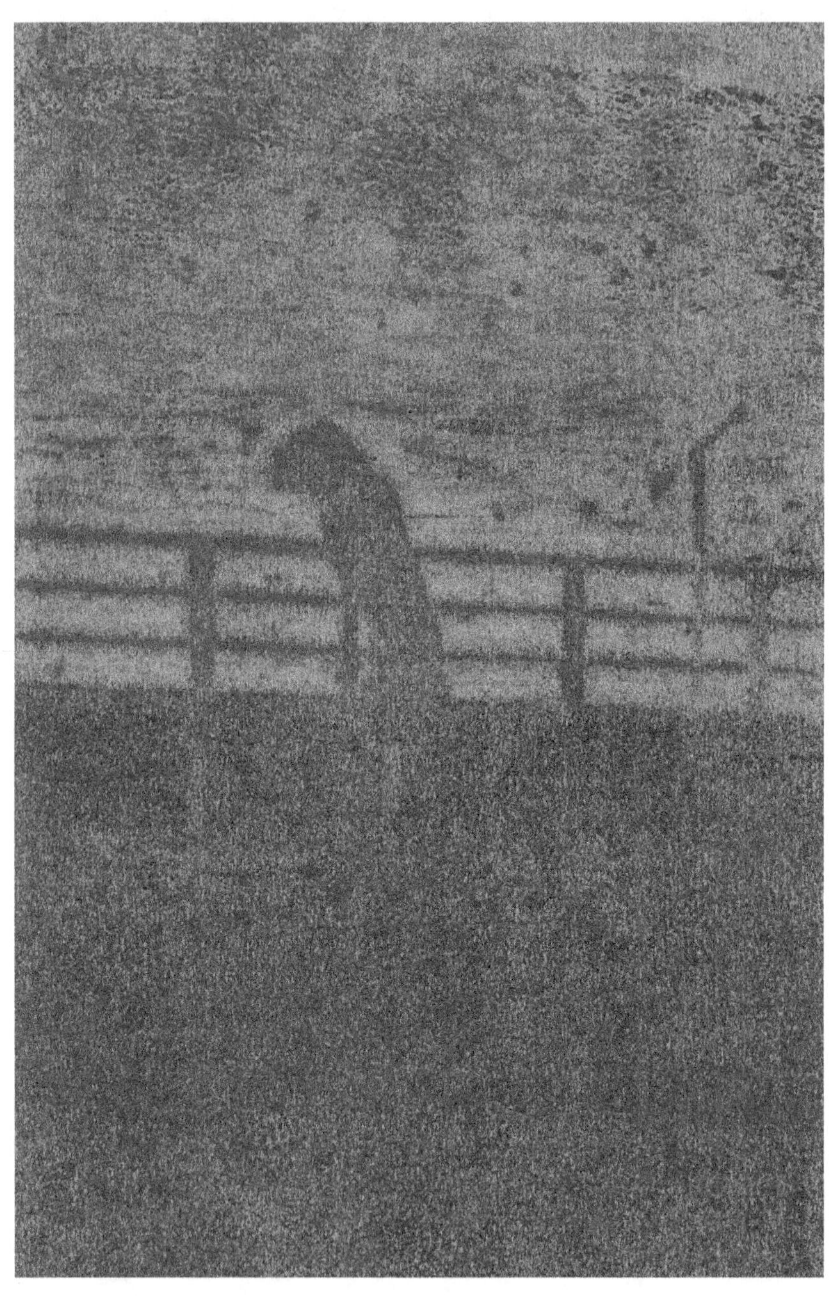

38. Arched Over The Melancholy

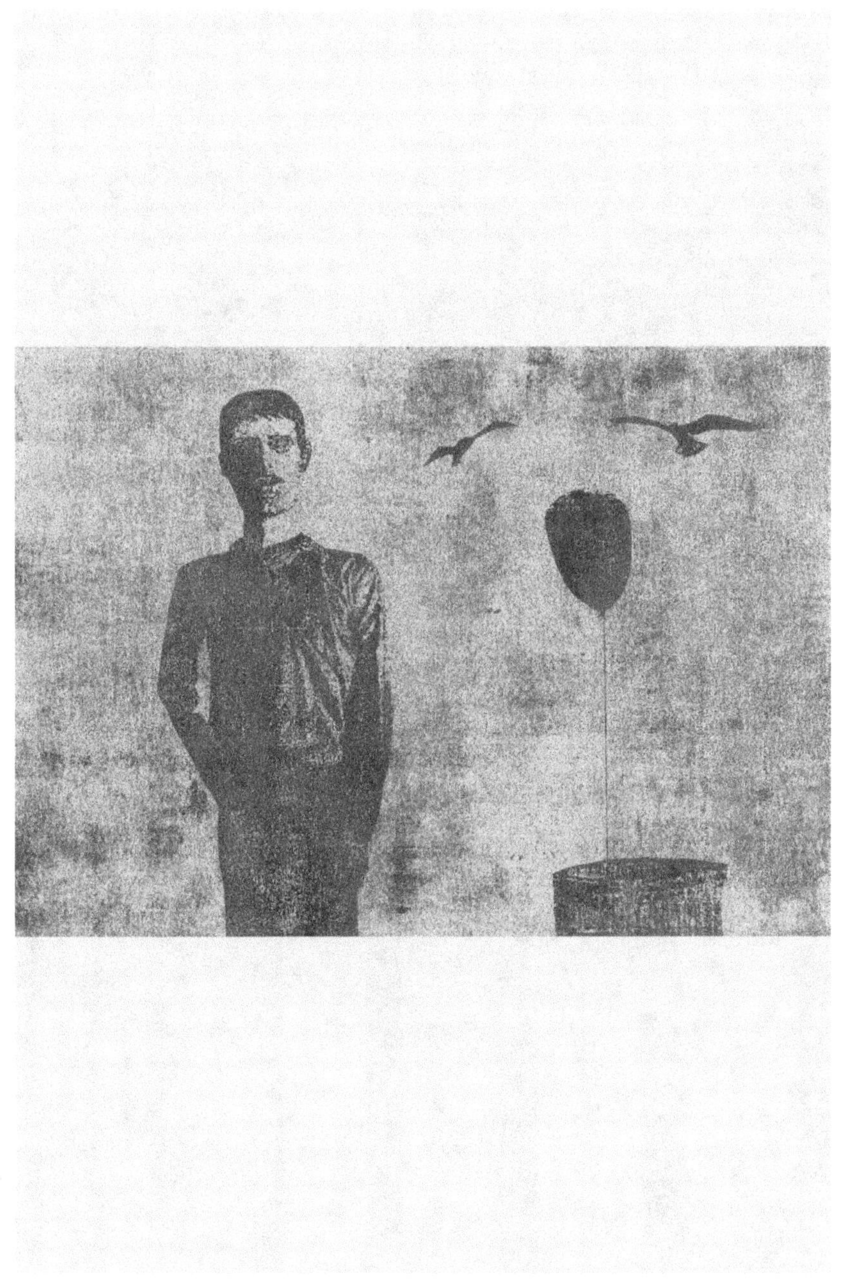

39. The Balloon Popped Away

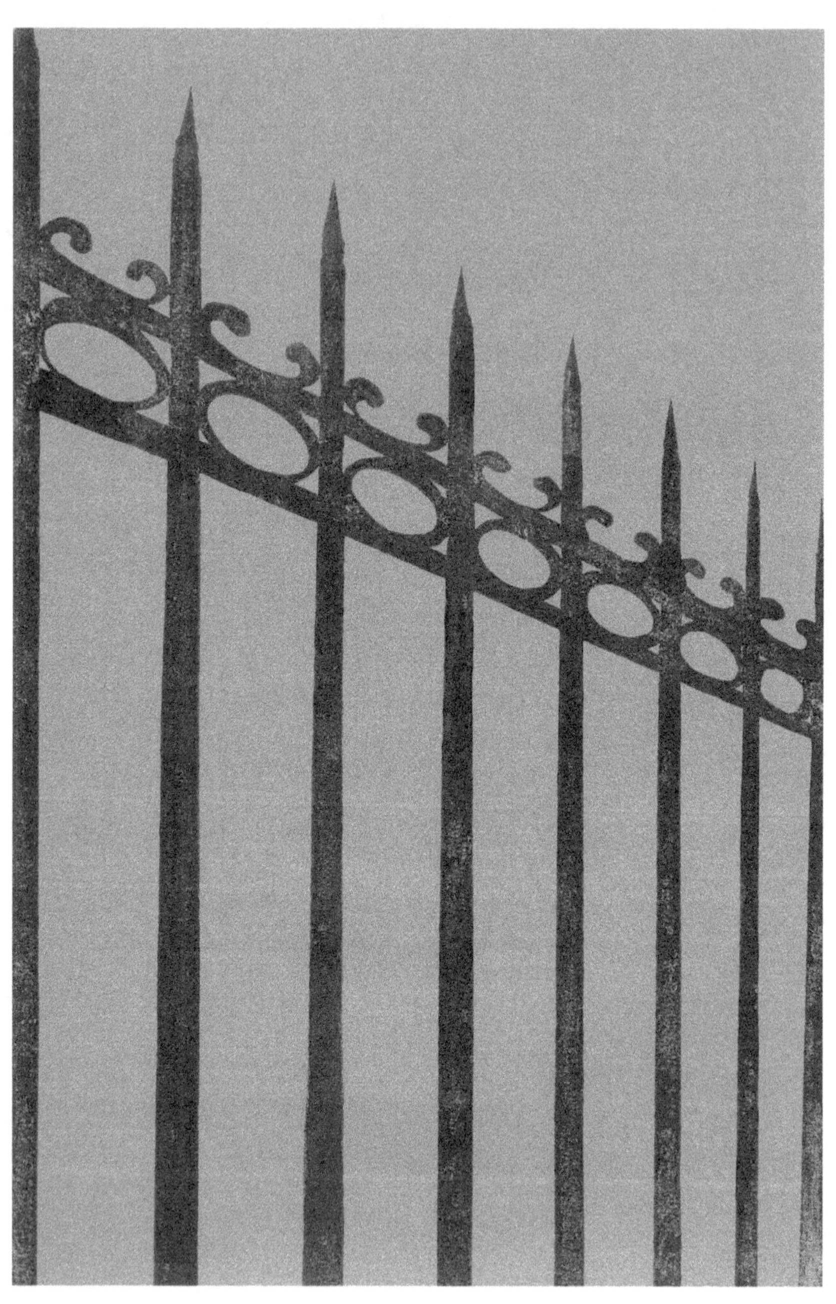

40. The Fence

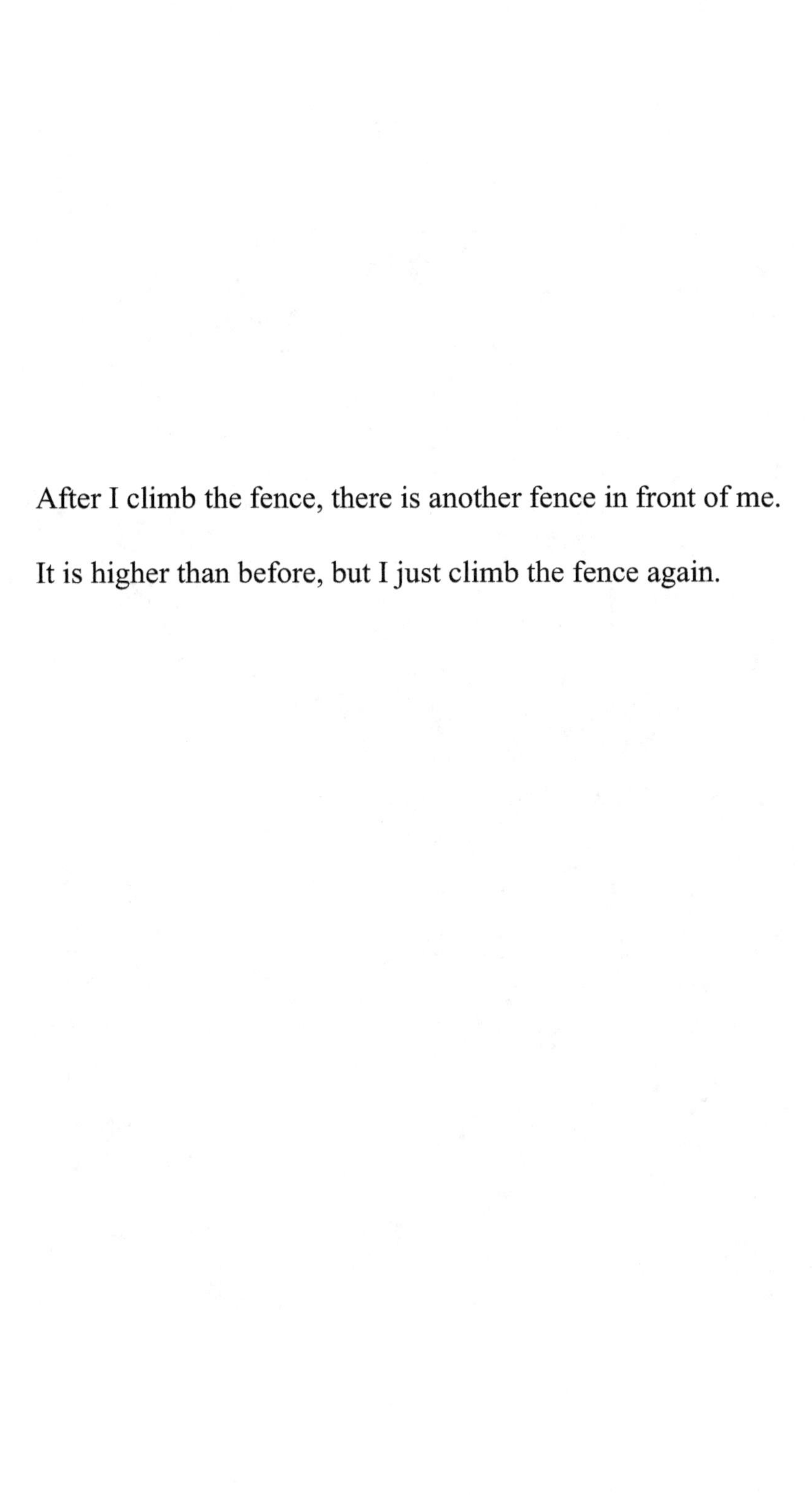

After I climb the fence, there is another fence in front of me.

It is higher than before, but I just climb the fence again.

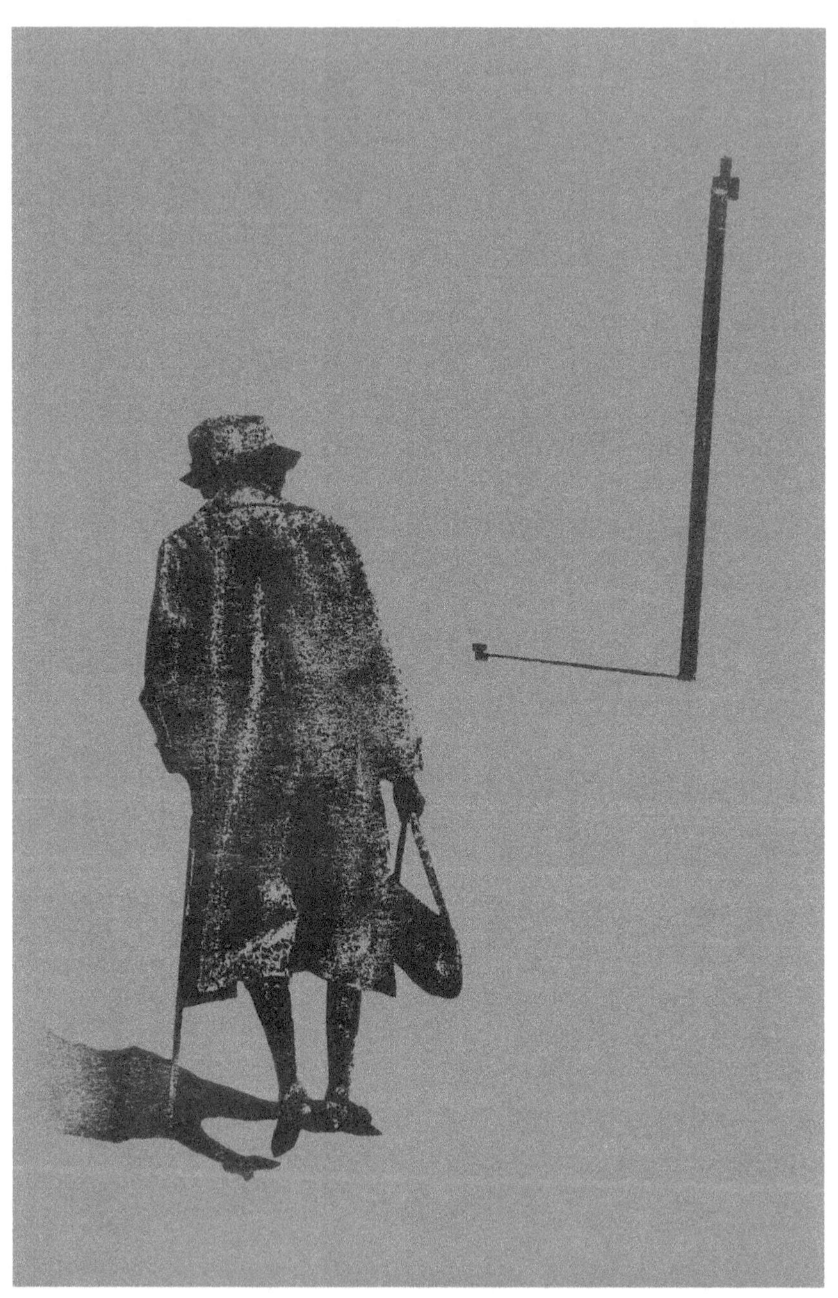

41. Someone's Grandmother

42. Nonfiction

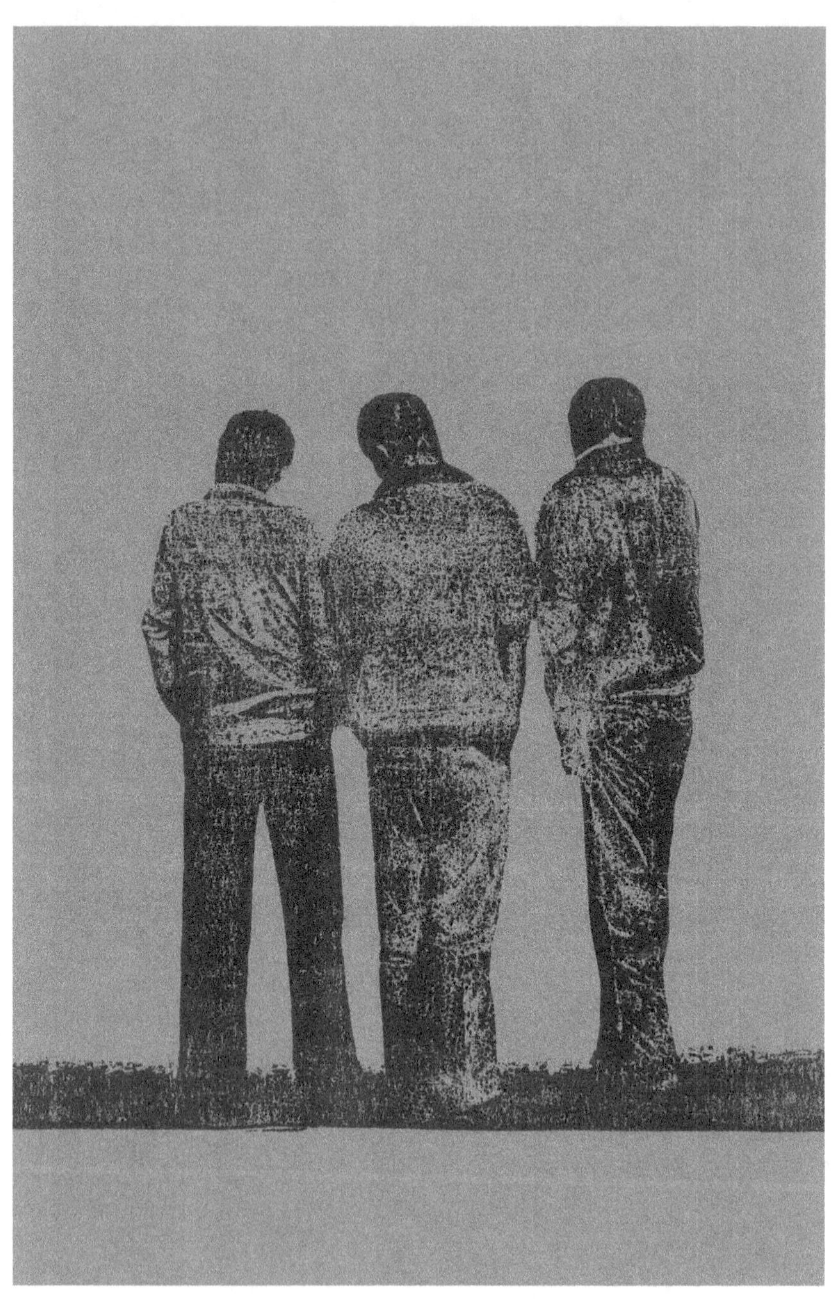

43. Stylish Kids

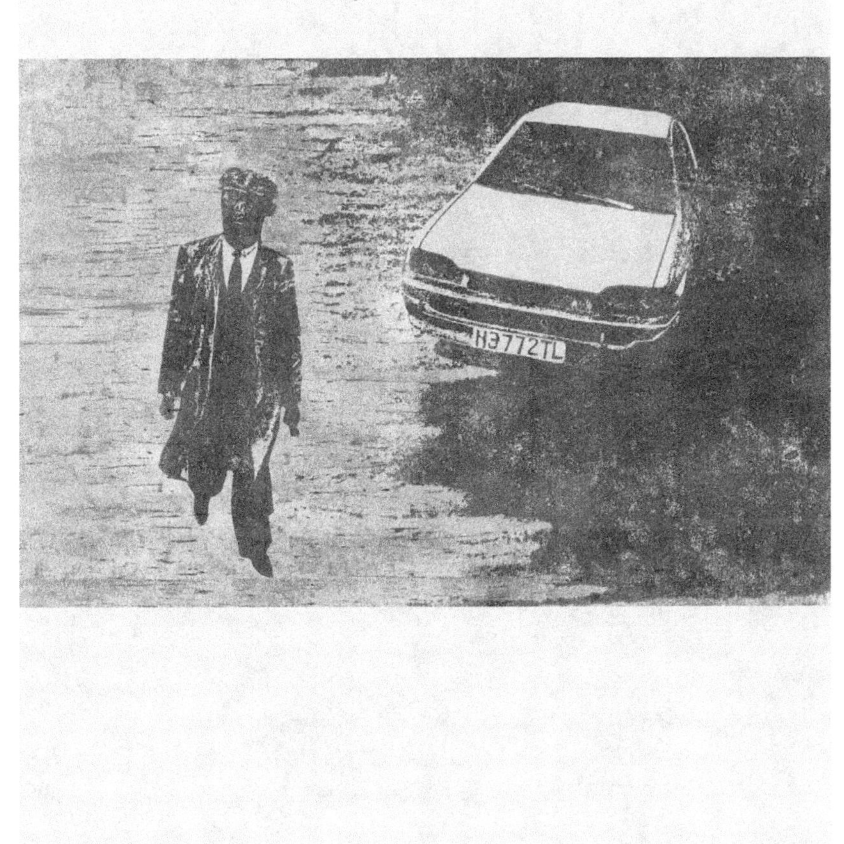

44. Disused Car

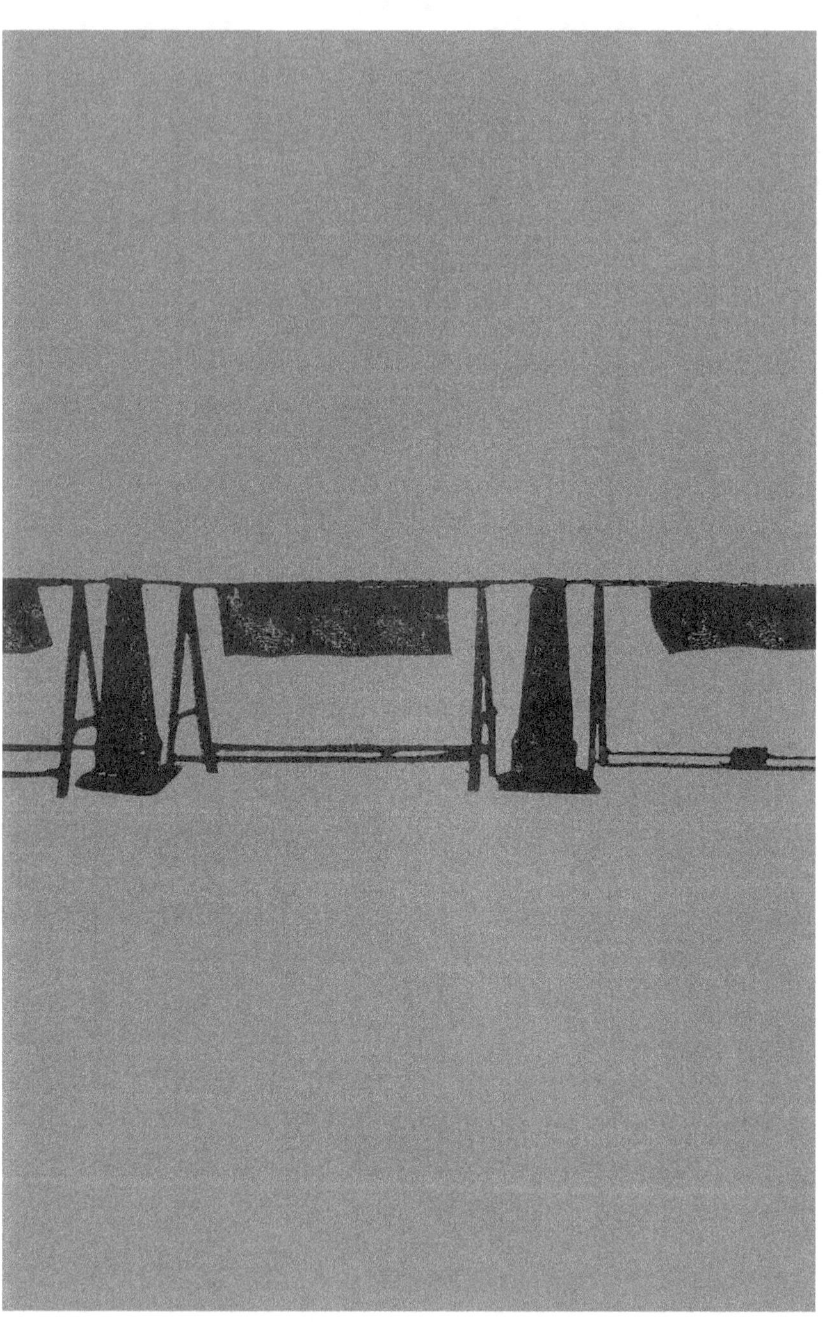

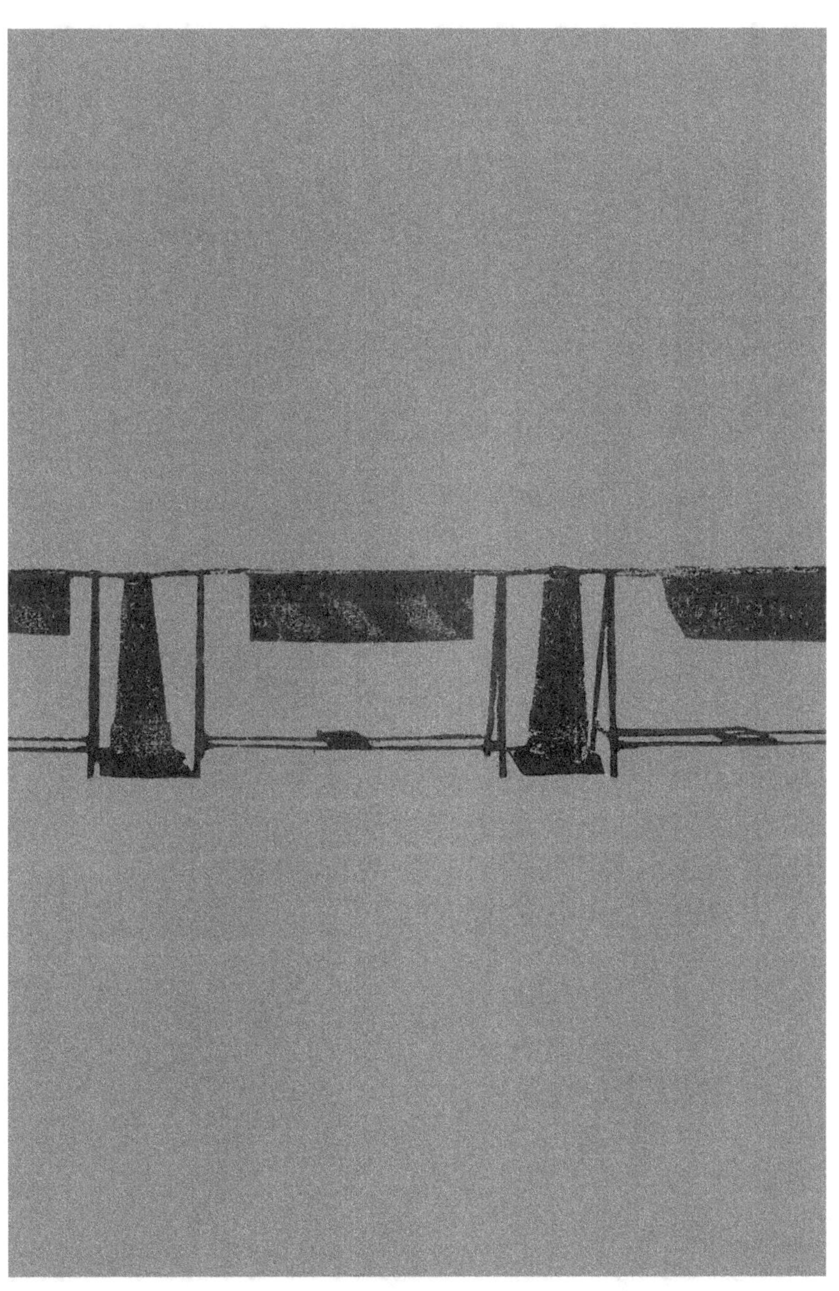

45. No Trespassing

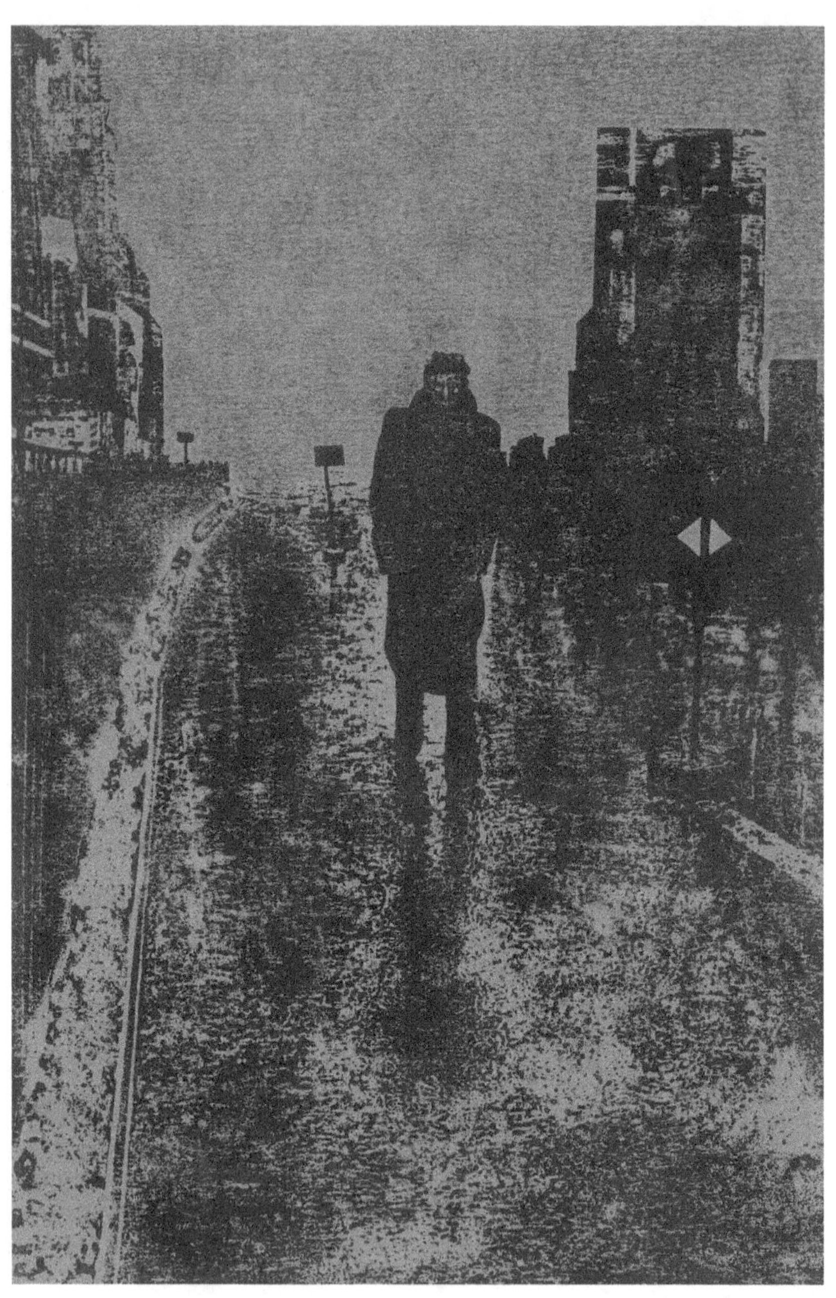

46. Jimmy

I like James Dean. I am 24 years old now, and he was same age as me when he passed away. It's a shame that we lost him but we should appreciate that we still can see him in his wonderful movies.

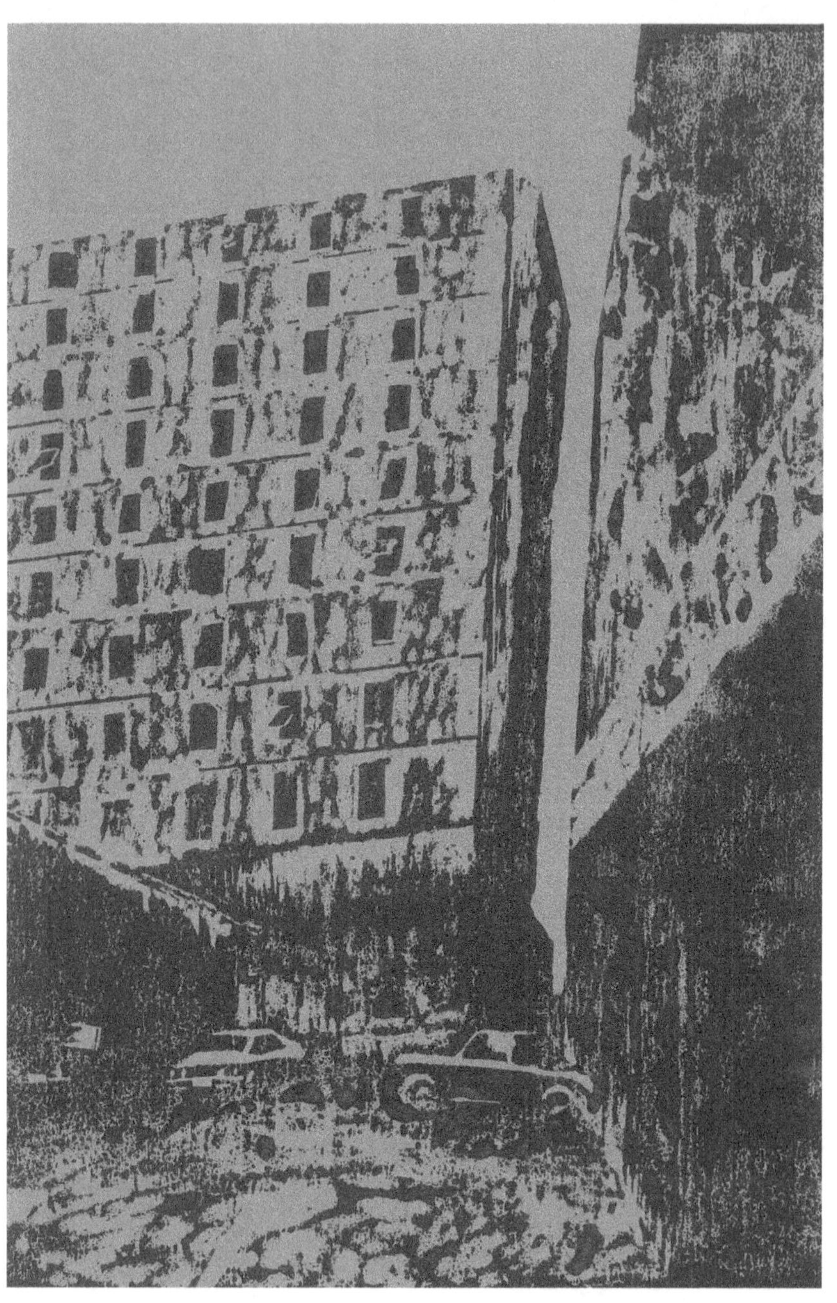

47. Ruins

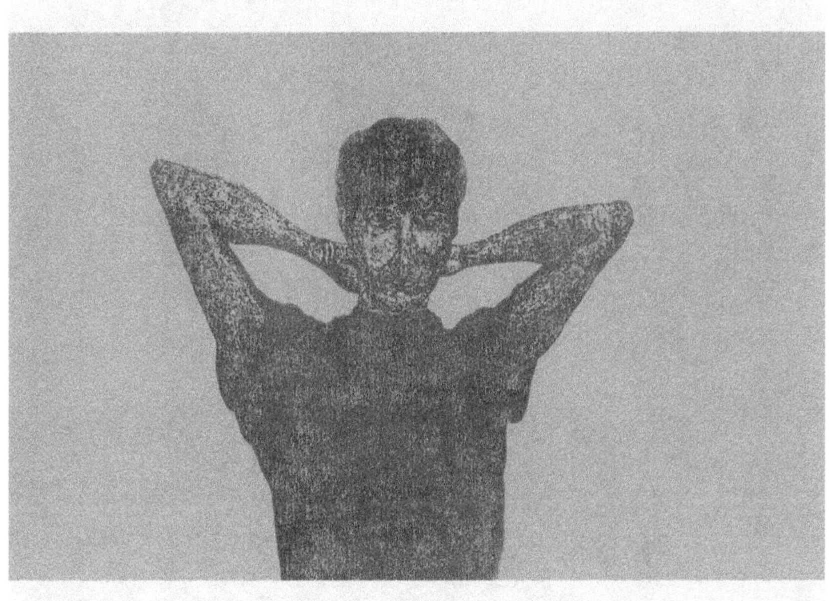

48. Nothing To Do

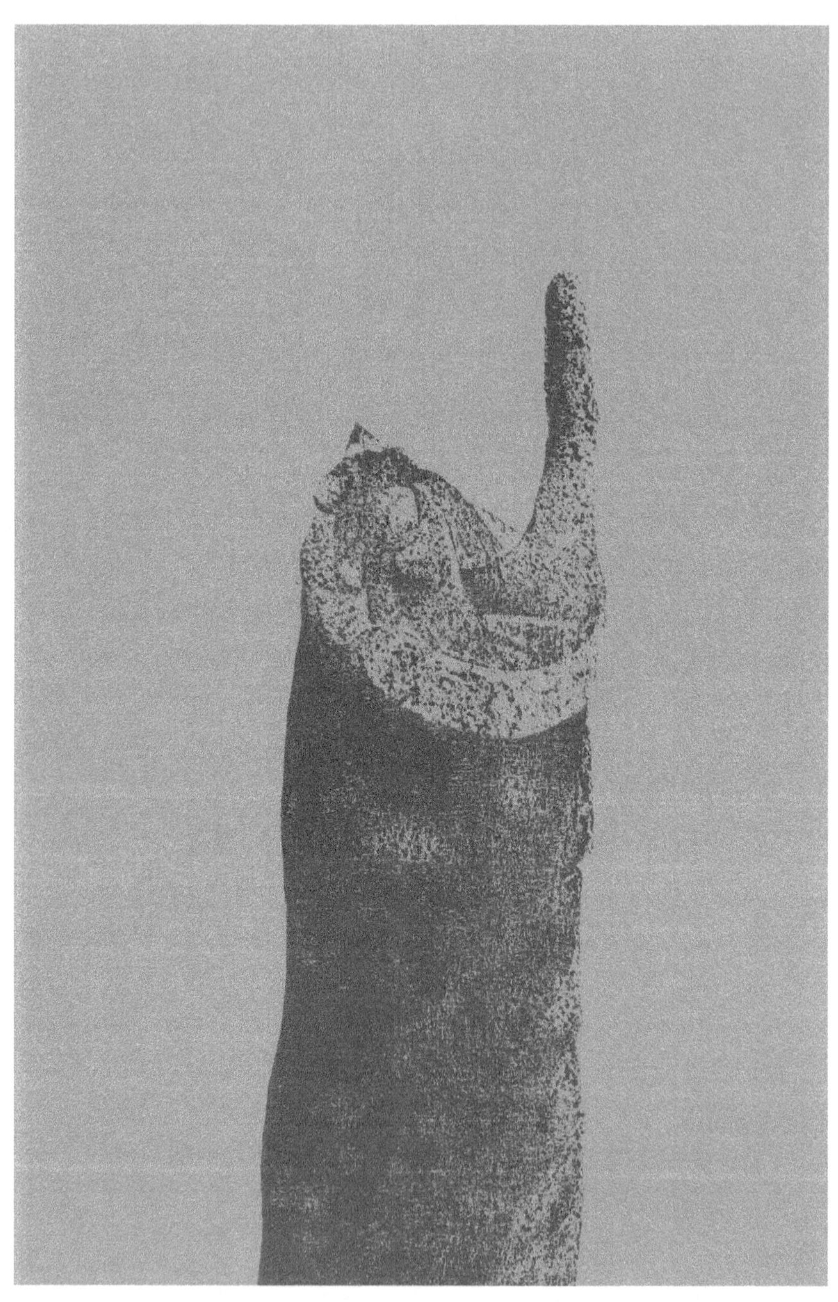

49. Communist's Finger

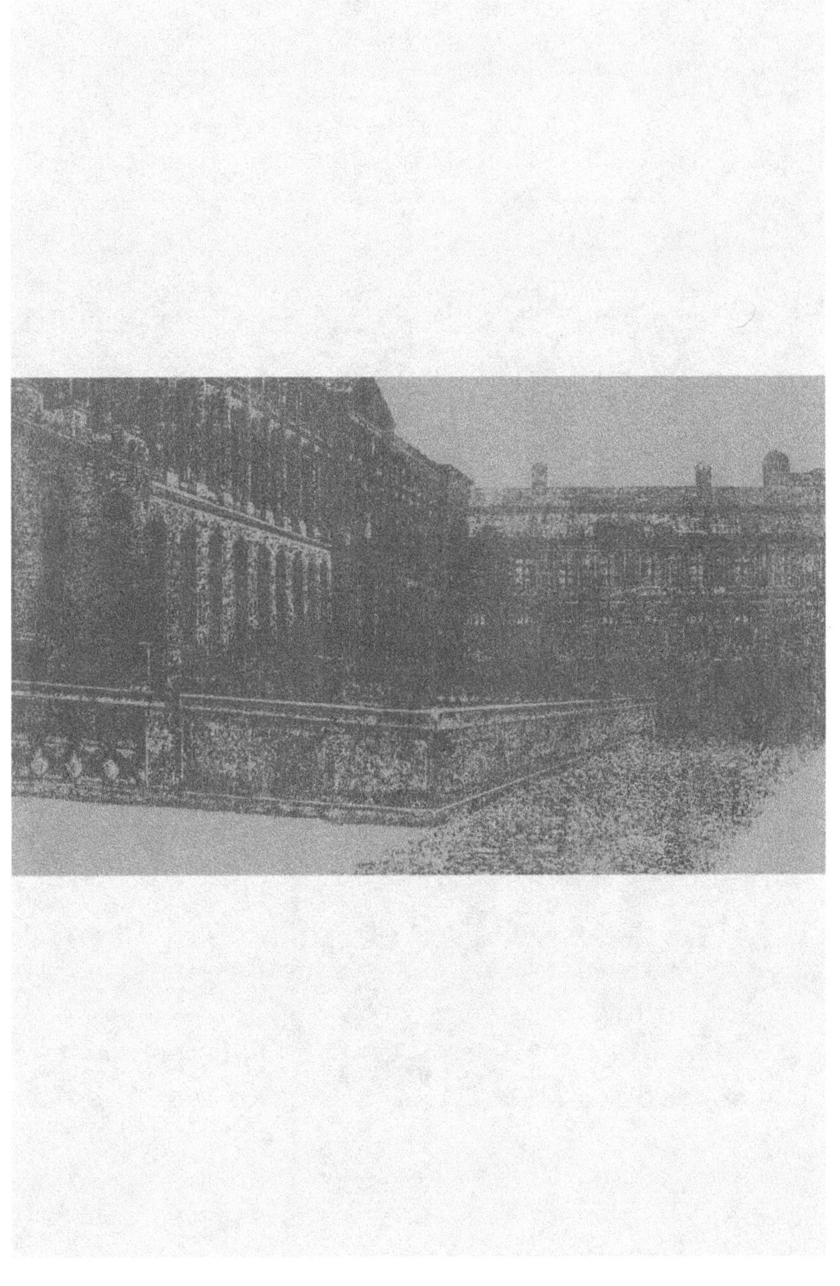

50. A Tourist Attraction

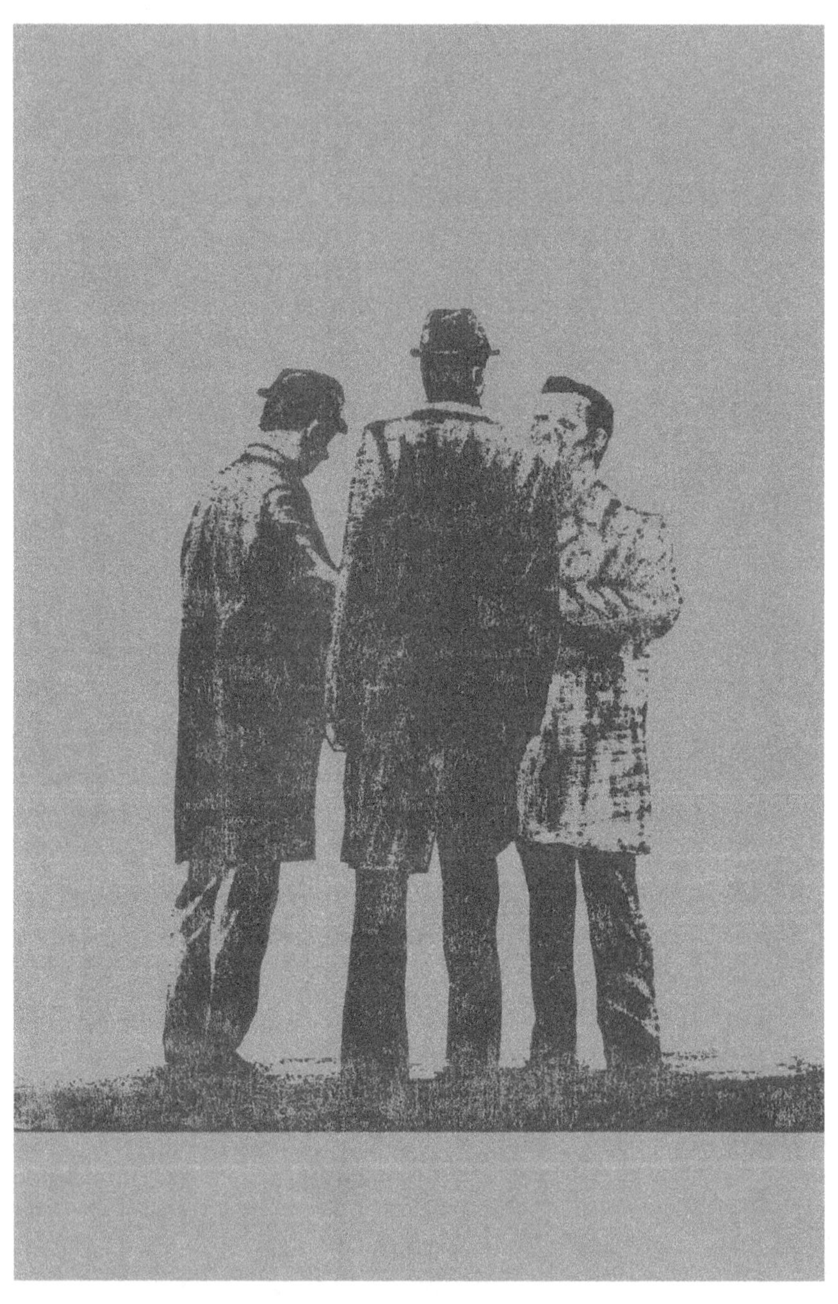

51. Did You See Those Stylish Kids

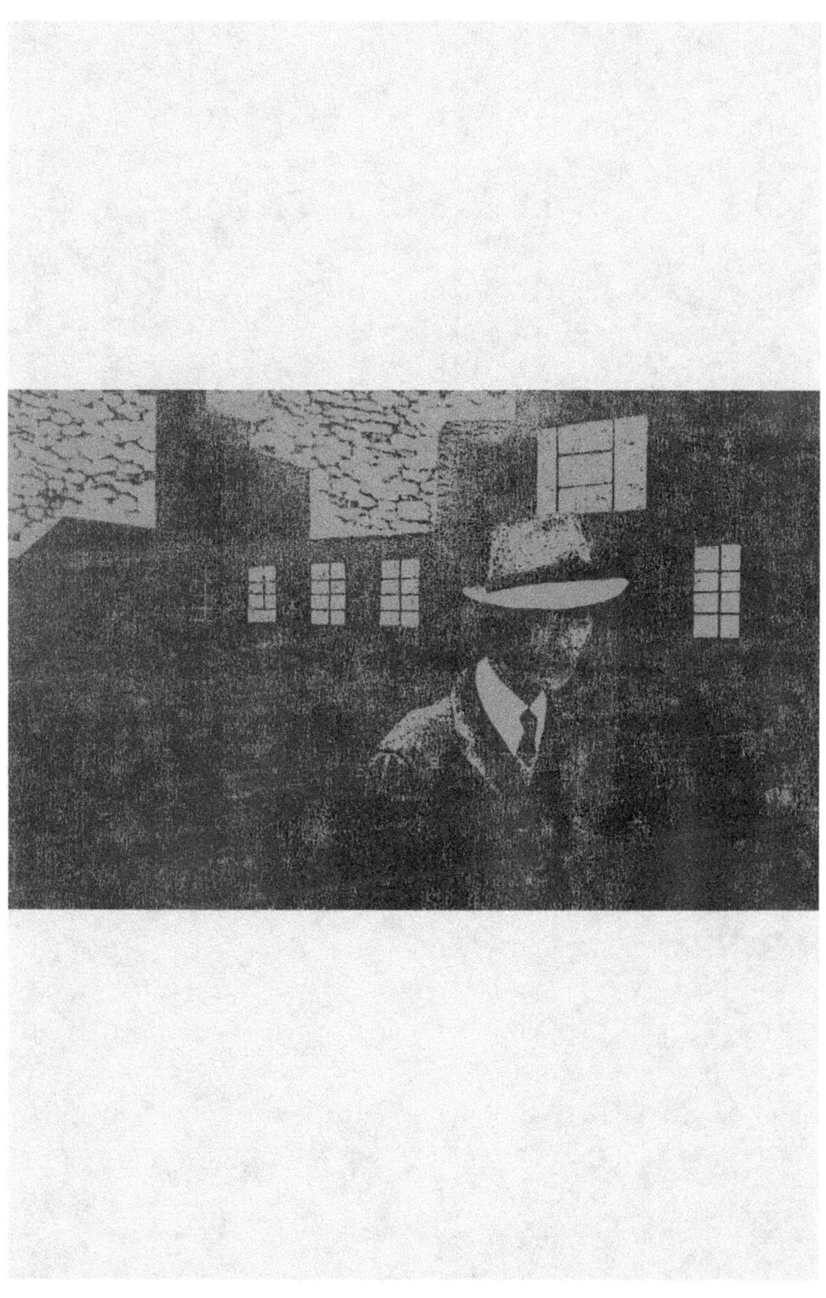

52. Wandering The Midnight

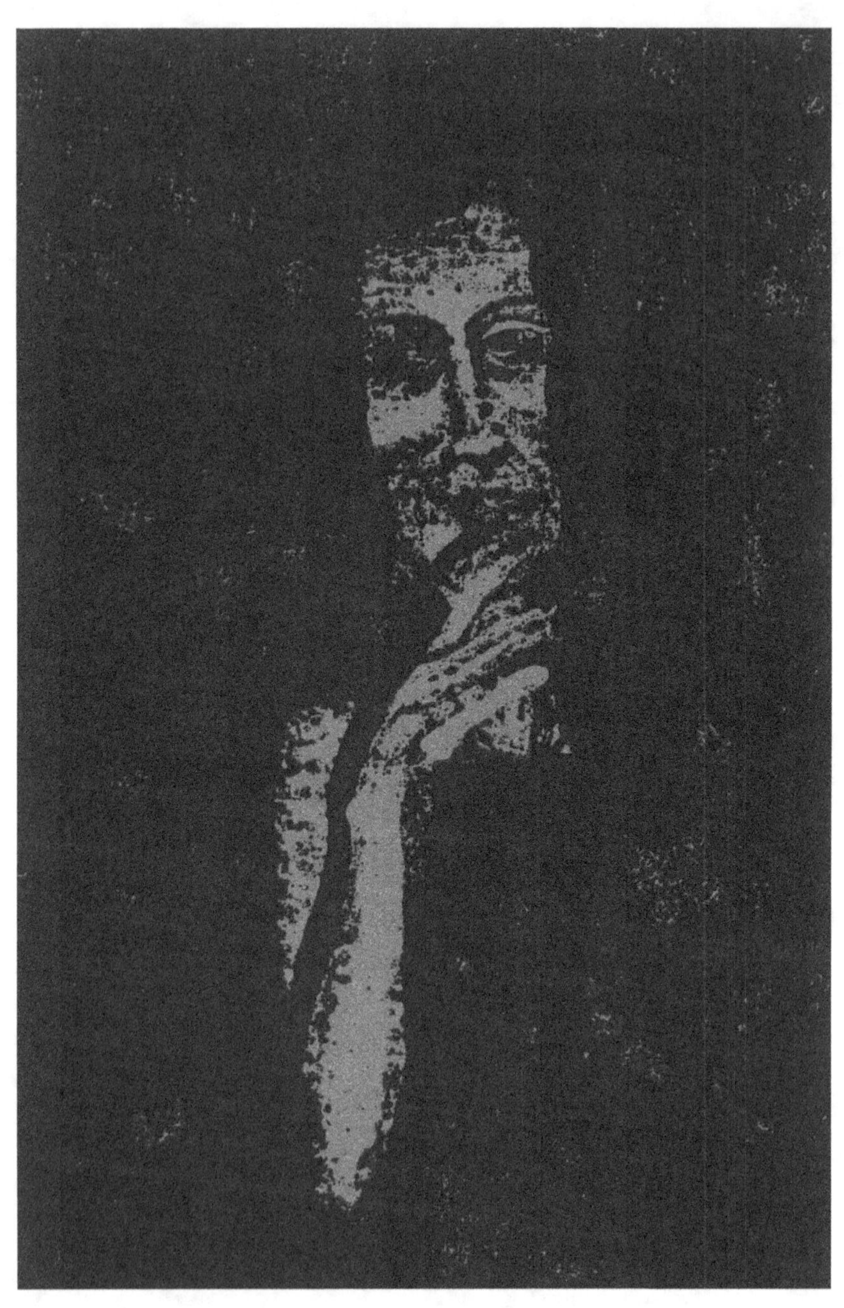

53. Late At Night

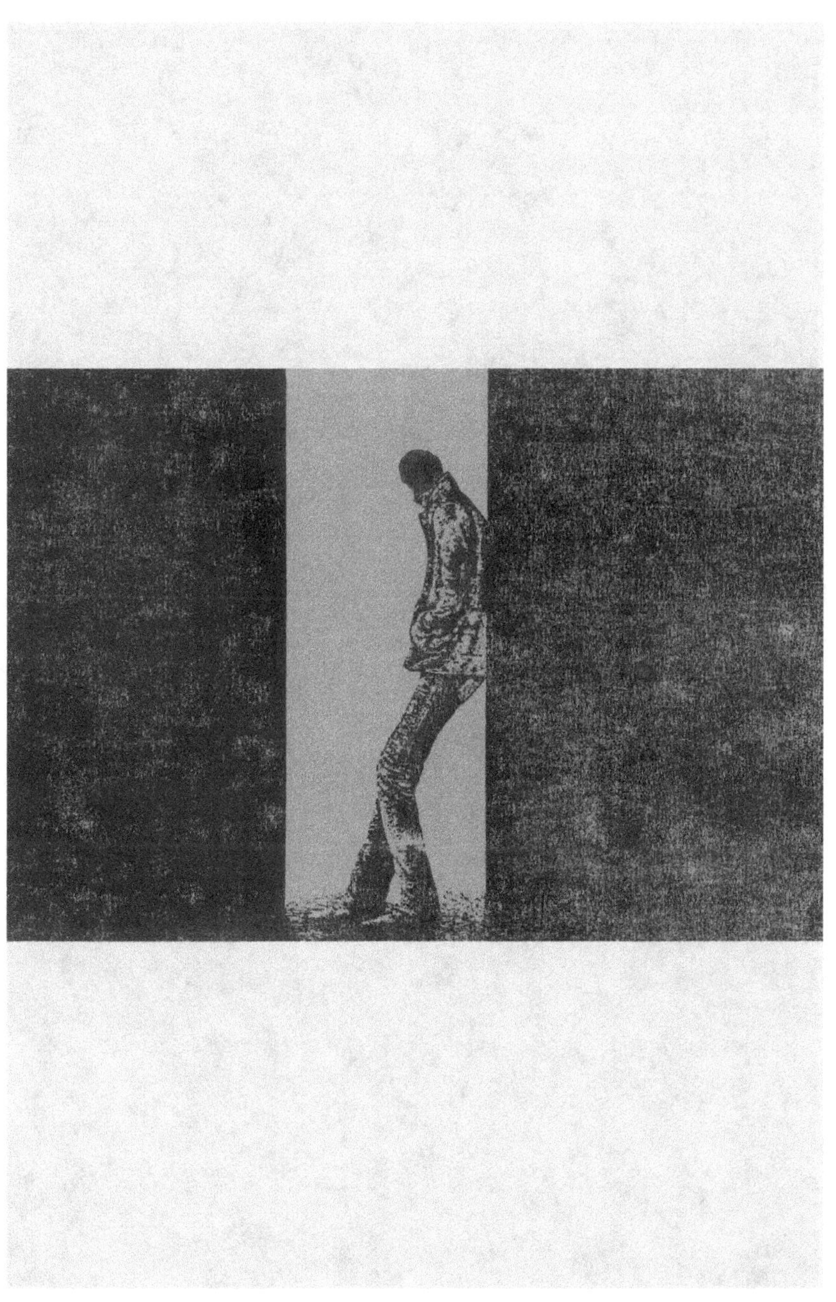

54. My Funny Christmas

55. On The Wall

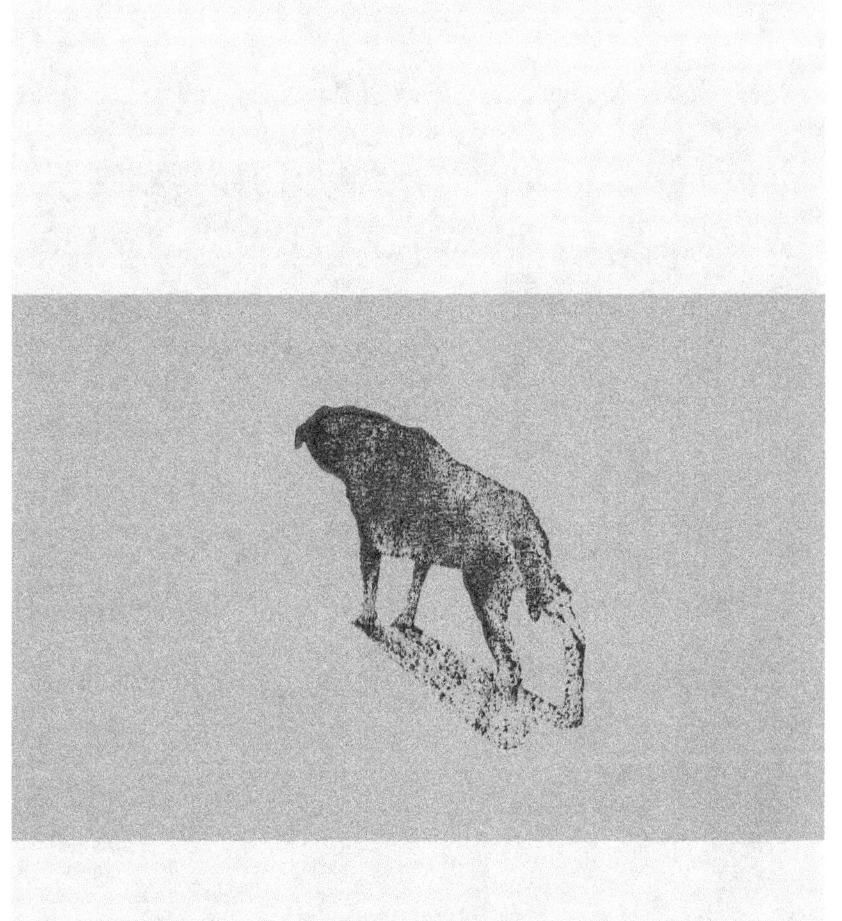

56. Shibaken

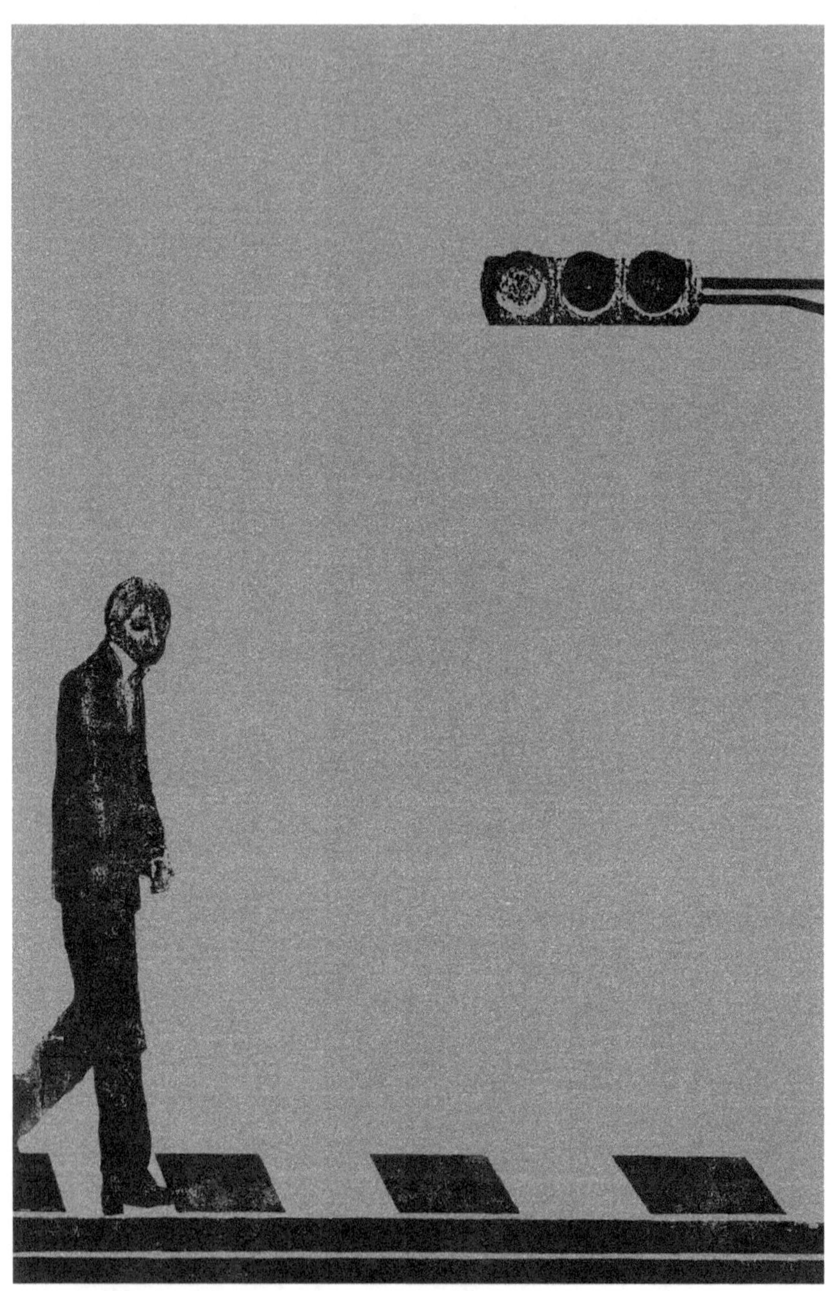

57. Gloomy Man

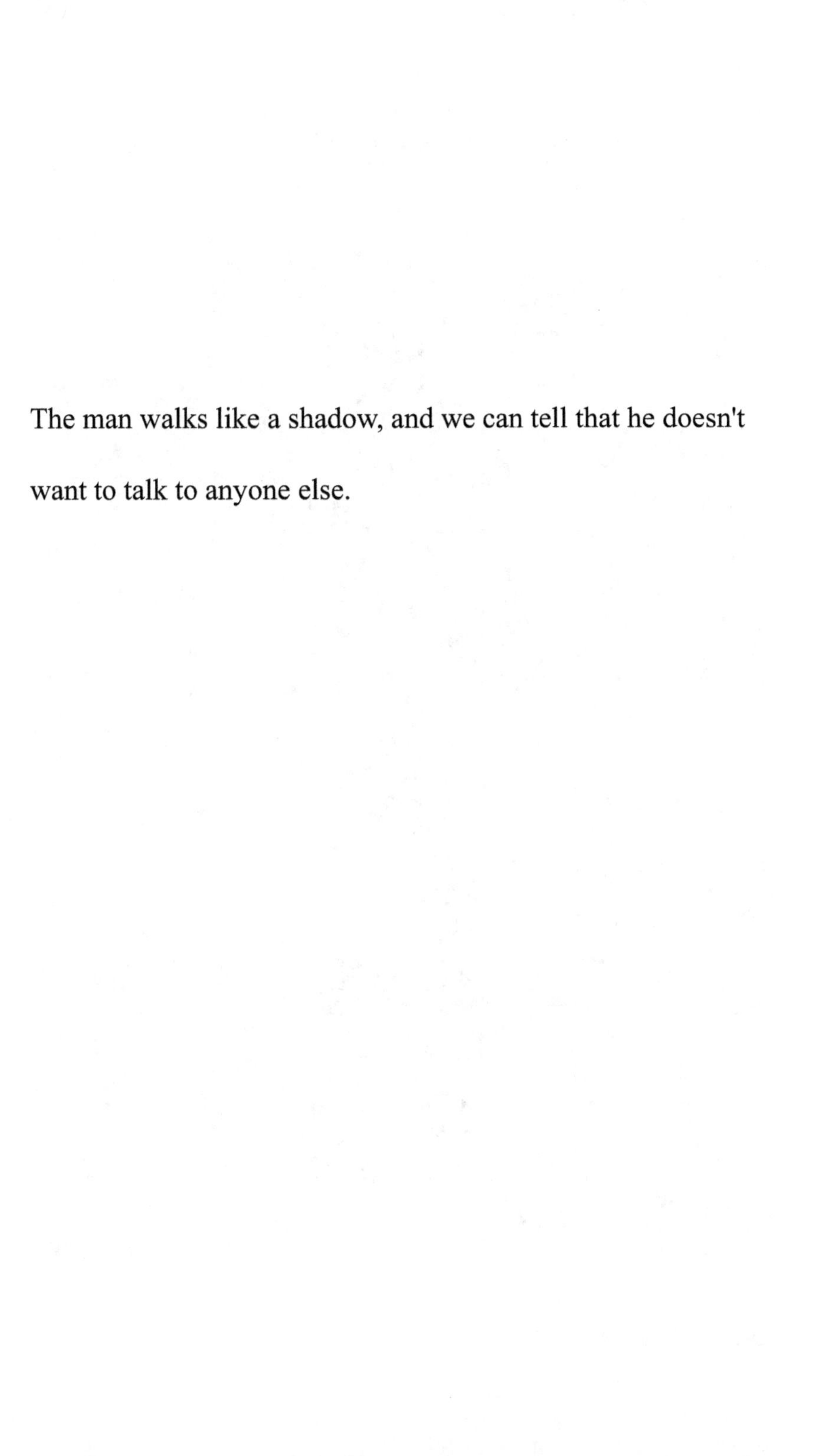

The man walks like a shadow, and we can tell that he doesn't want to talk to anyone else.

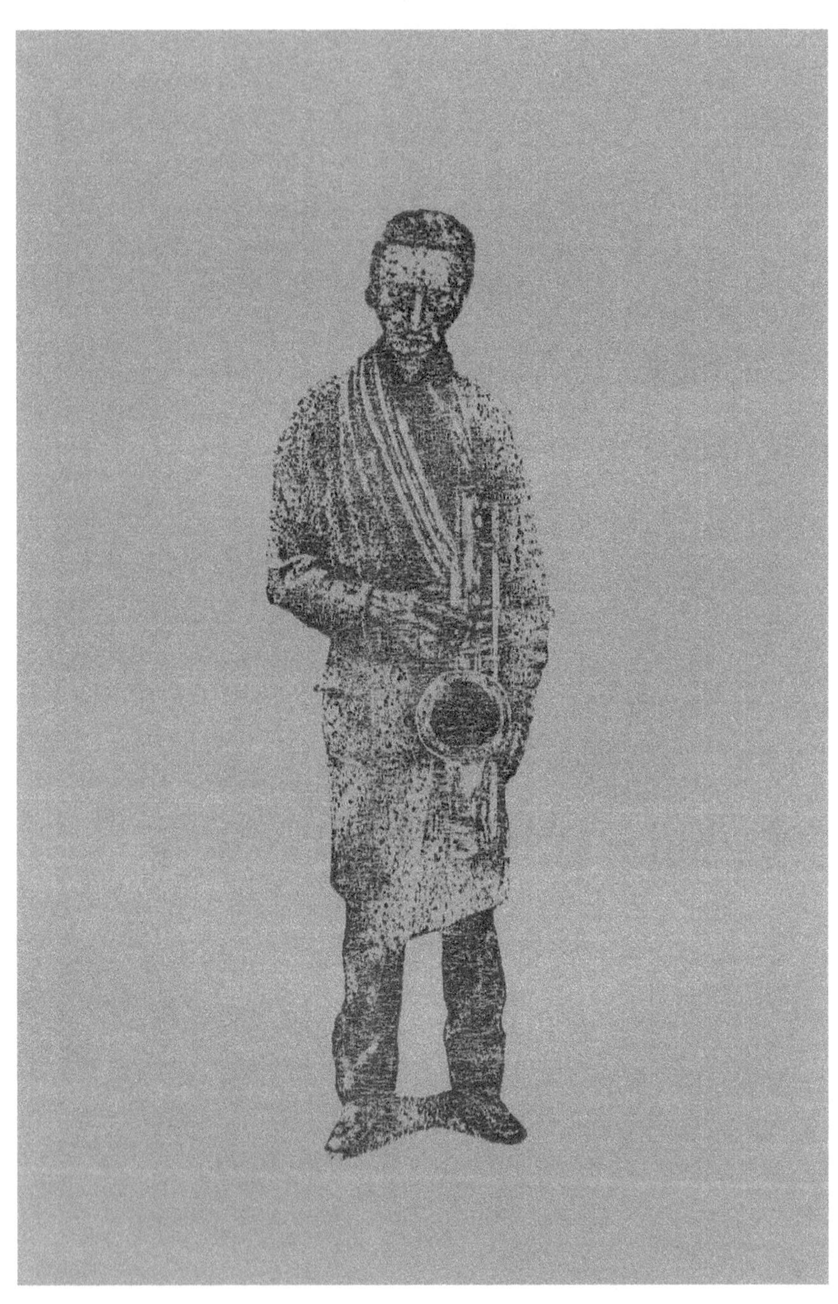

58. I Hate Jazz

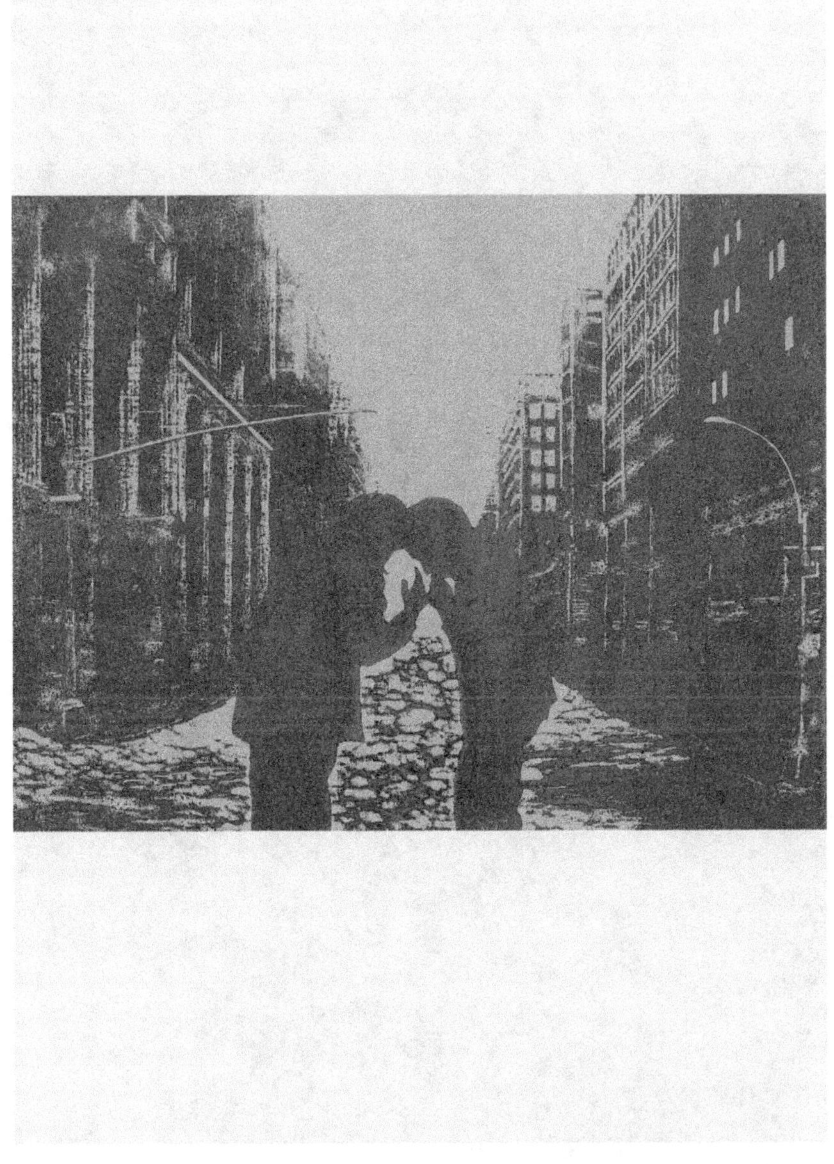

59. AM 6:00

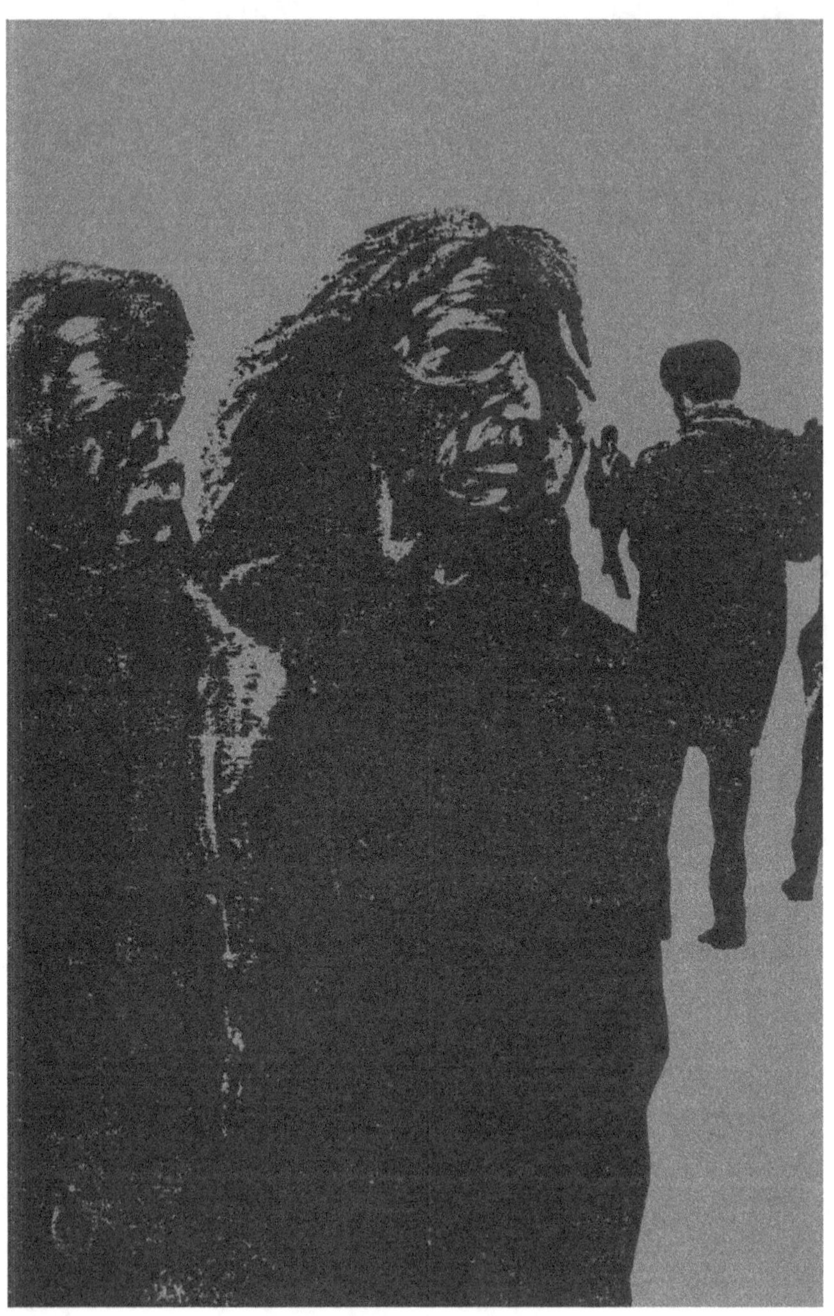

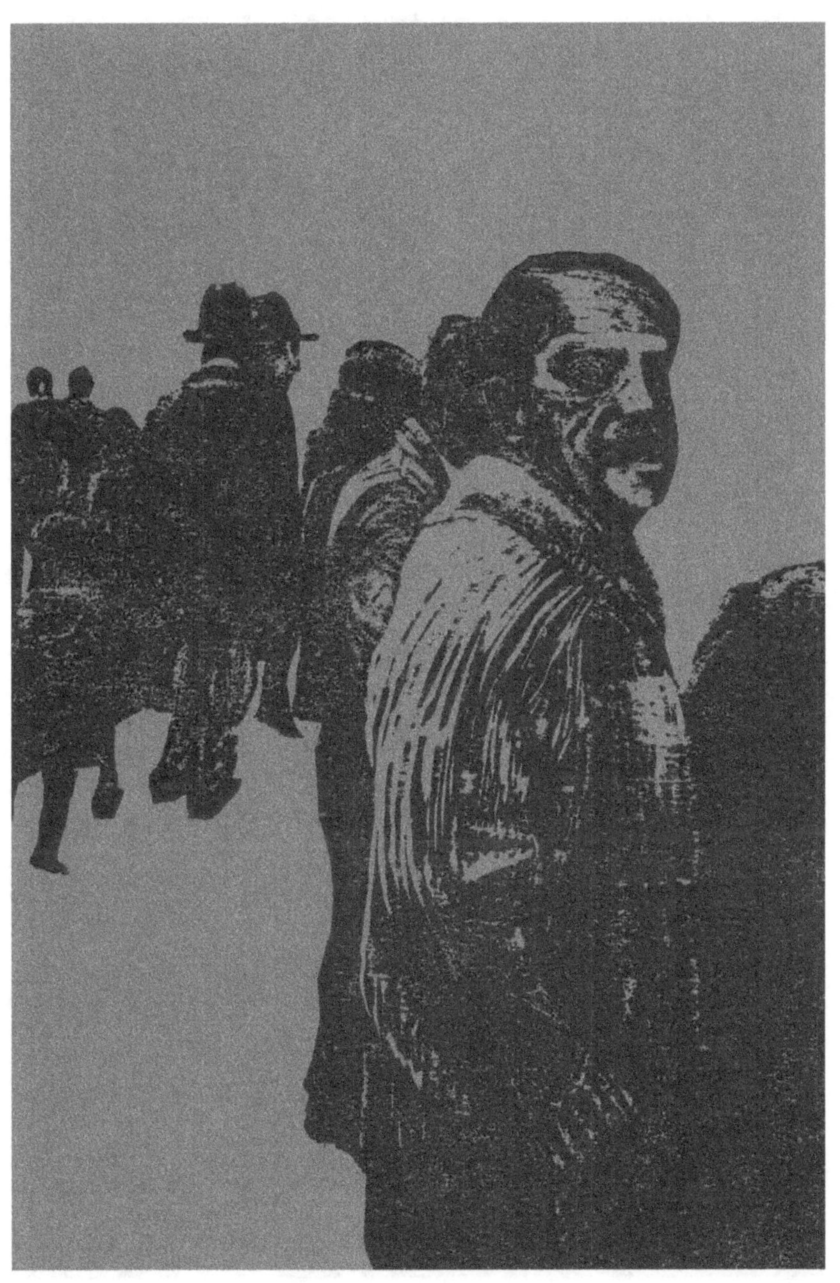

60. The Crowd

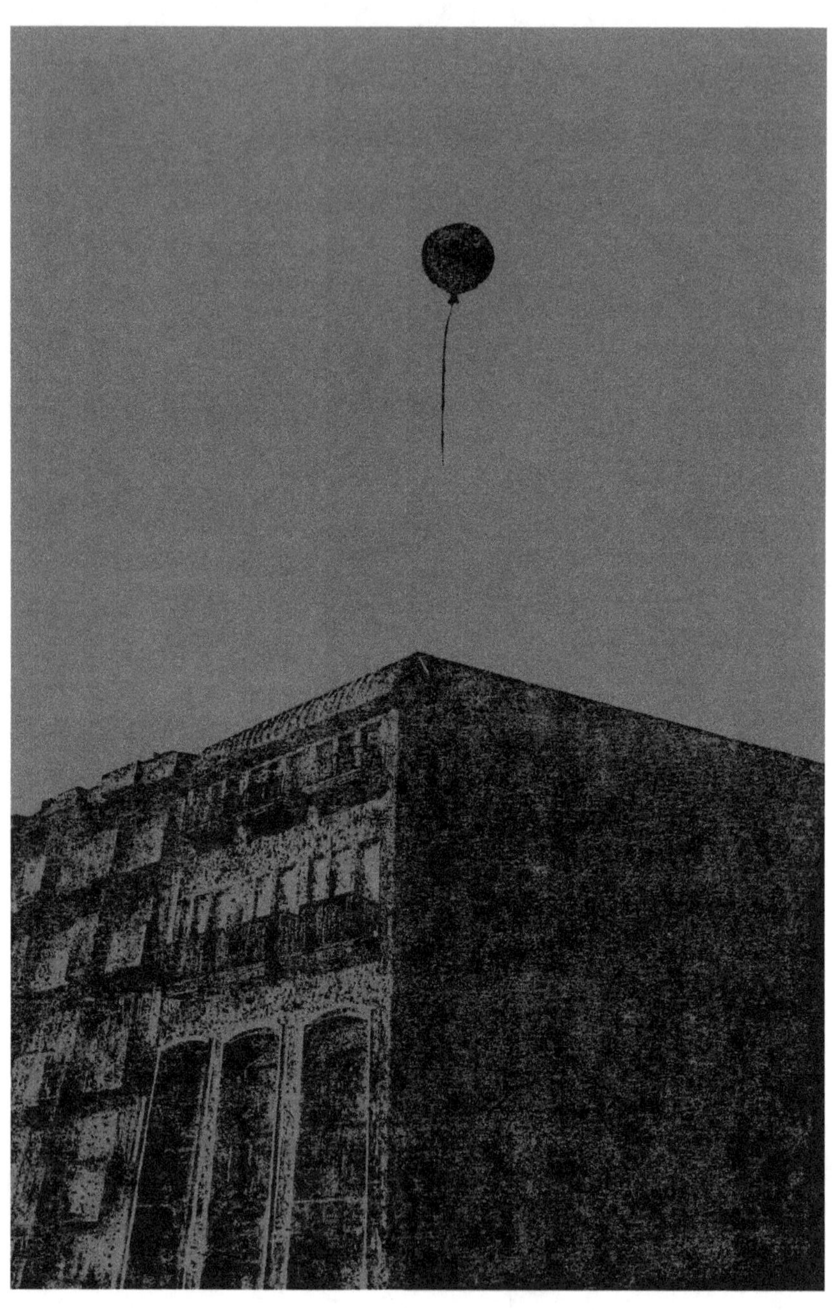

61. A Happy New Year

A man saw this engraving and said, "You expressed death on this work, right?" I didn't mean death but I don't care what people think of my works because I have no thought with my artworks.

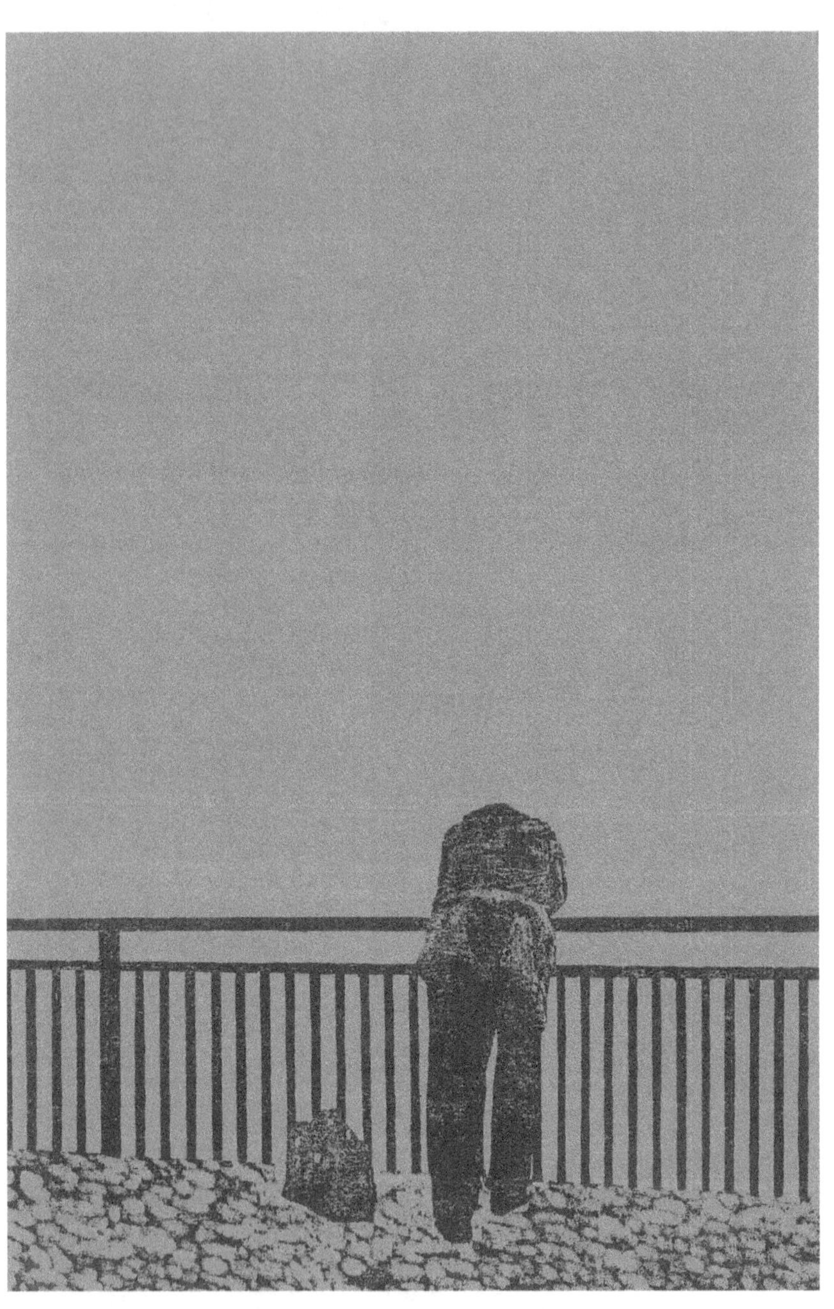

62. Running Away

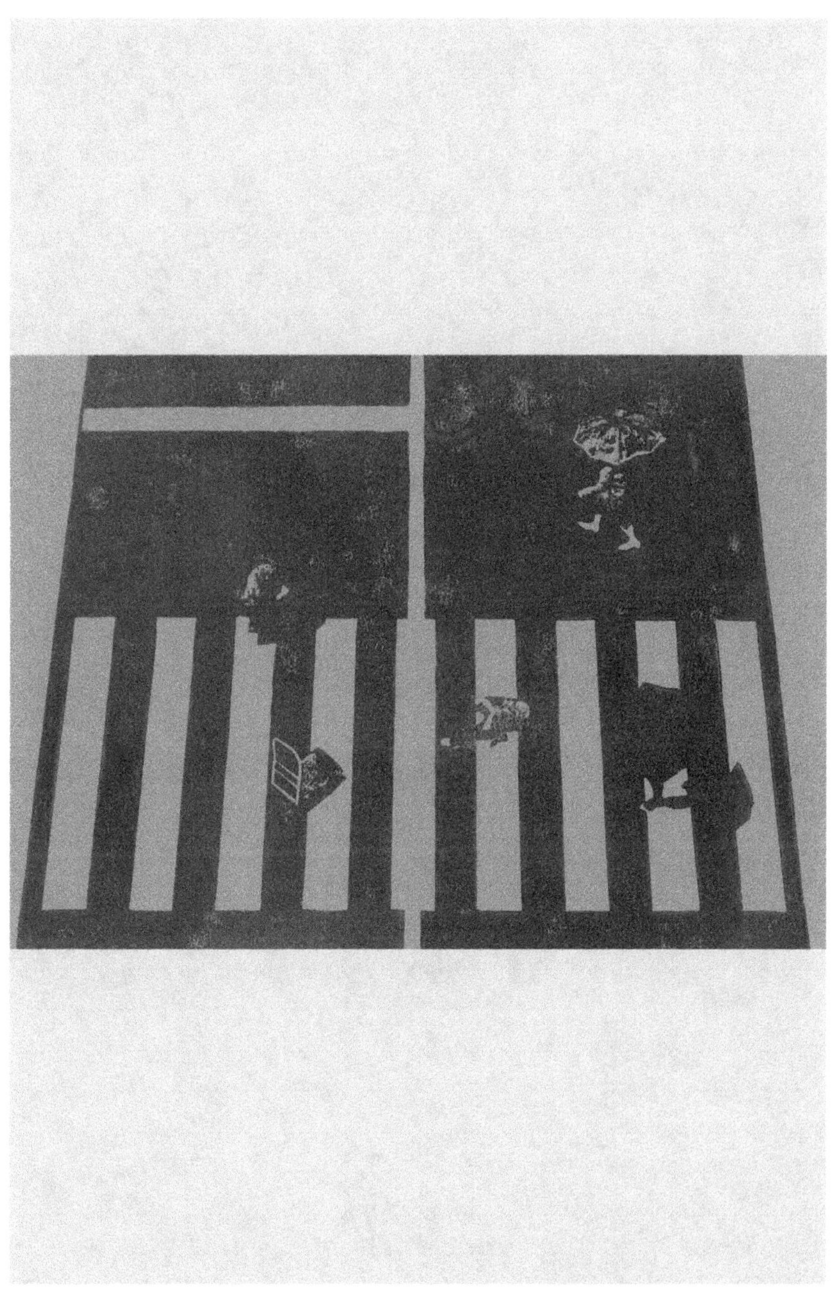

63. Zebra Crossing

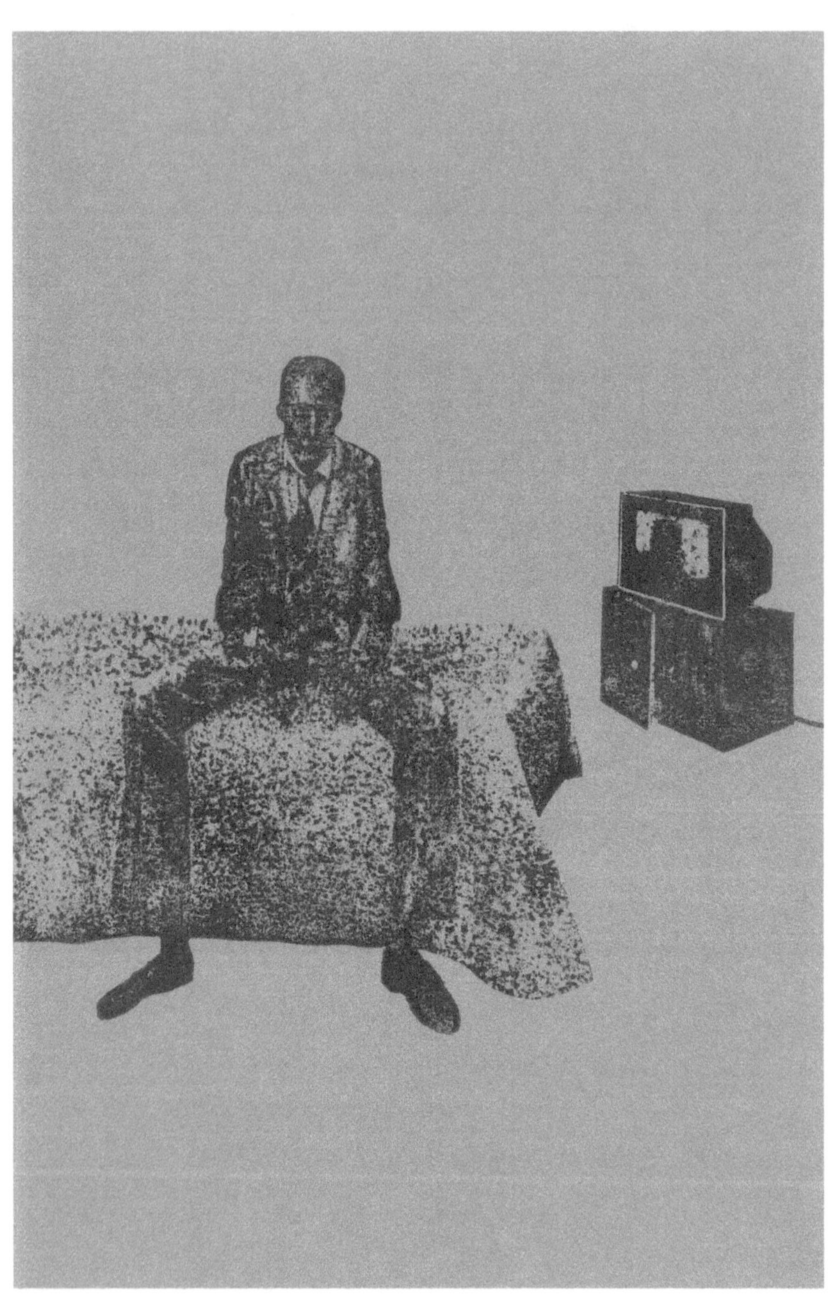

64. Room 304

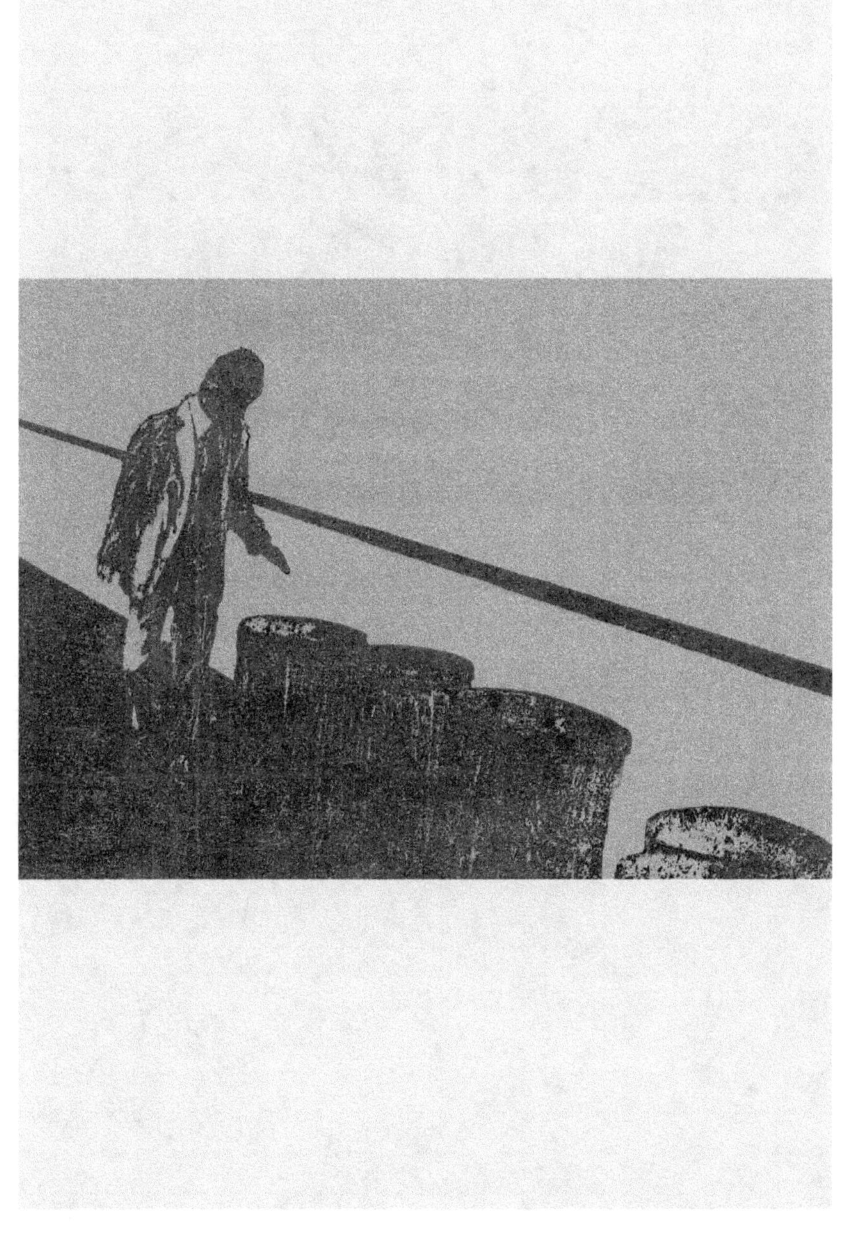

65. Looking For My Dinner

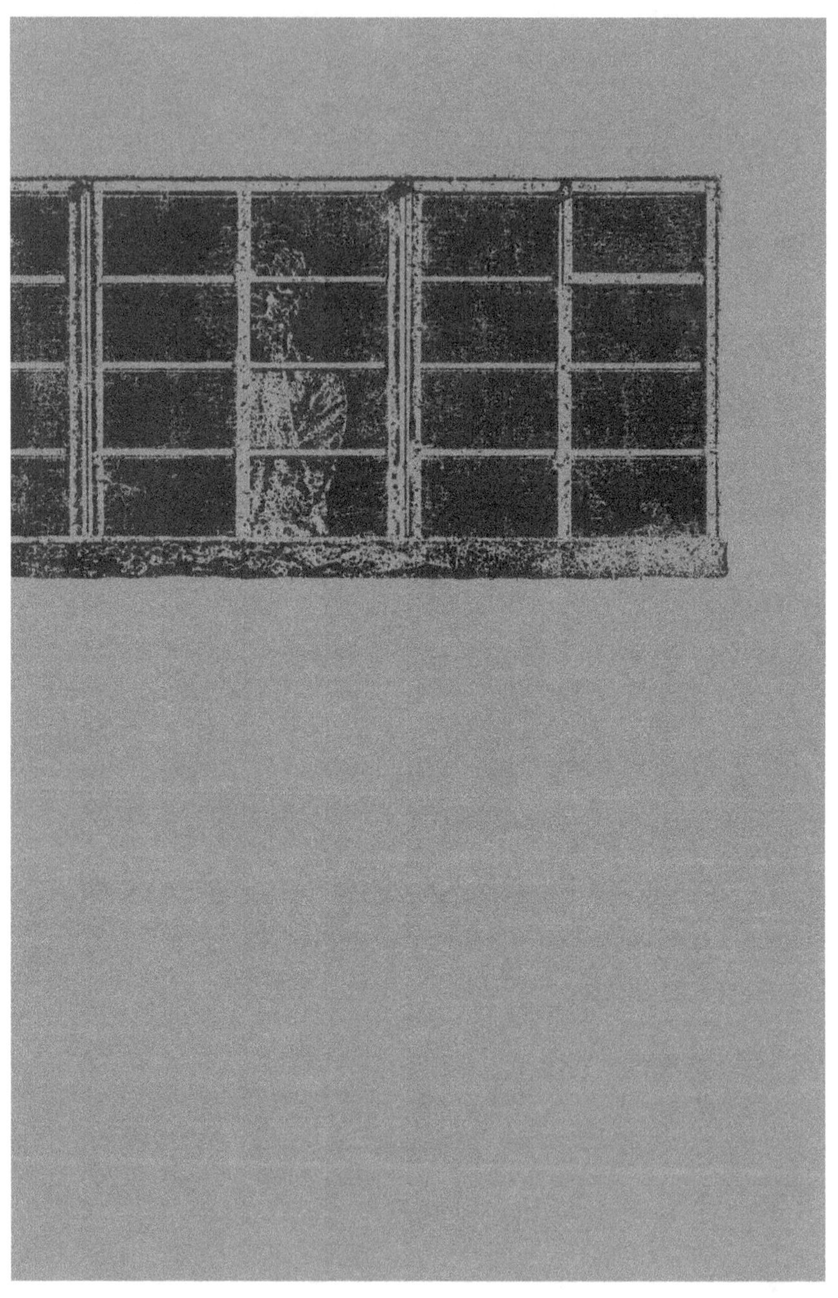

66. Narcissist

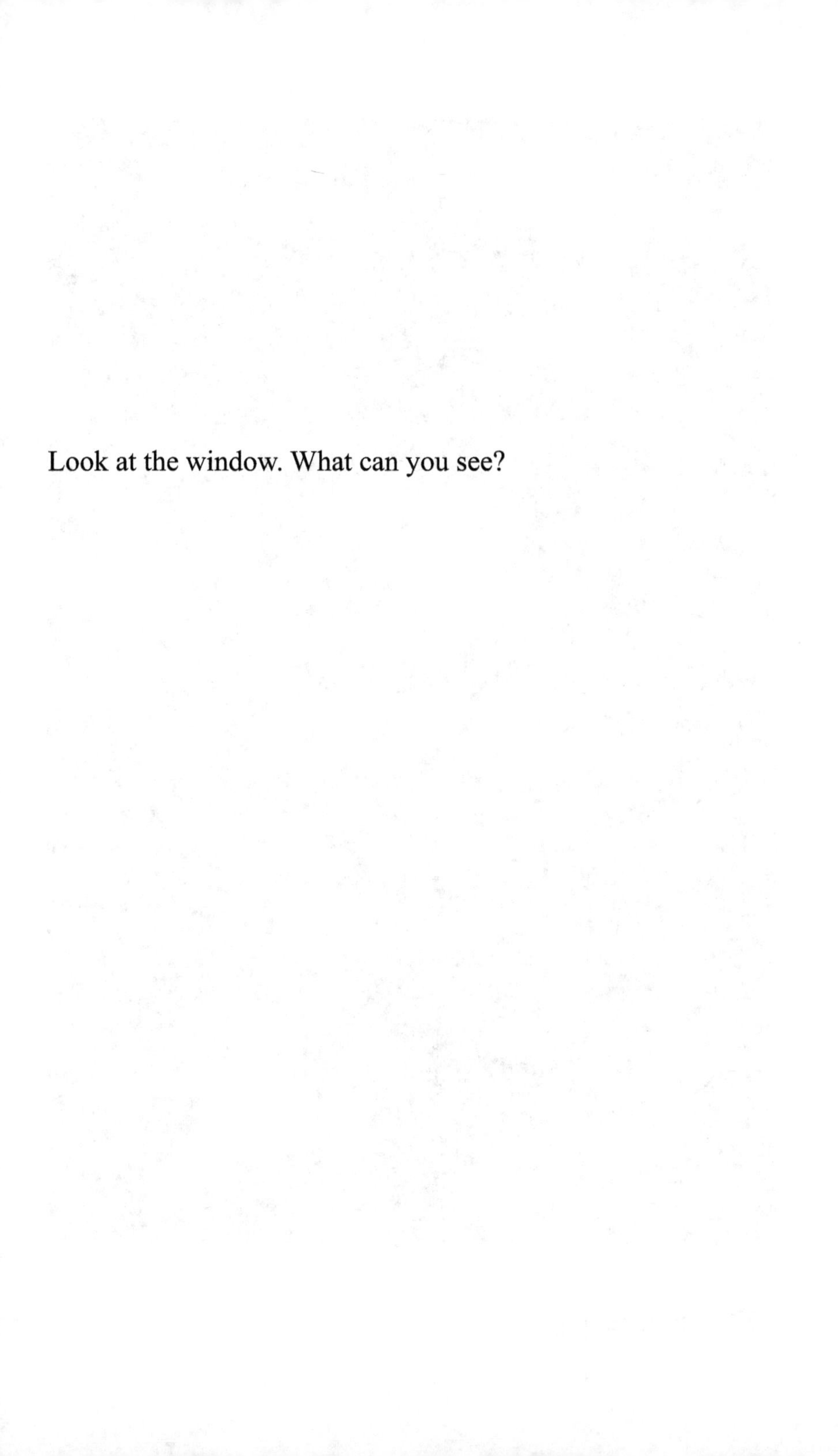

Look at the window. What can you see?

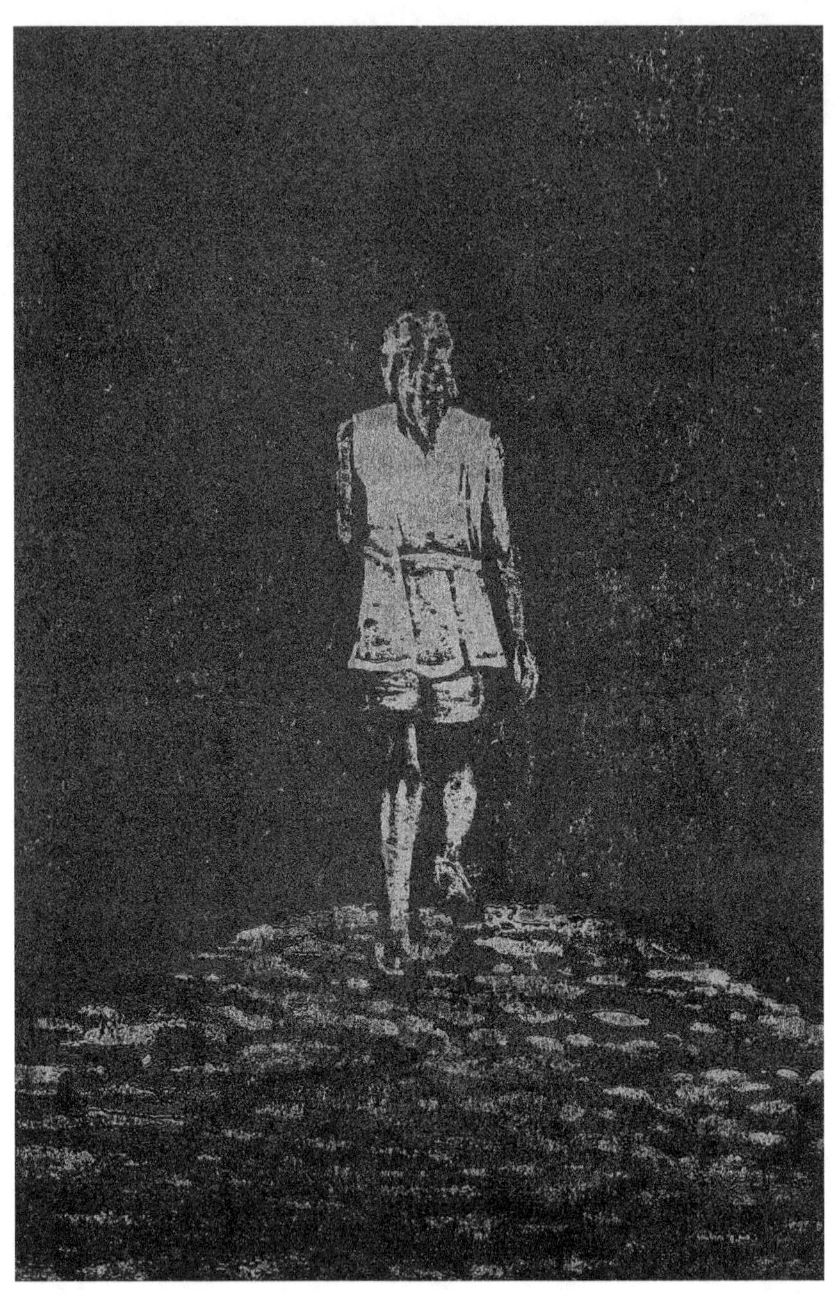

67. Fancy Girl

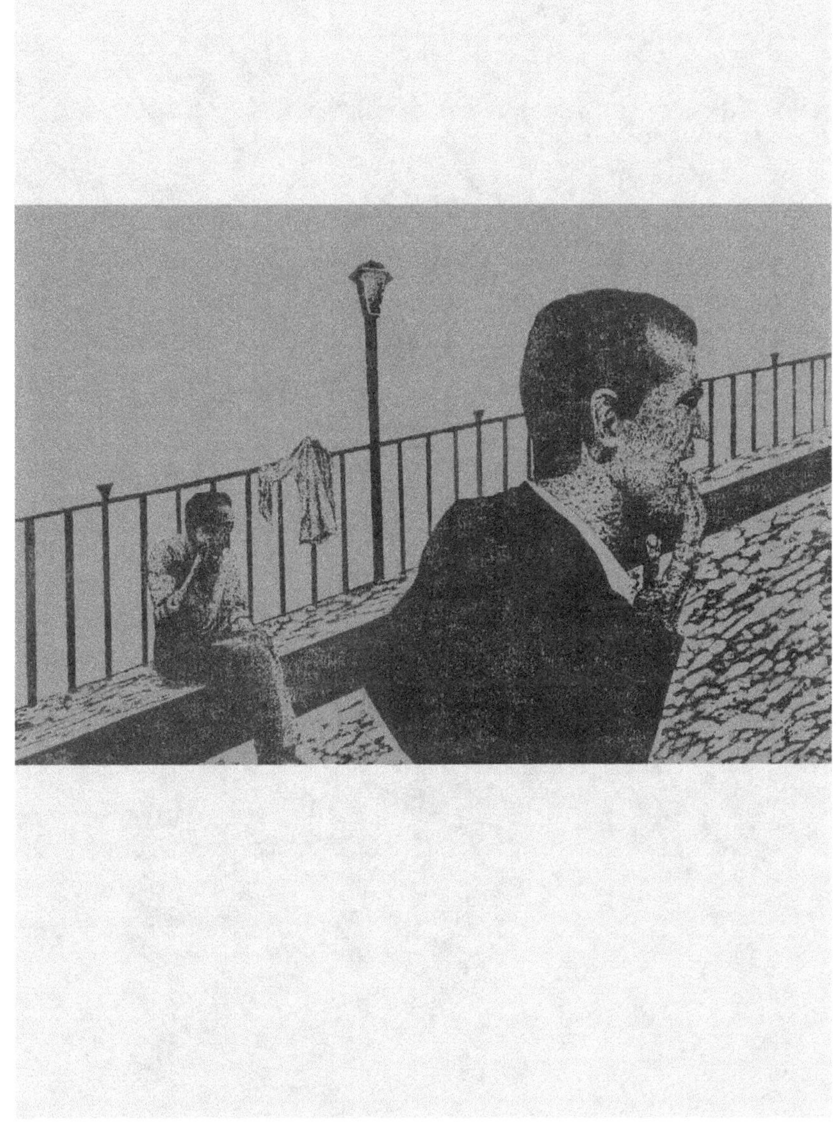

68. Gossip

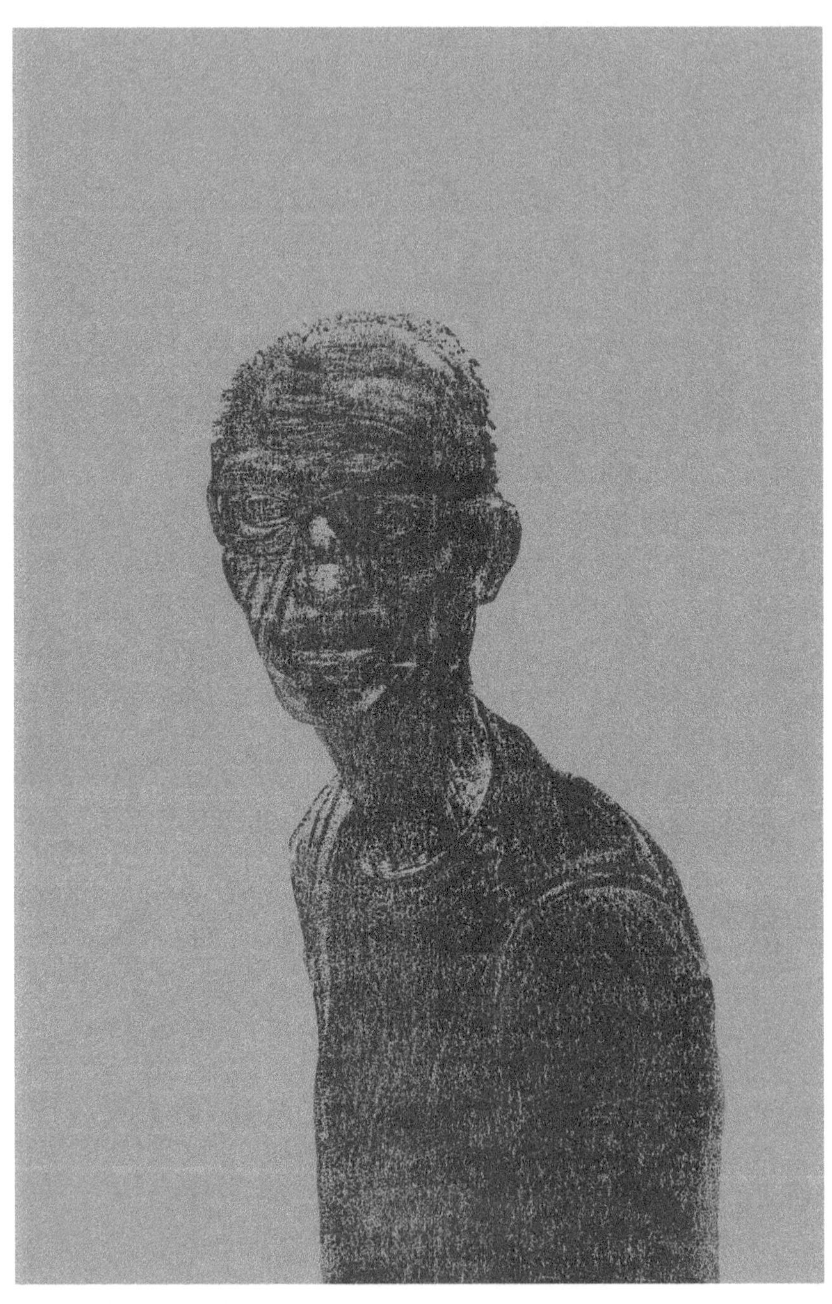

69. Strange Man

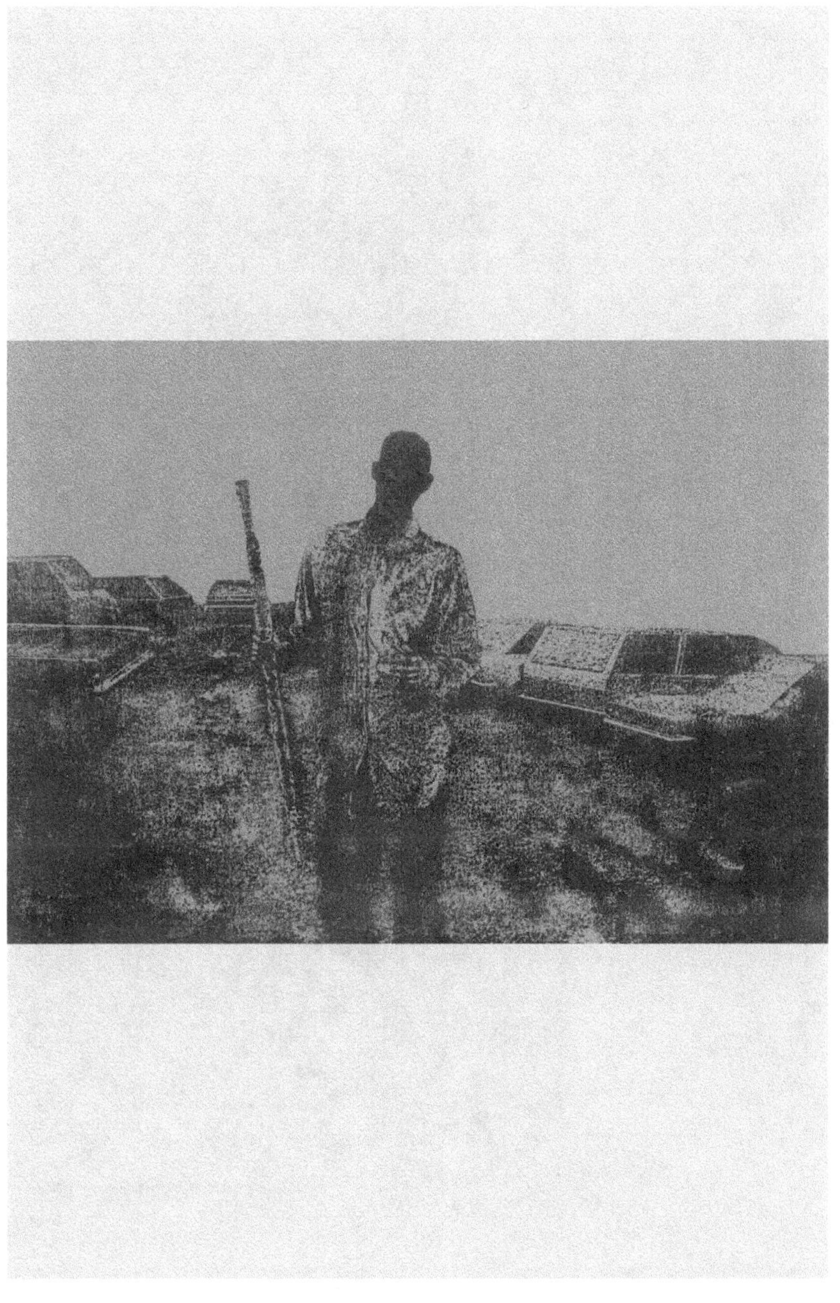

70. An Auto Graveyard

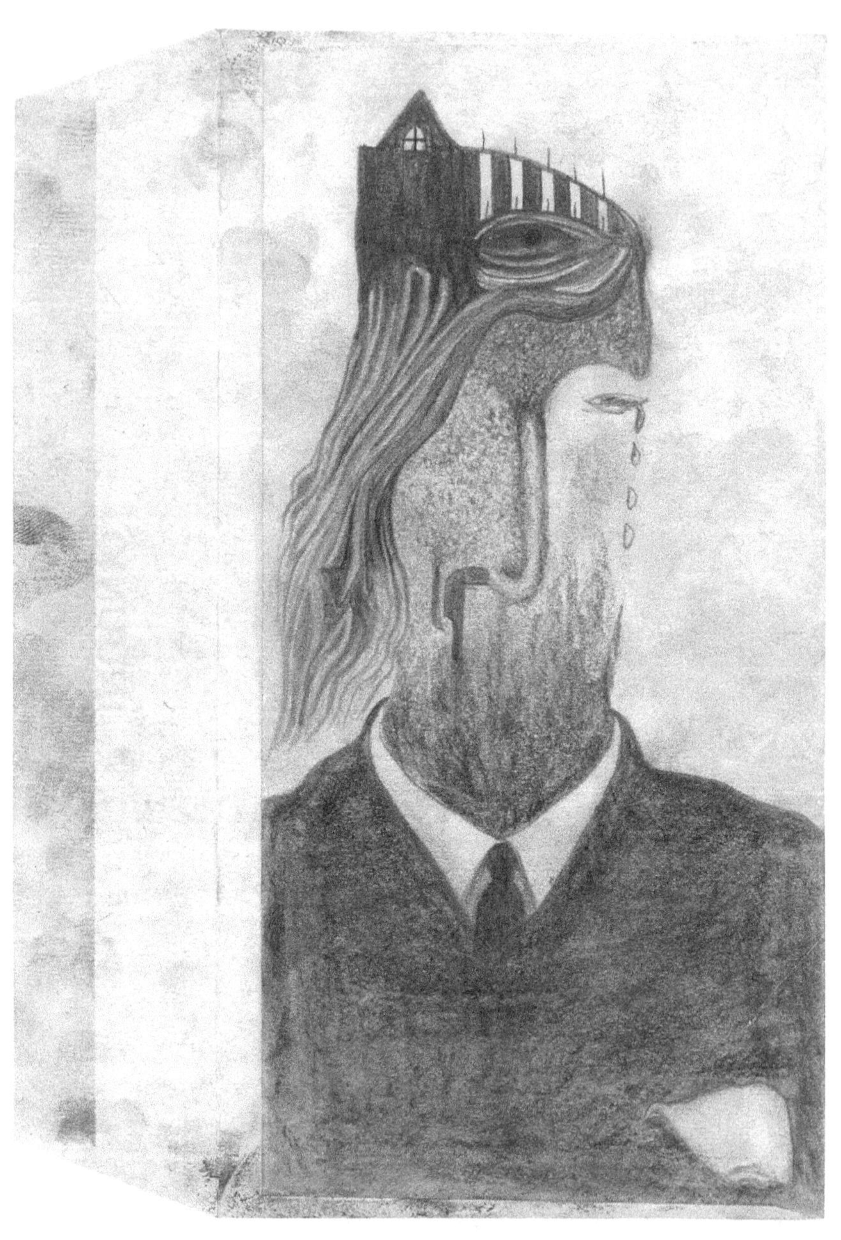

71. King With Sorrow

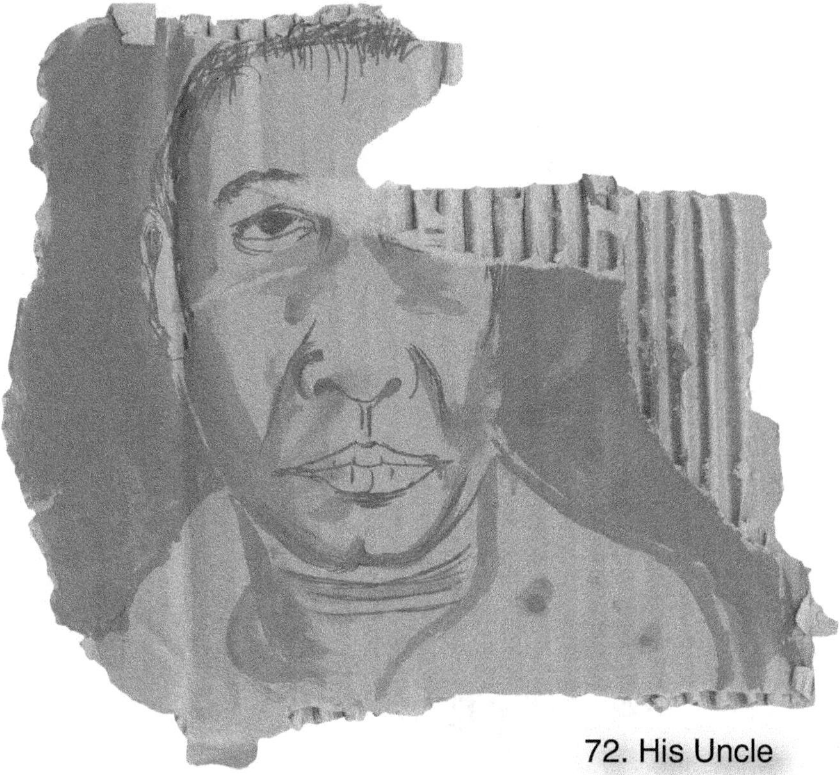

72. His Uncle

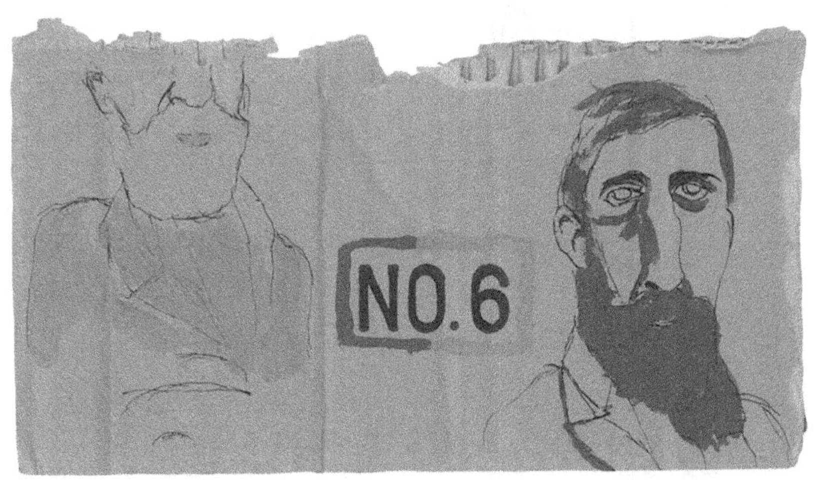

73. An American Philosopher

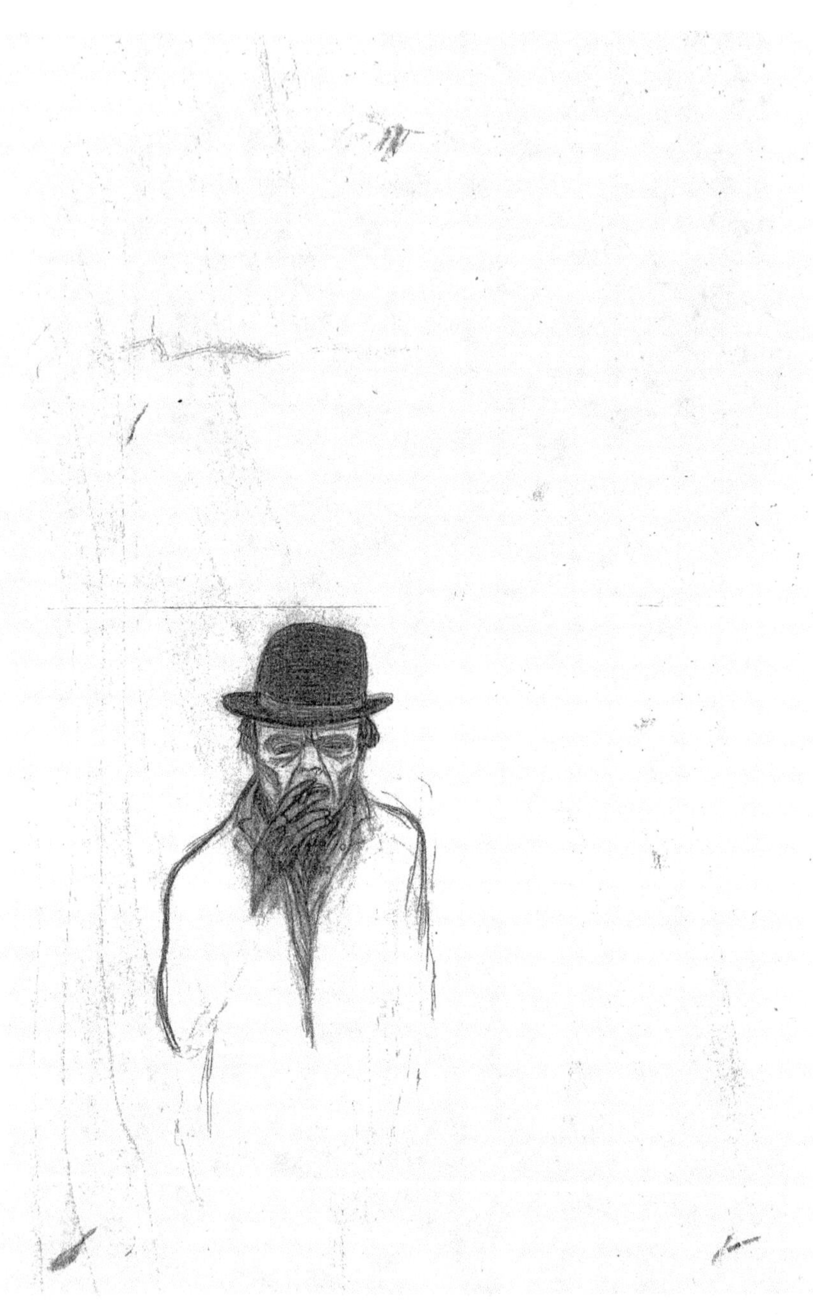

74. Pierrot Has A Break

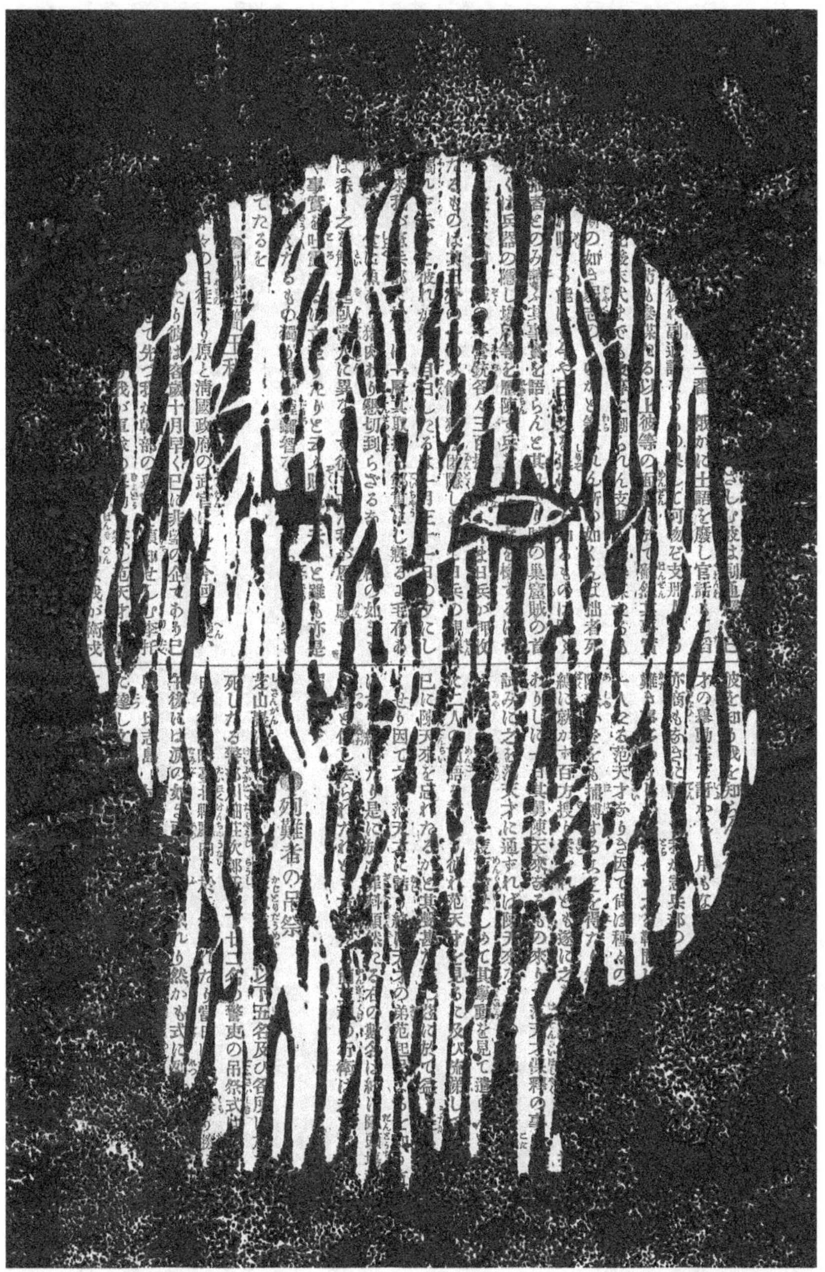

75. My War

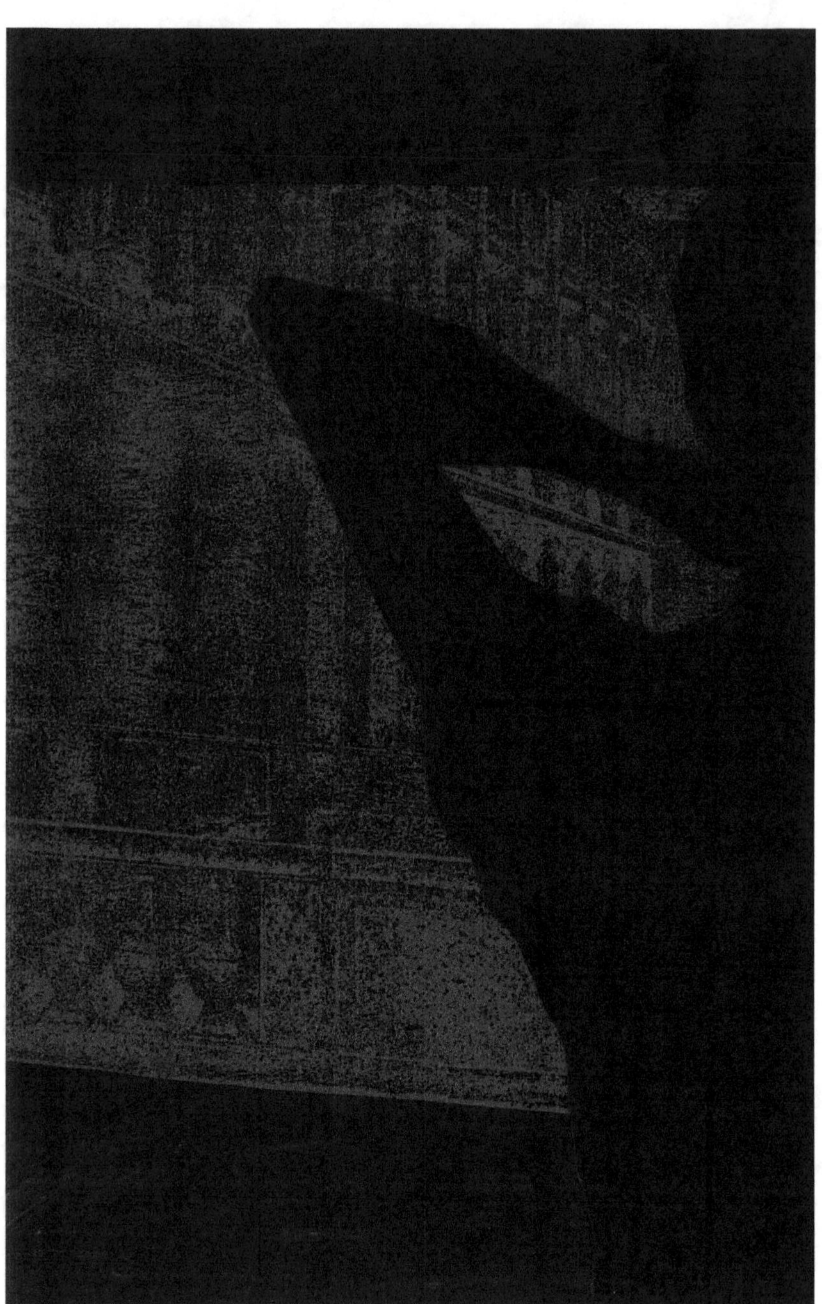

76. No One Knows That I'm Gone

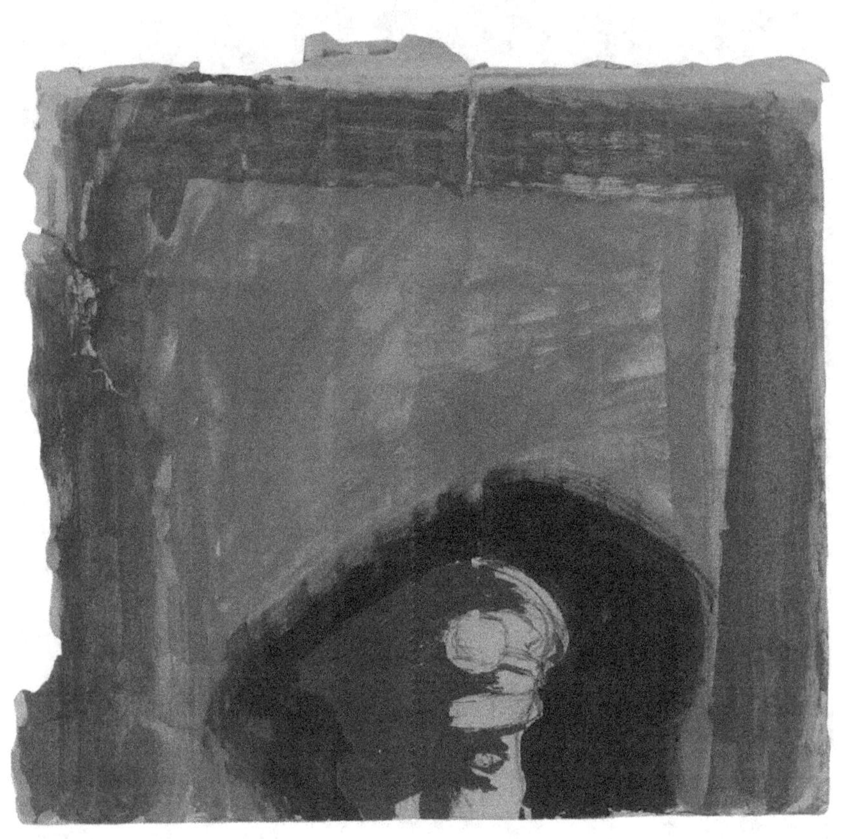

77. A Student

When I was an elementary school student, going to school was my pleasure because the school served us lunch. Eating the school lunch was my purpose in going to school.

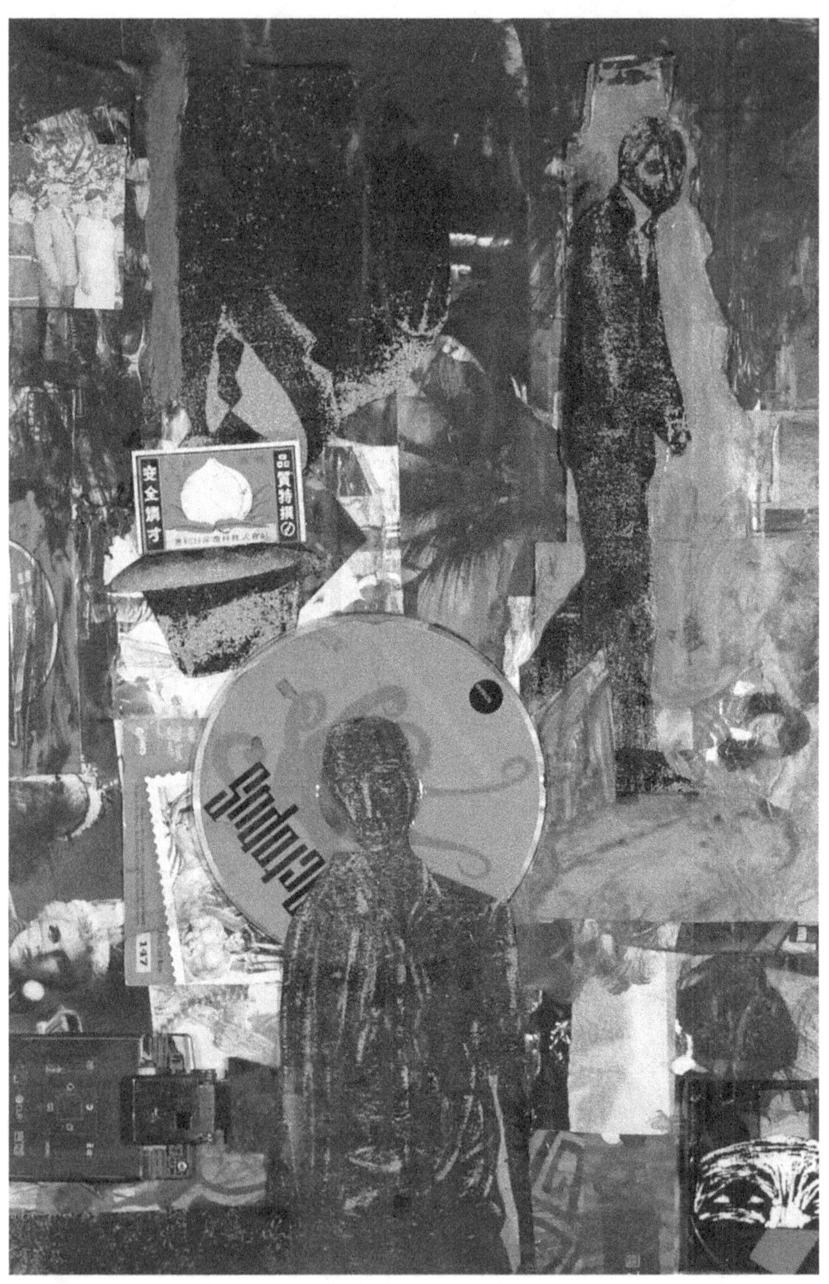

78. Hawaii

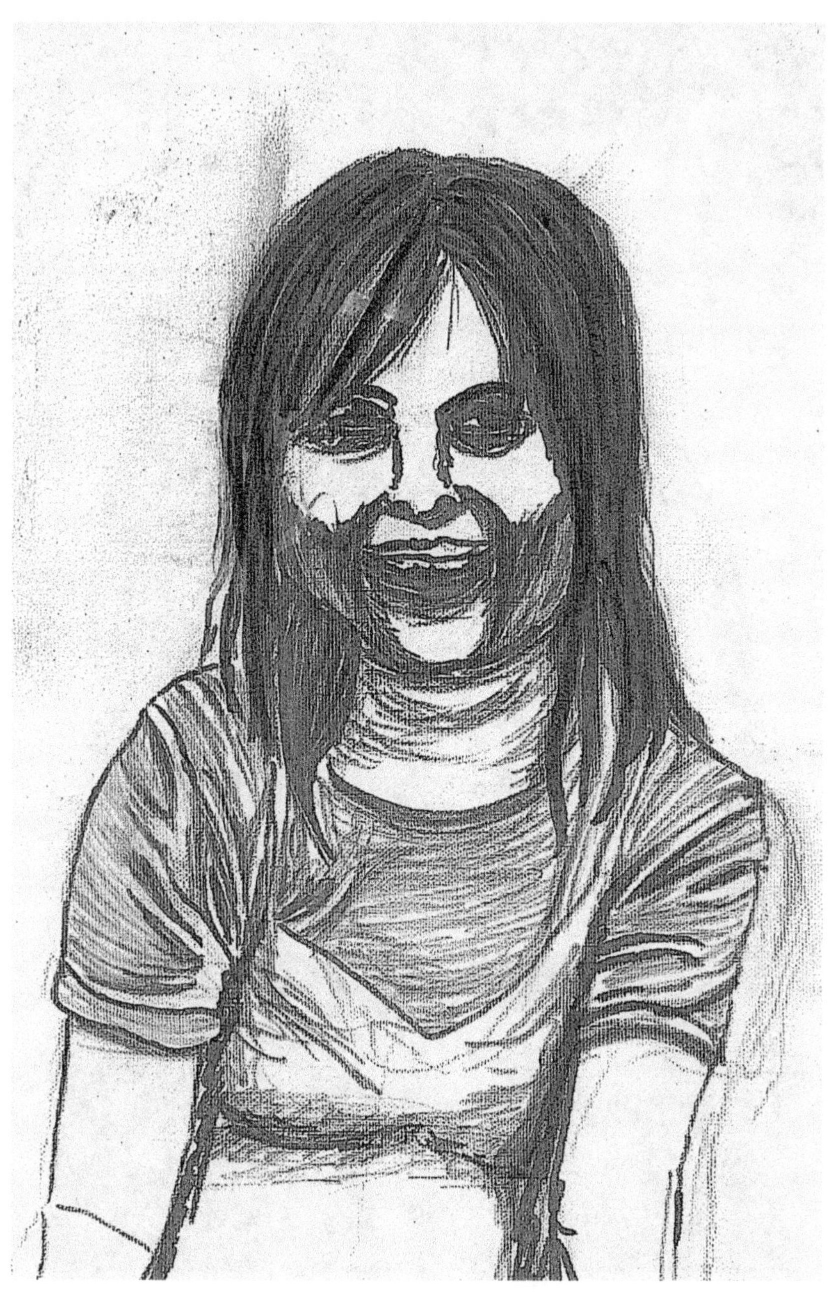

79. Miss Kuribayashi

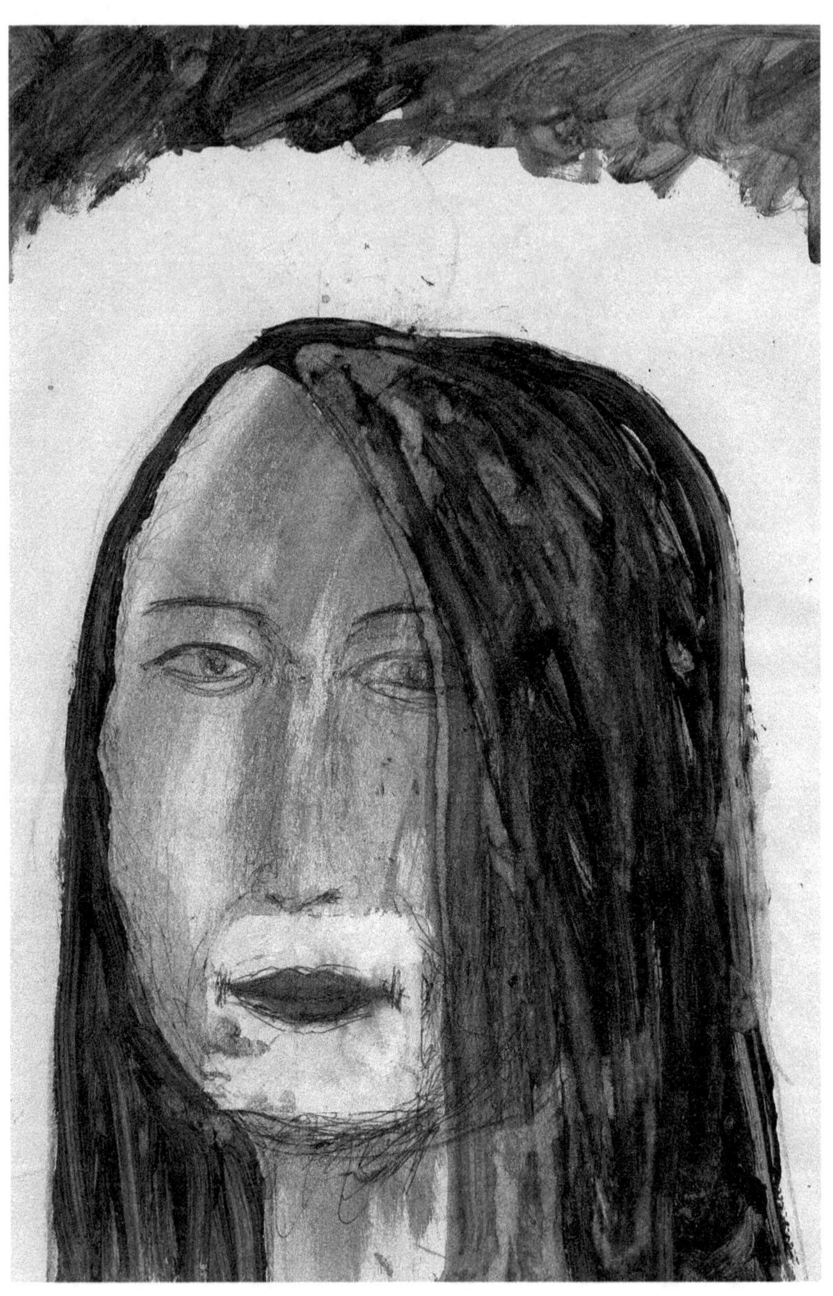

80. Miss Murakami

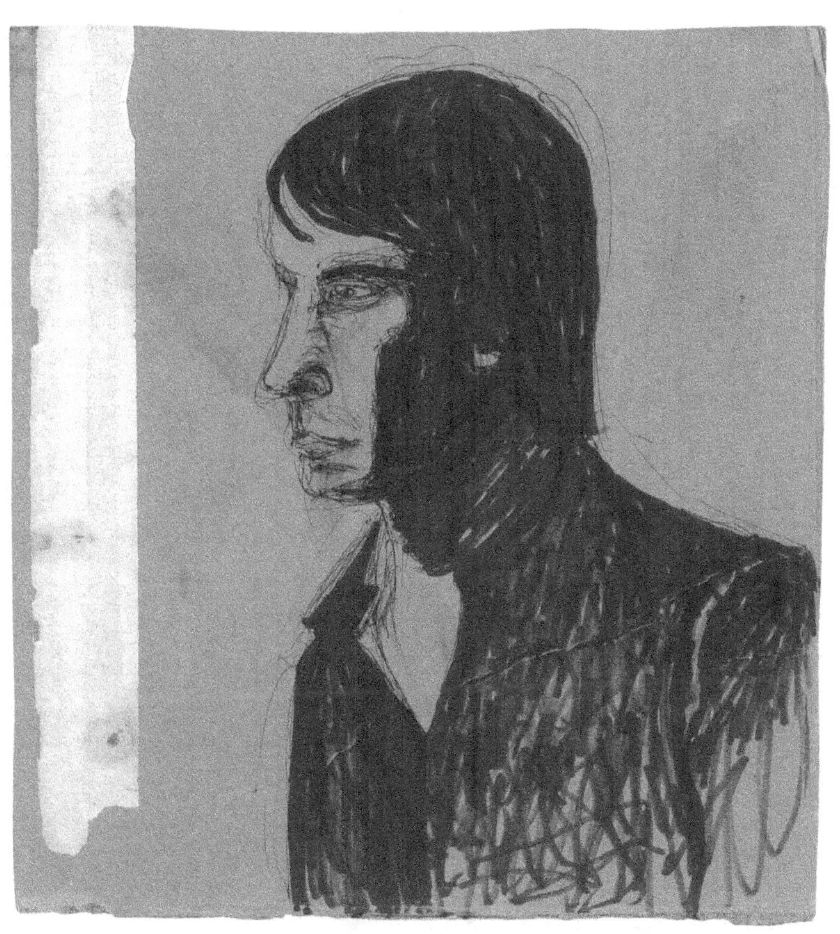

81. All The Wind Blows

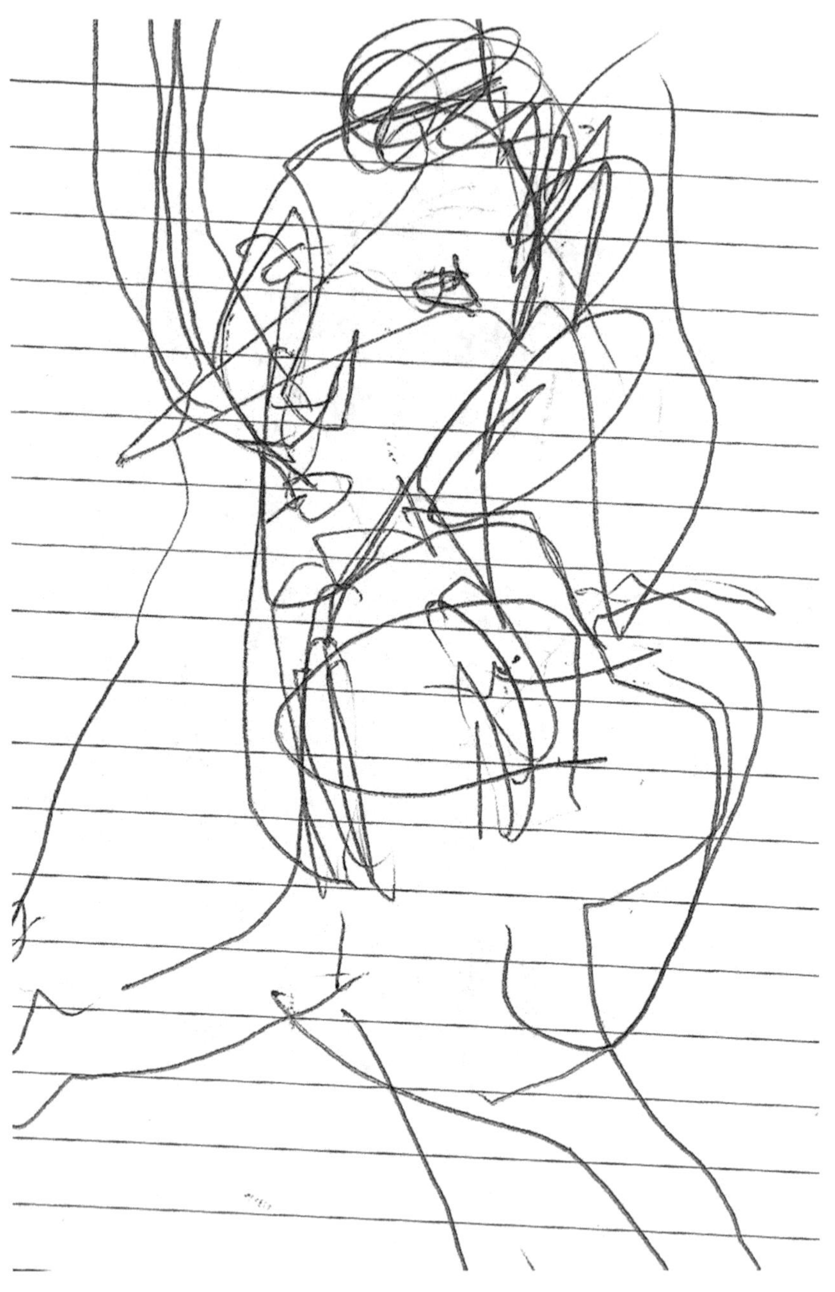

82. Mr. Amana

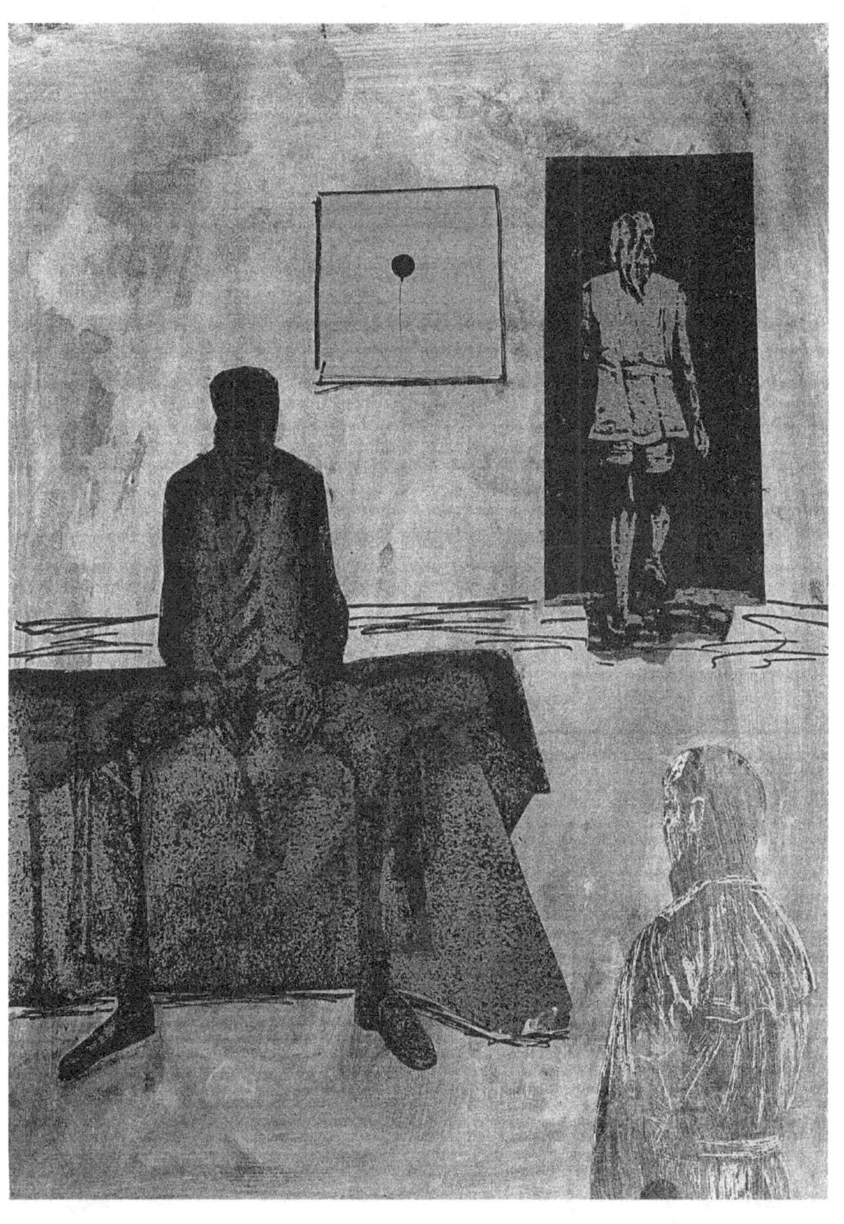

83. Love Is Lies

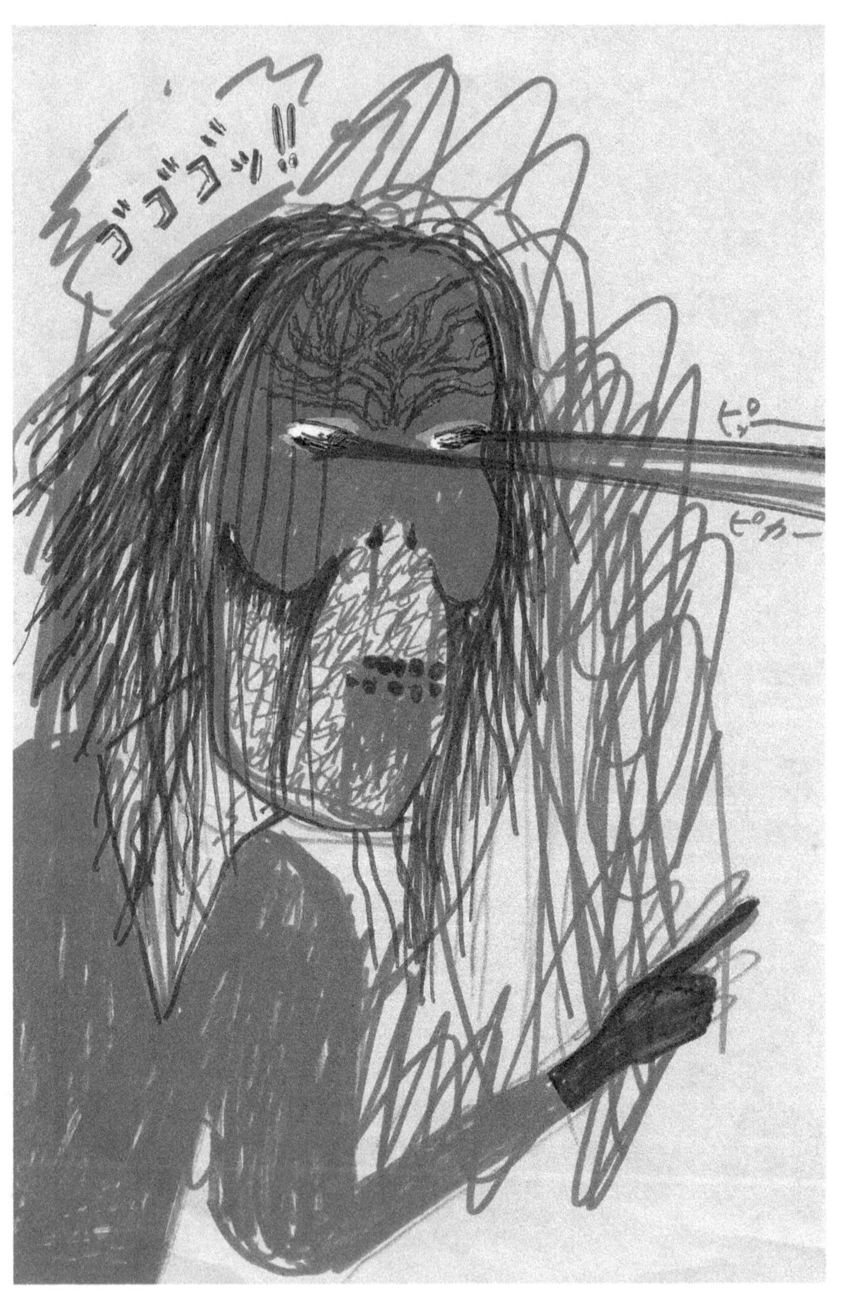

84. Miss Saitou

Her face is like a skull. She beams from her eyes, and eats the people whom she doesn't like, but becomes very quiet like a rabbit when she is in front of a man who she loves. Actually she is a very cute girl.

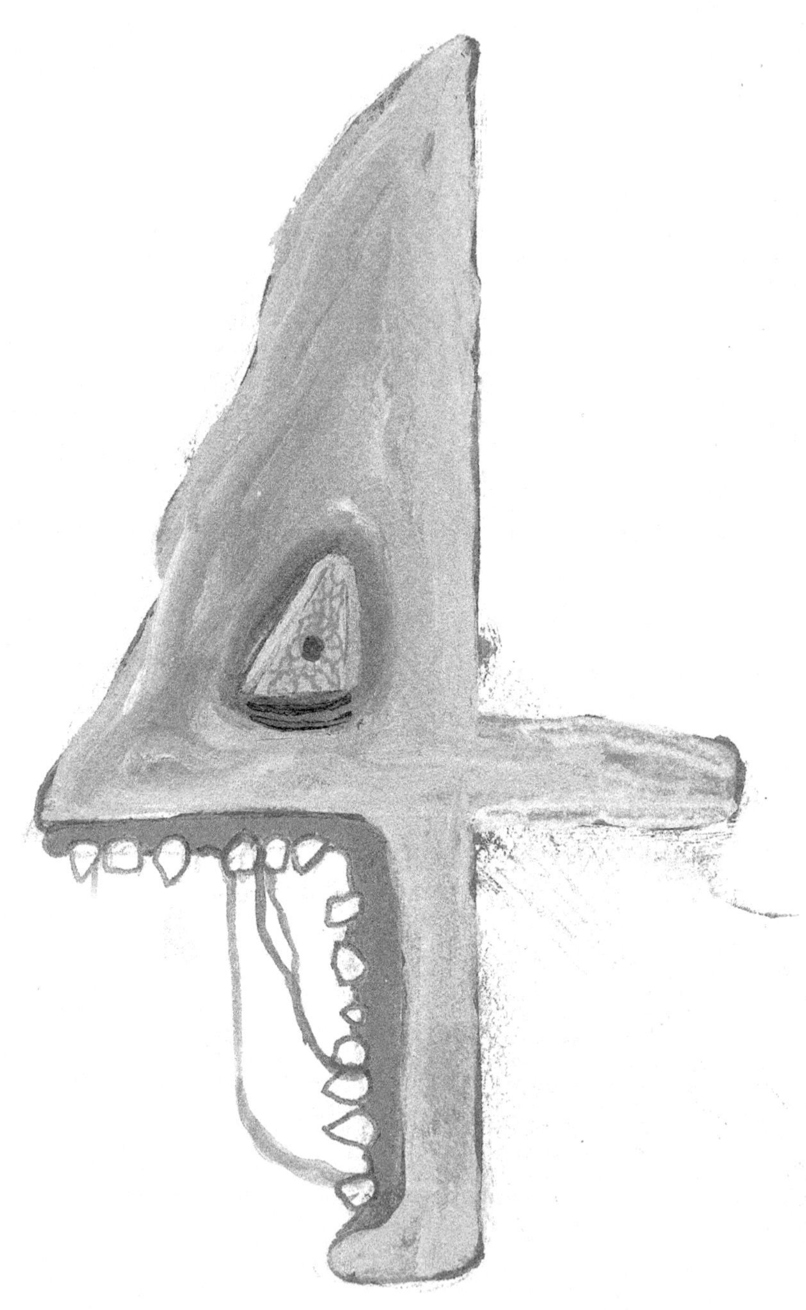

85. Four

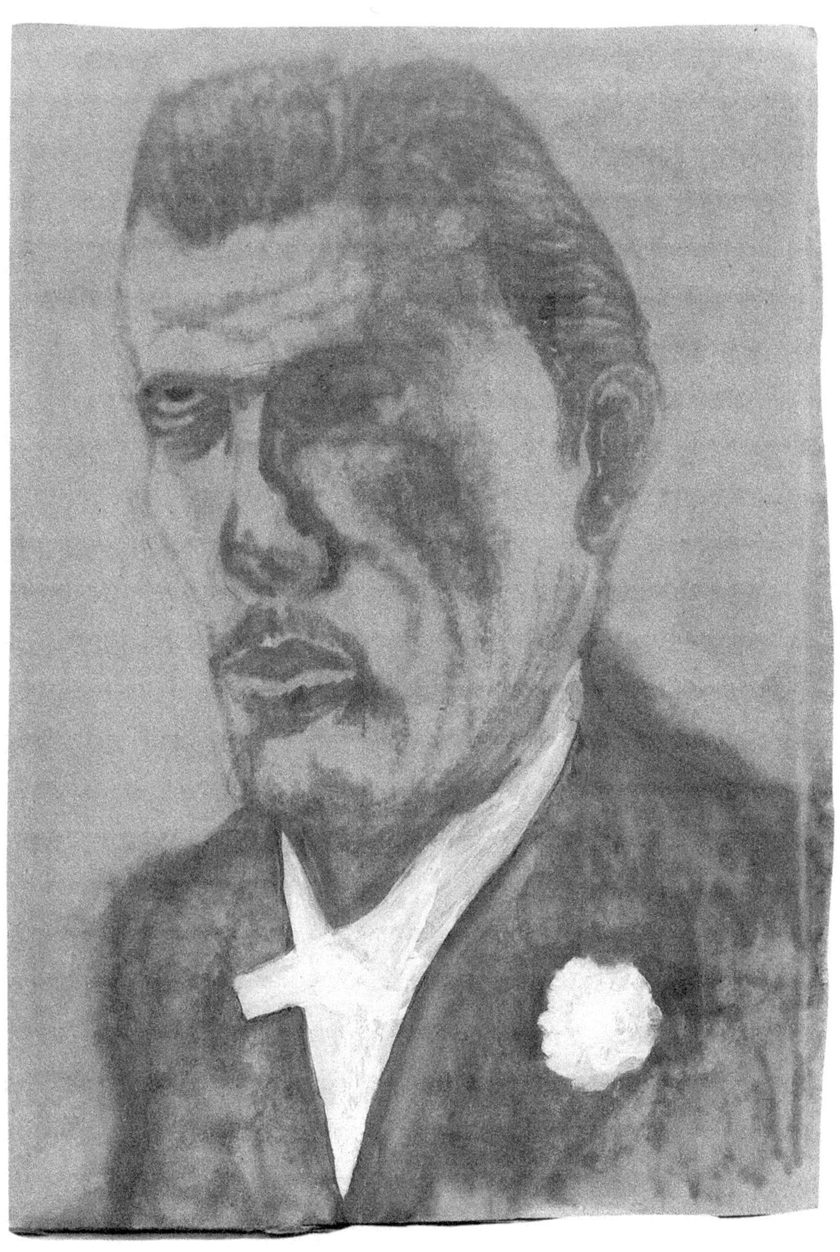

86. Gorilla

87. Going Mad

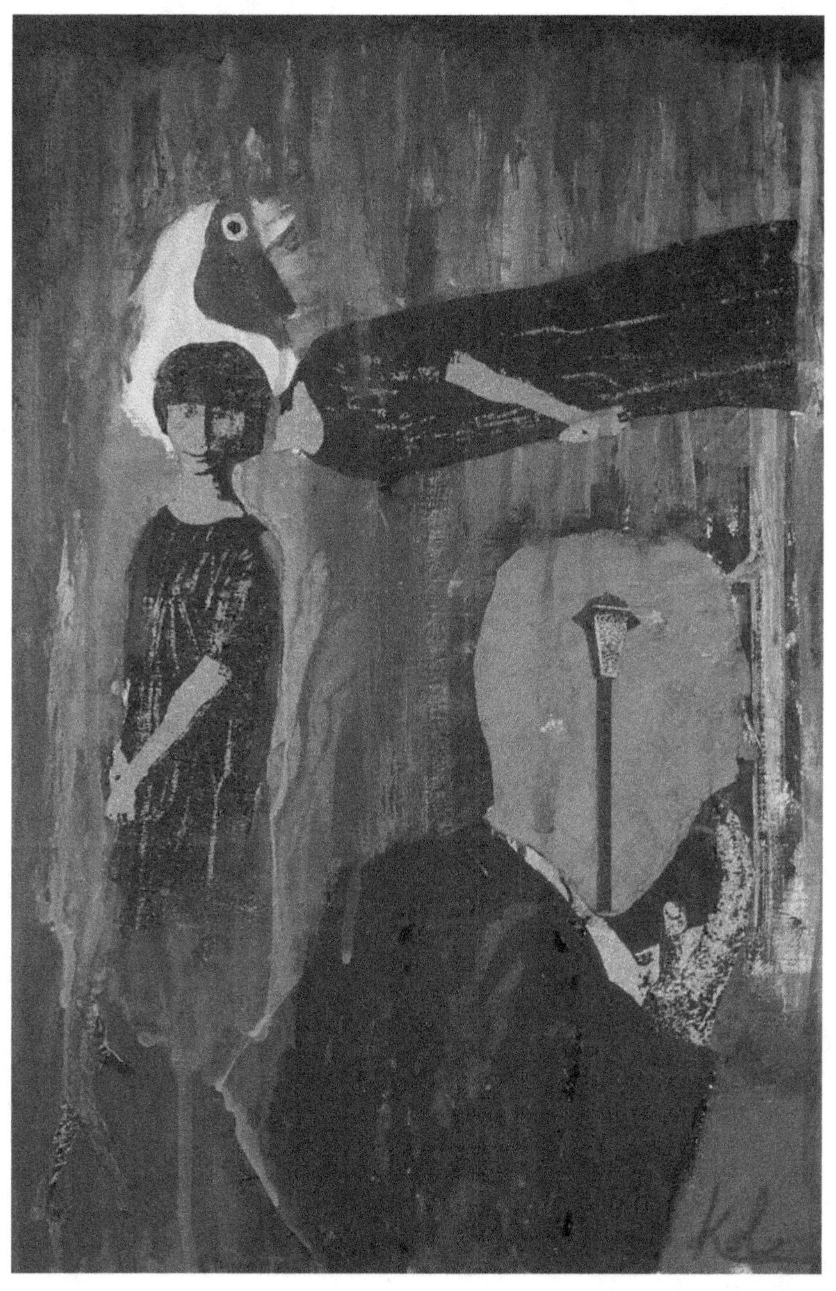

88. In His Head

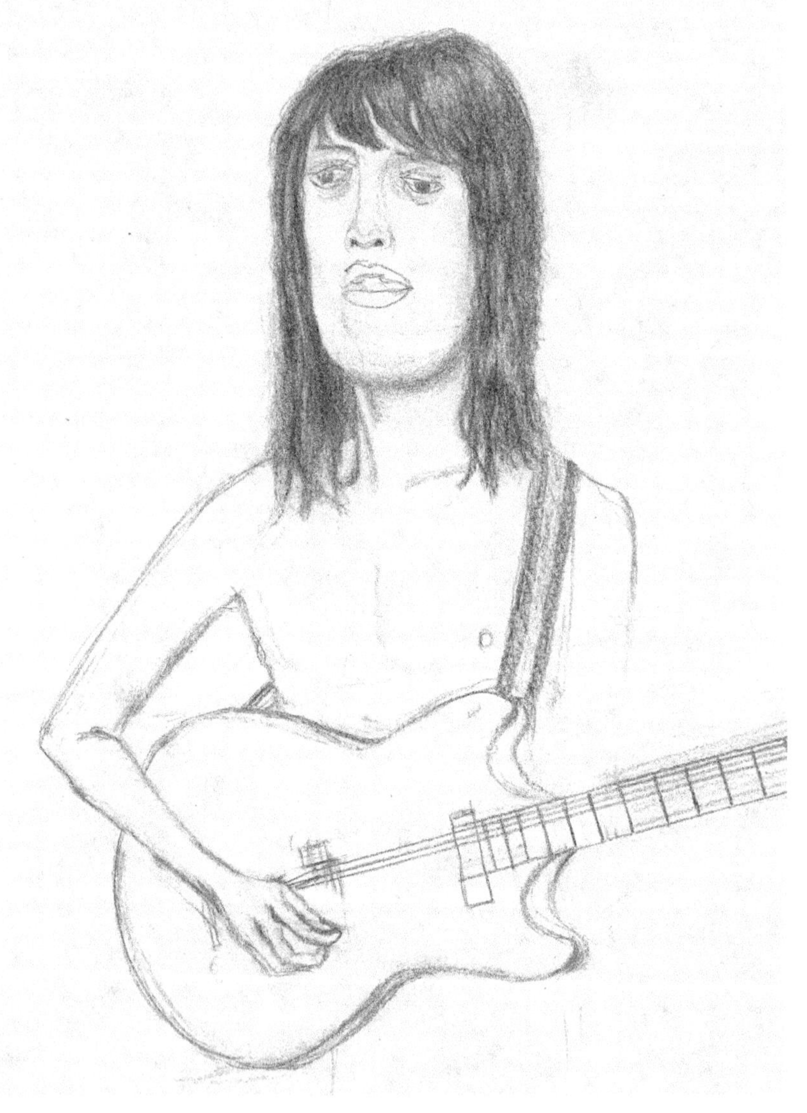

89. Boy

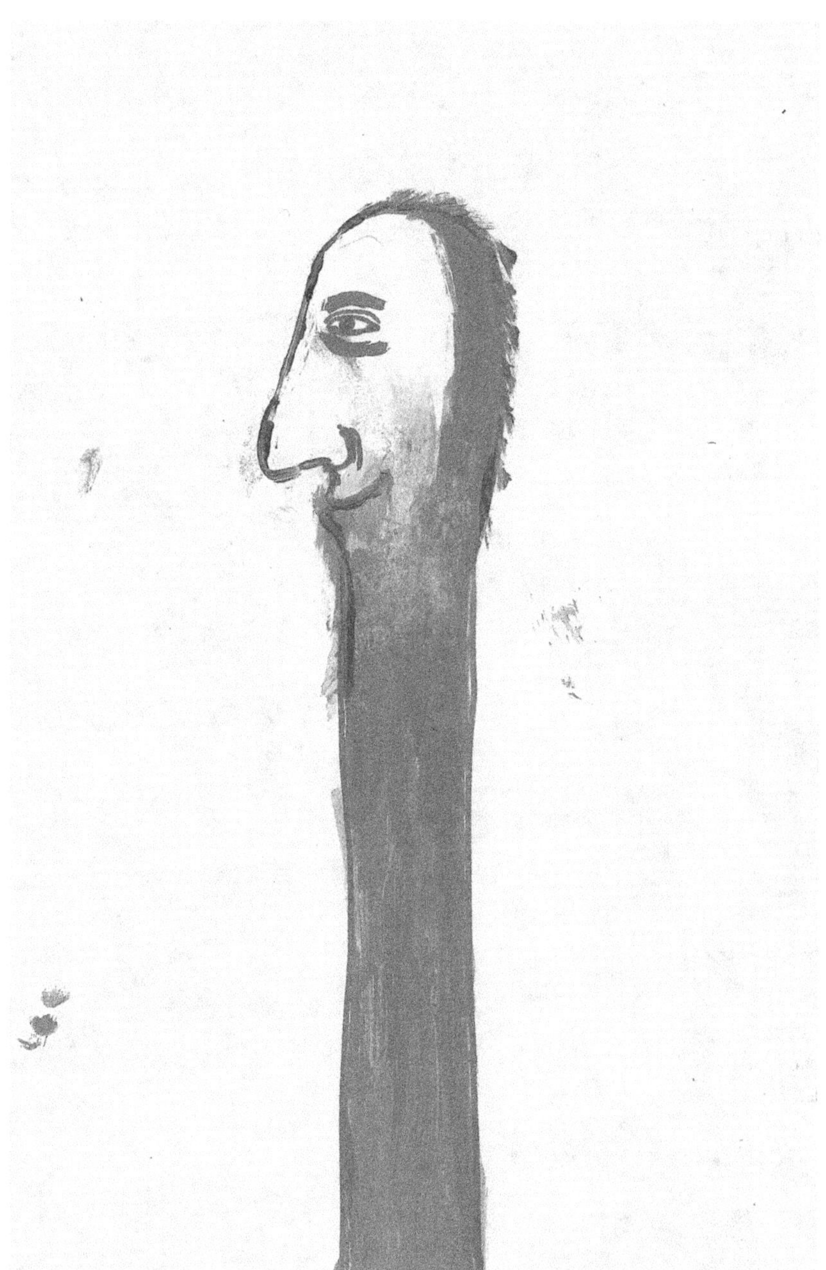

90. One

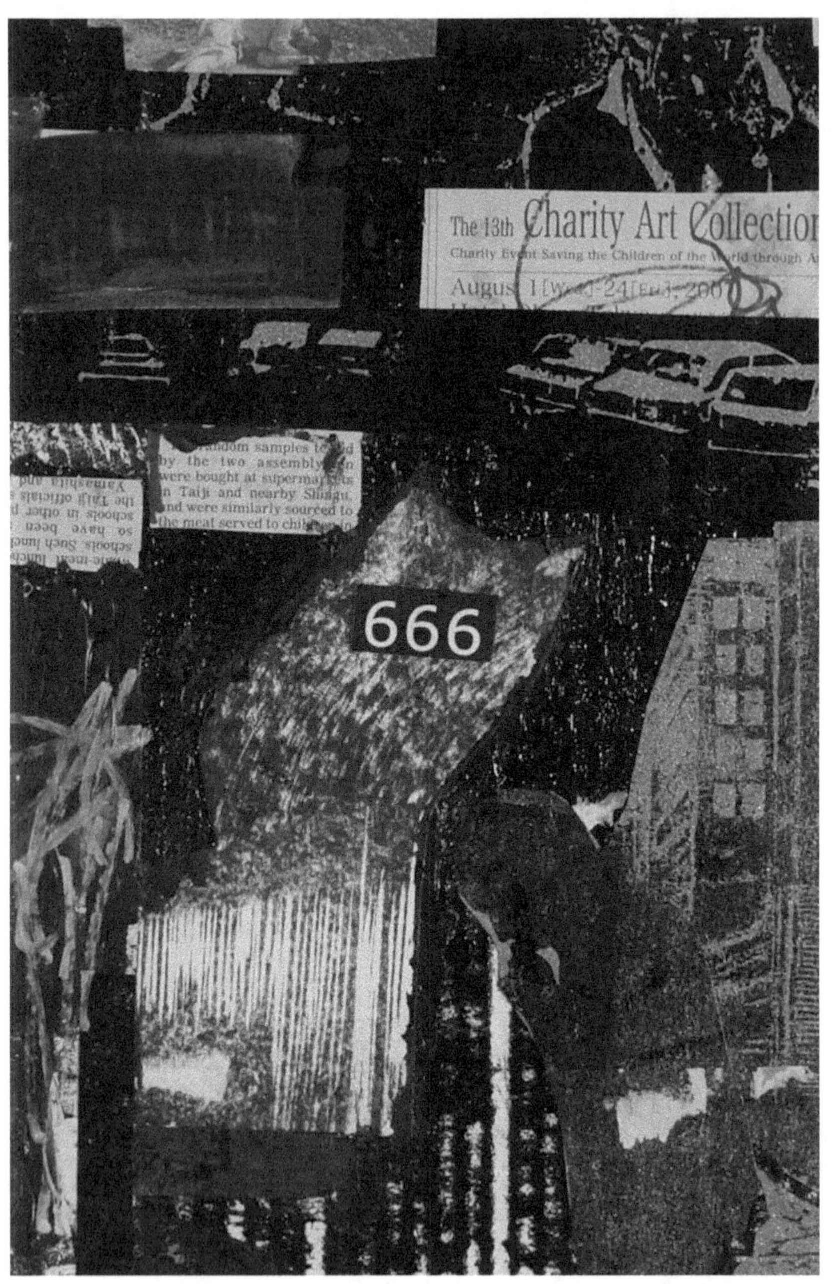

91. Back Street

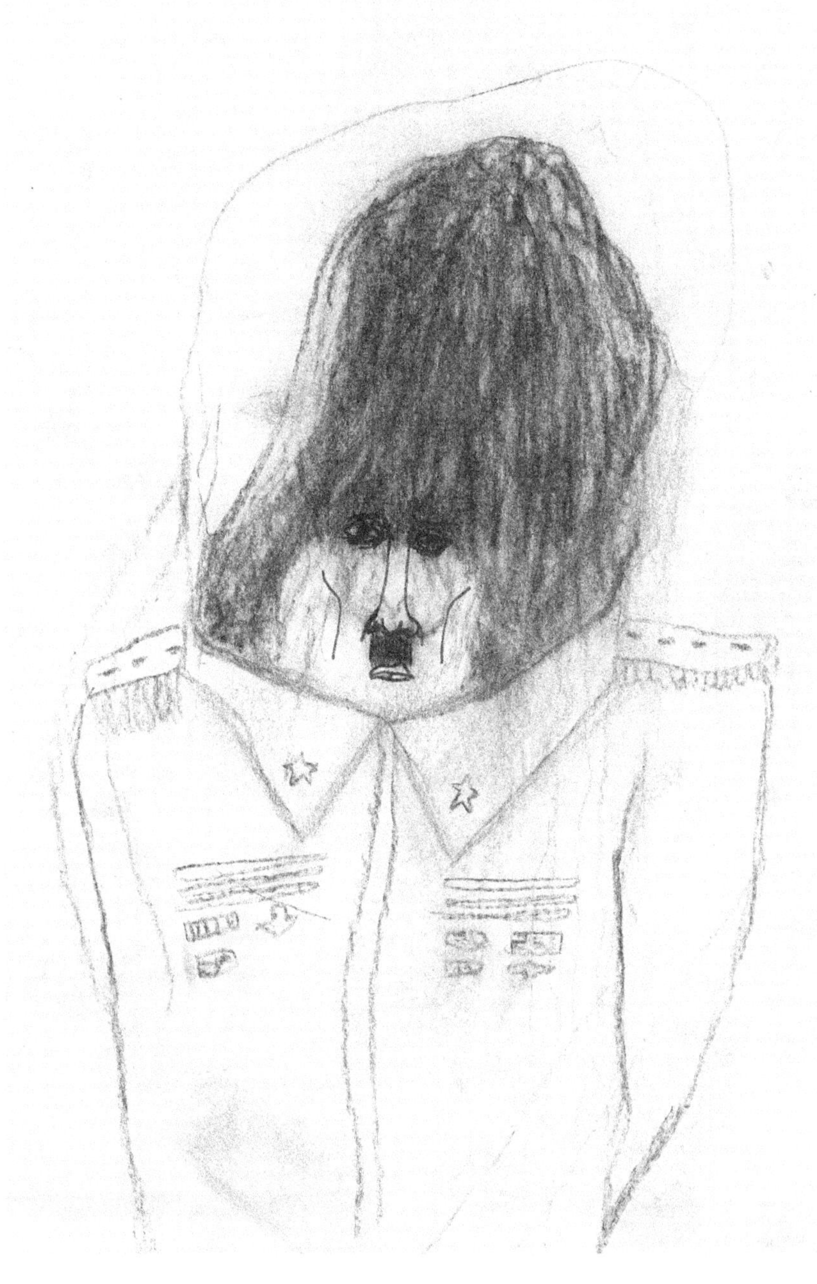

92. A General

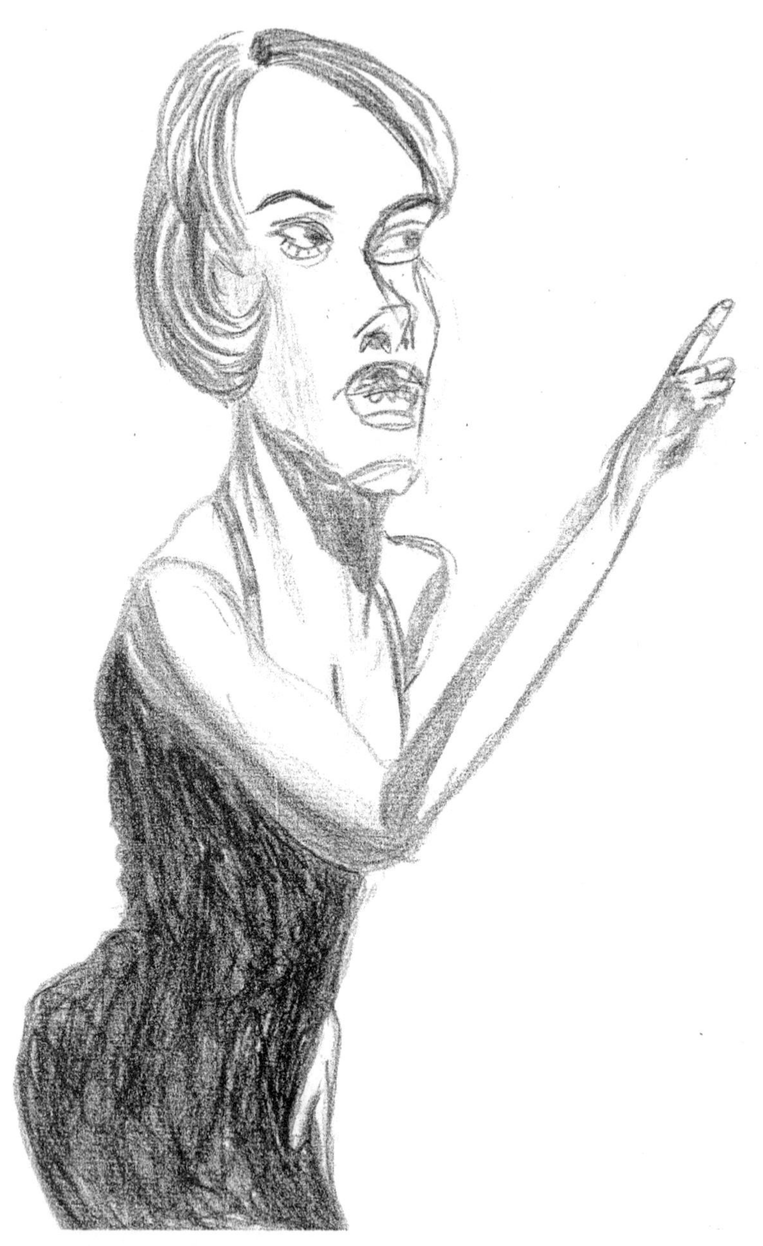

93. Singer

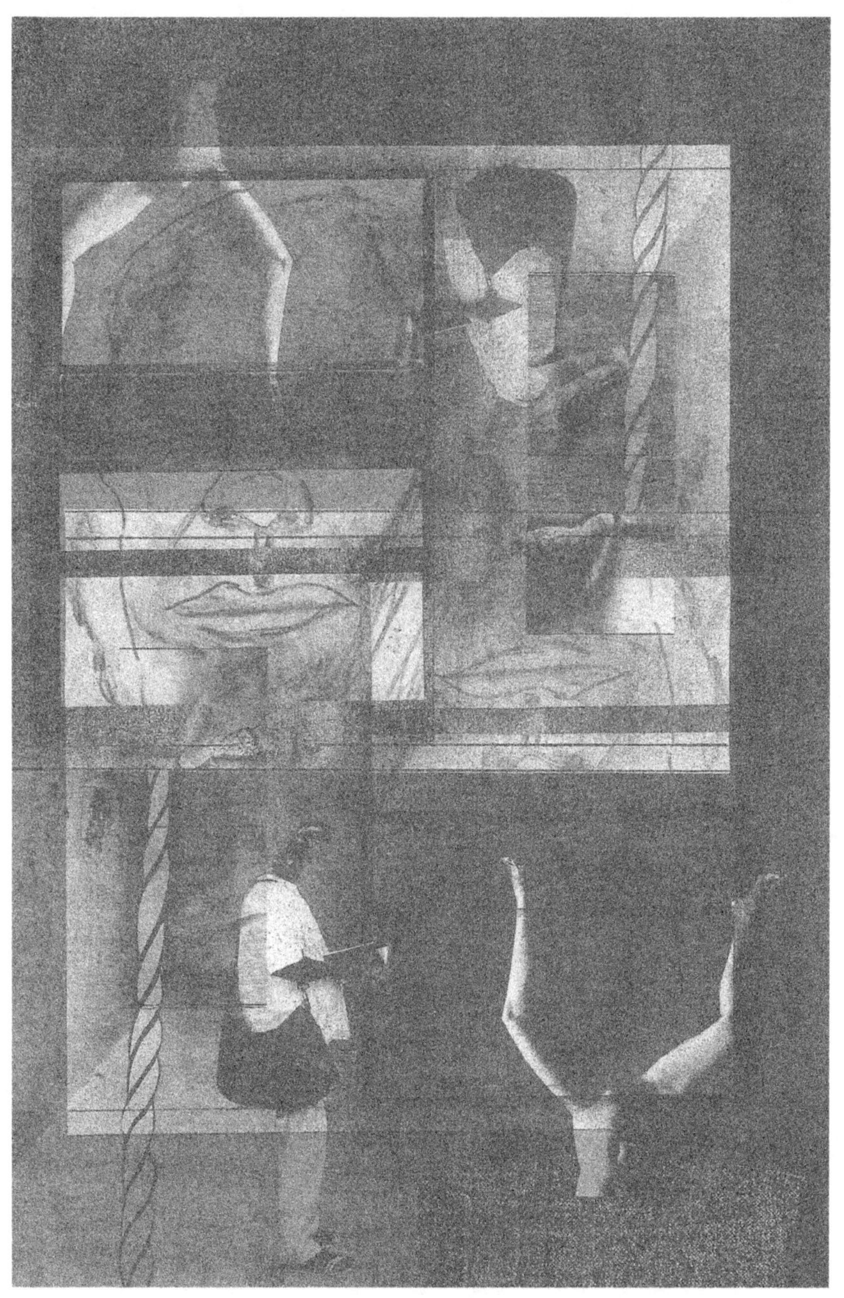

94. Excursion

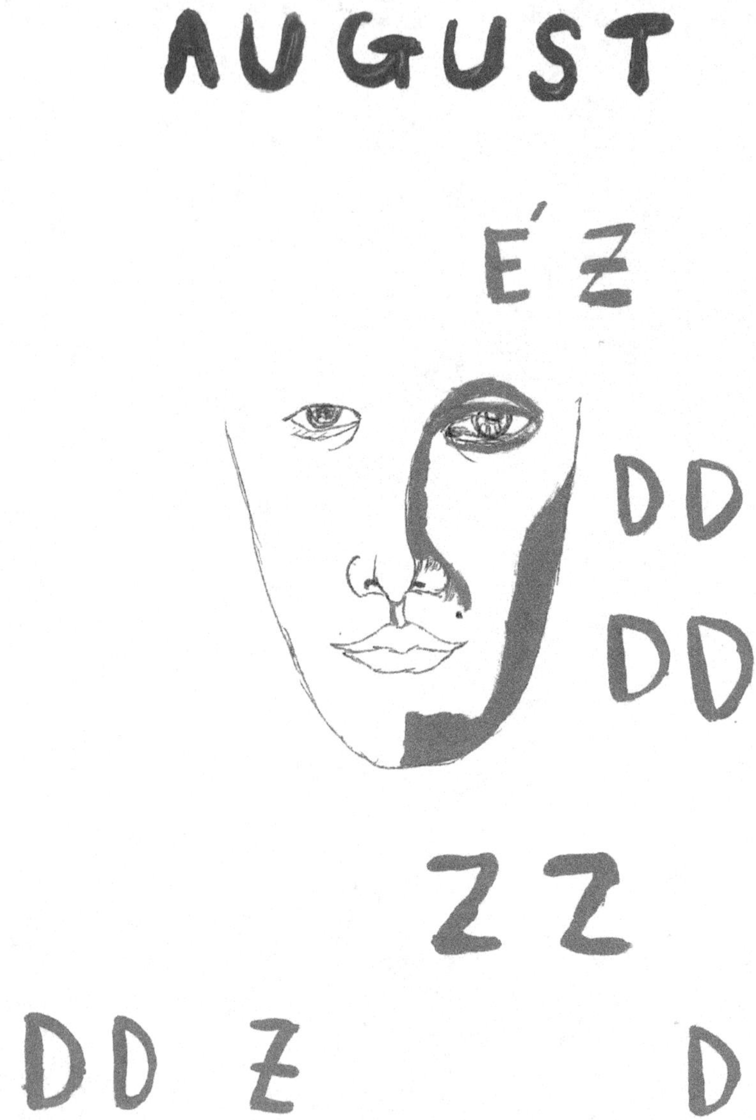

AUGUST

ÉZ

DD

DD

ZZ

DD Z D

95. My Schedule

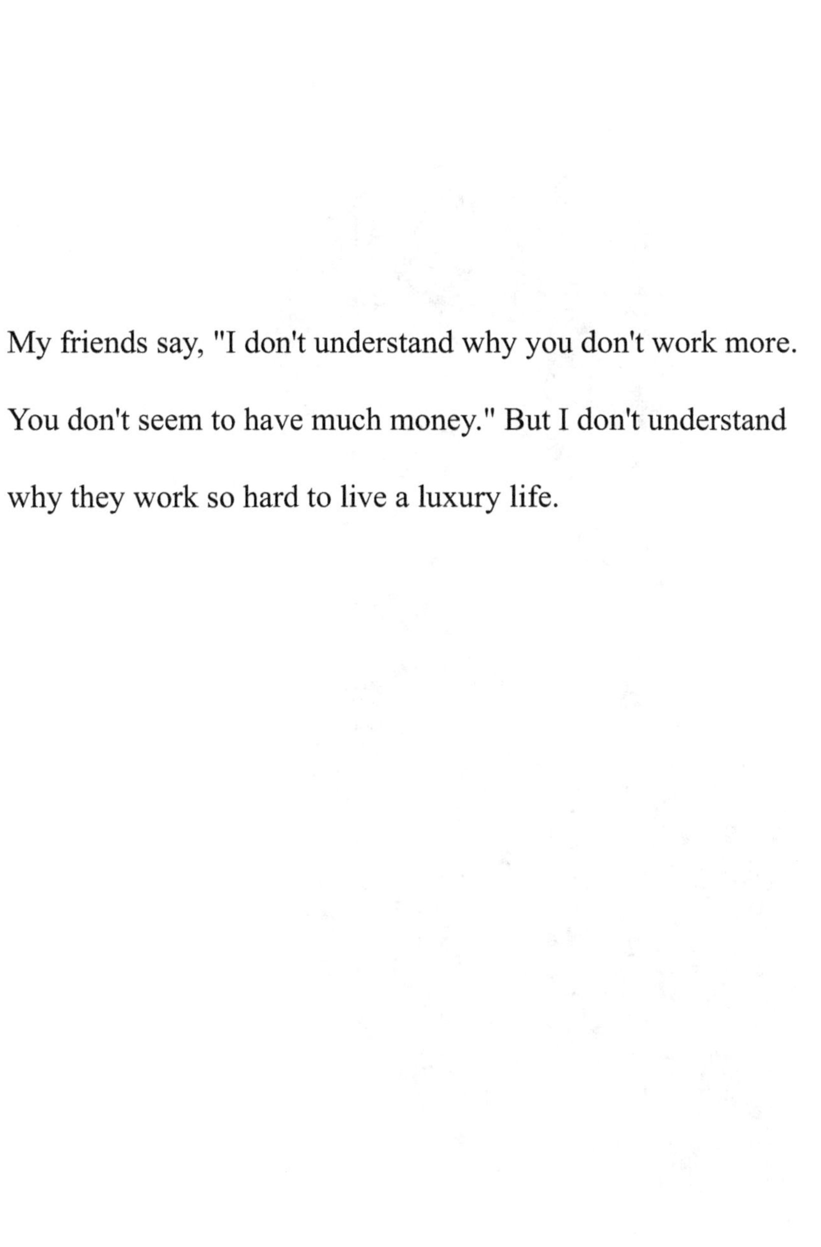

My friends say, "I don't understand why you don't work more. You don't seem to have much money." But I don't understand why they work so hard to live a luxury life.

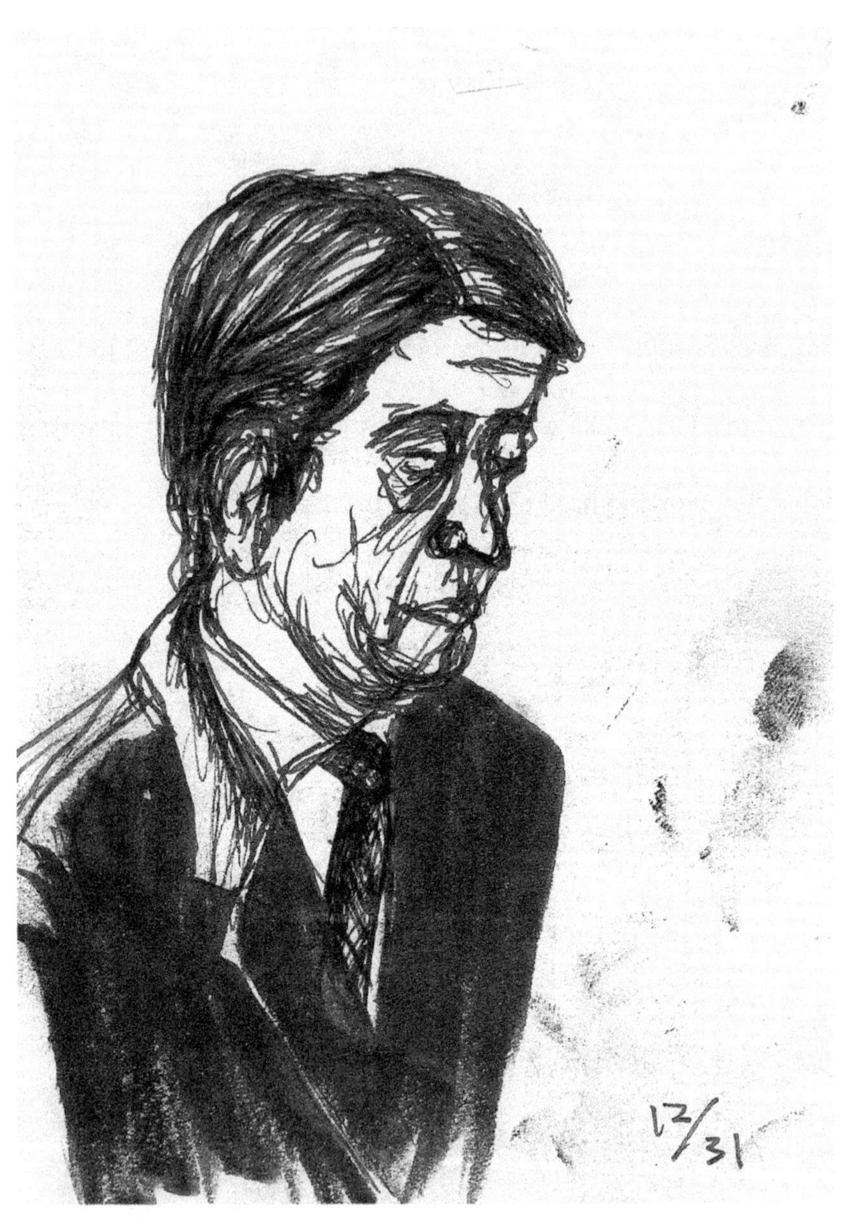

96. A Japanese President

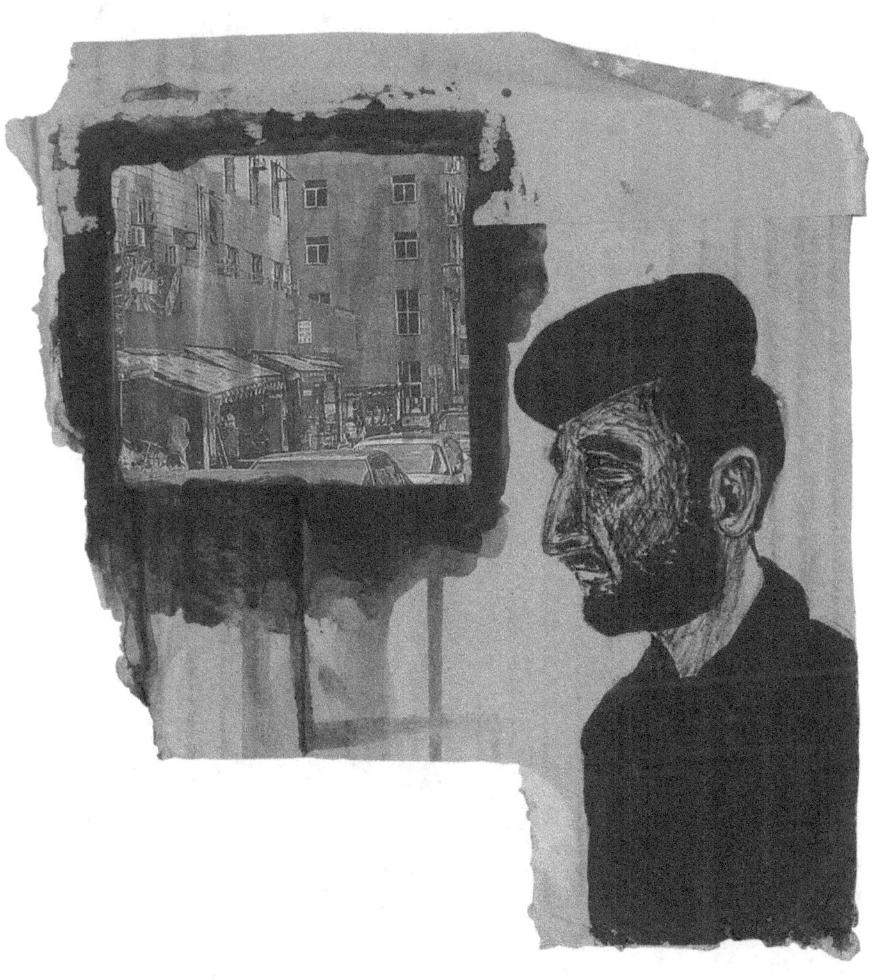

97. Information

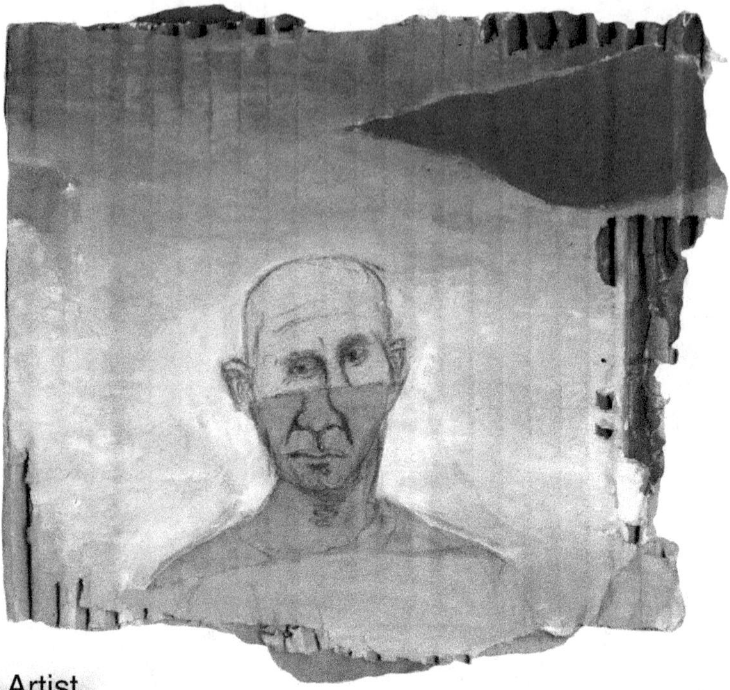

98. Artist

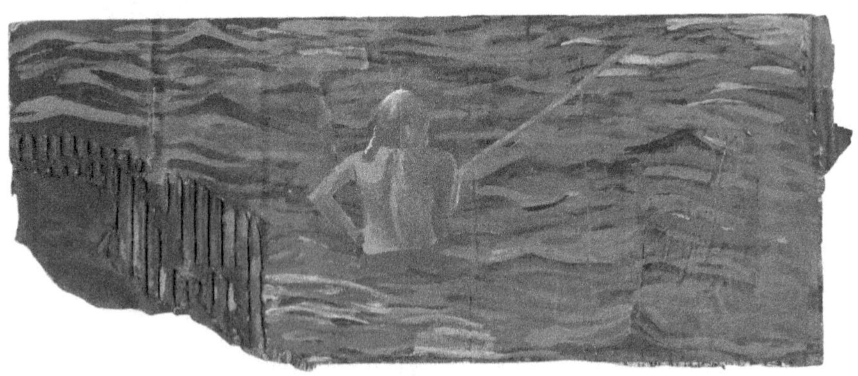

99. Wild Life

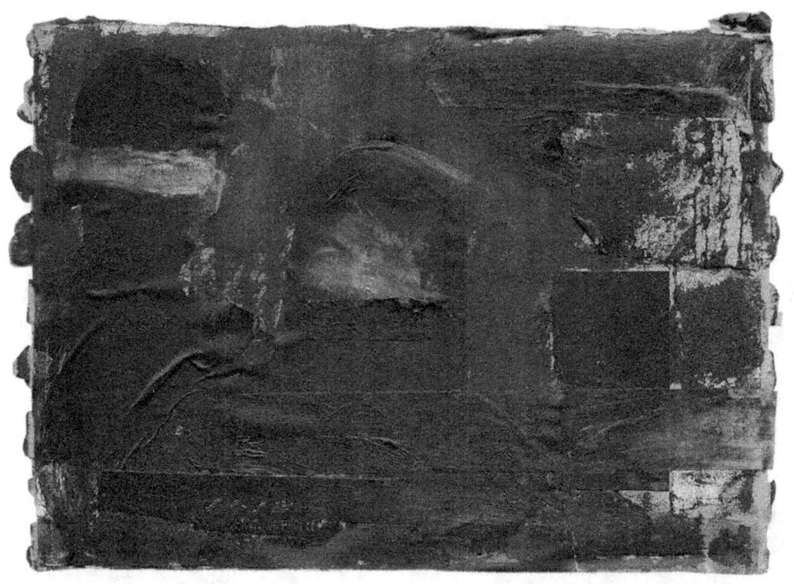

100. Two Ninjas

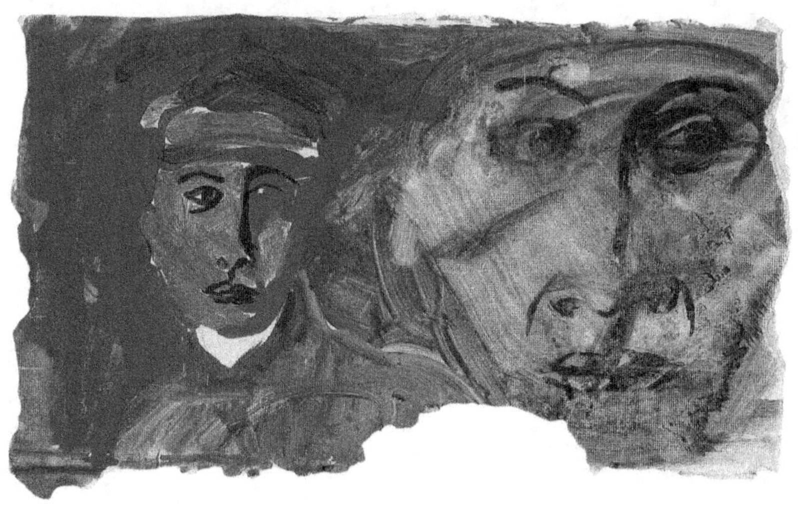

101. Adolescence

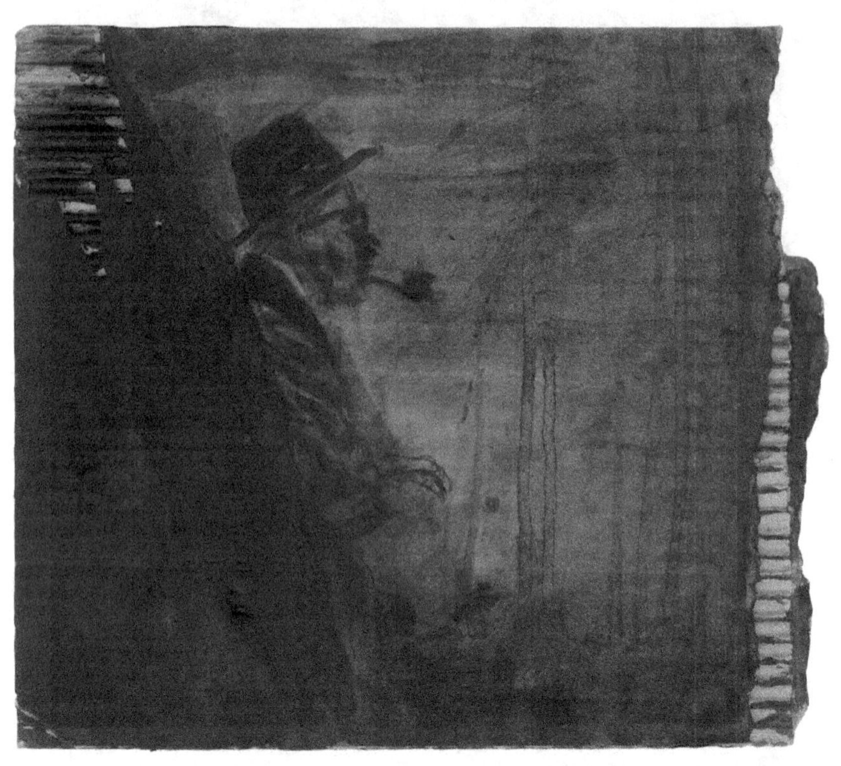

102. Novelist

I like to draw on cardboard. The best part of painting on cardboard is using a very small piece. I think it's similar to a can of tuna.

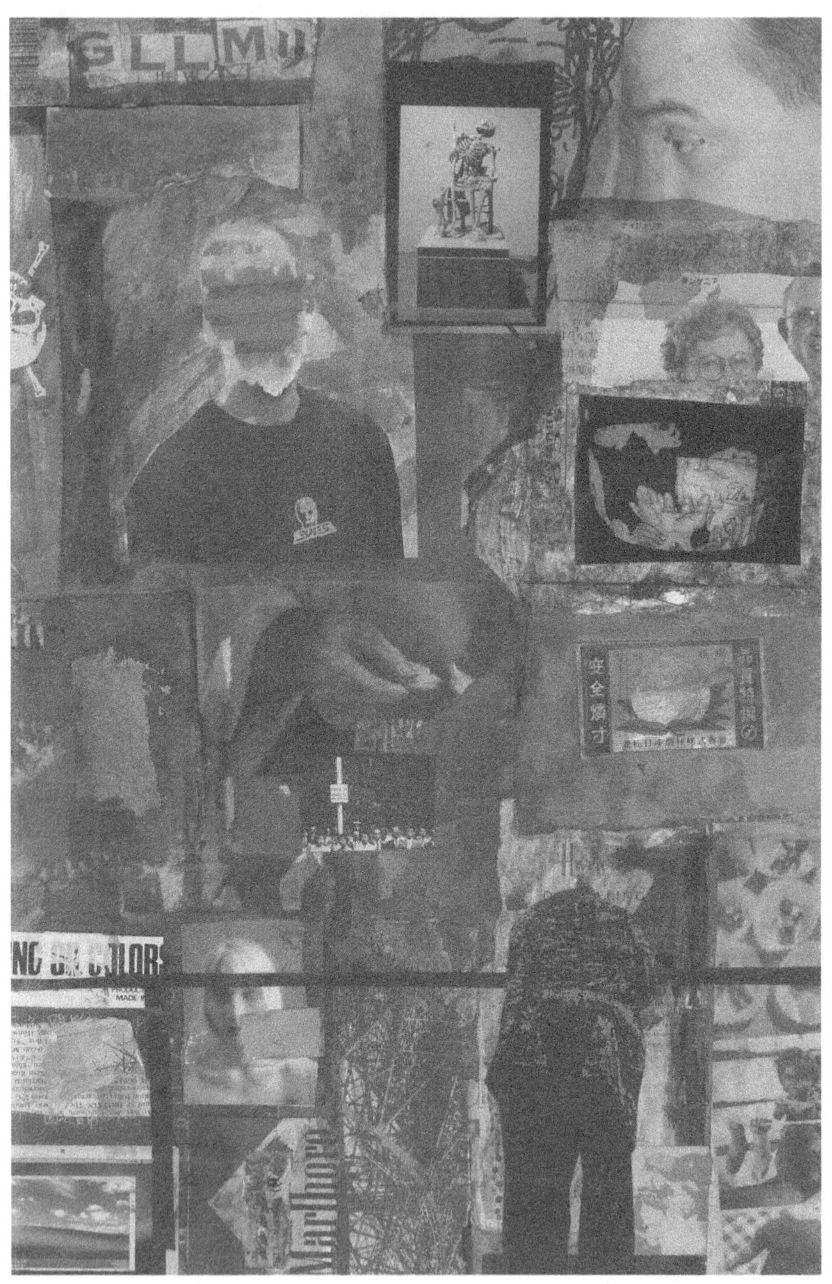

103. Hangover

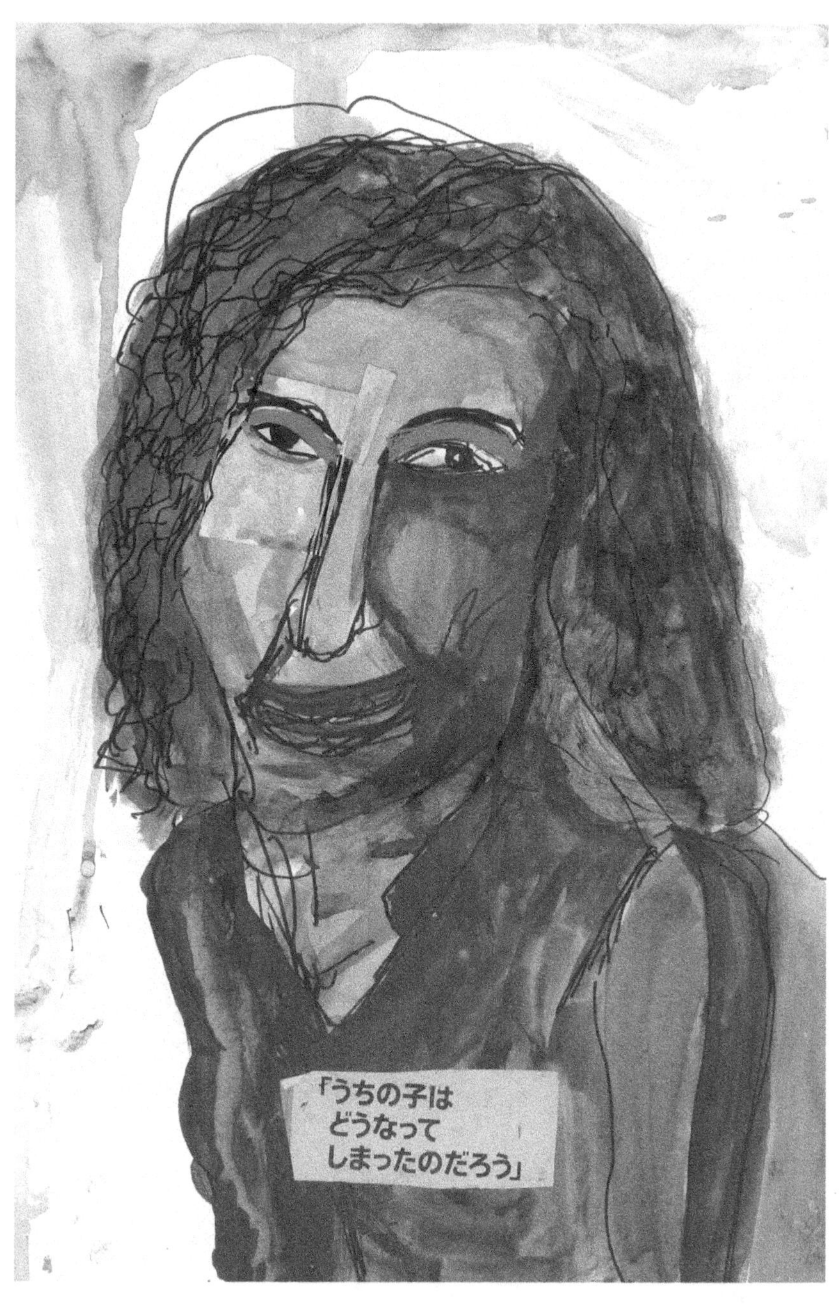

104. In Prison

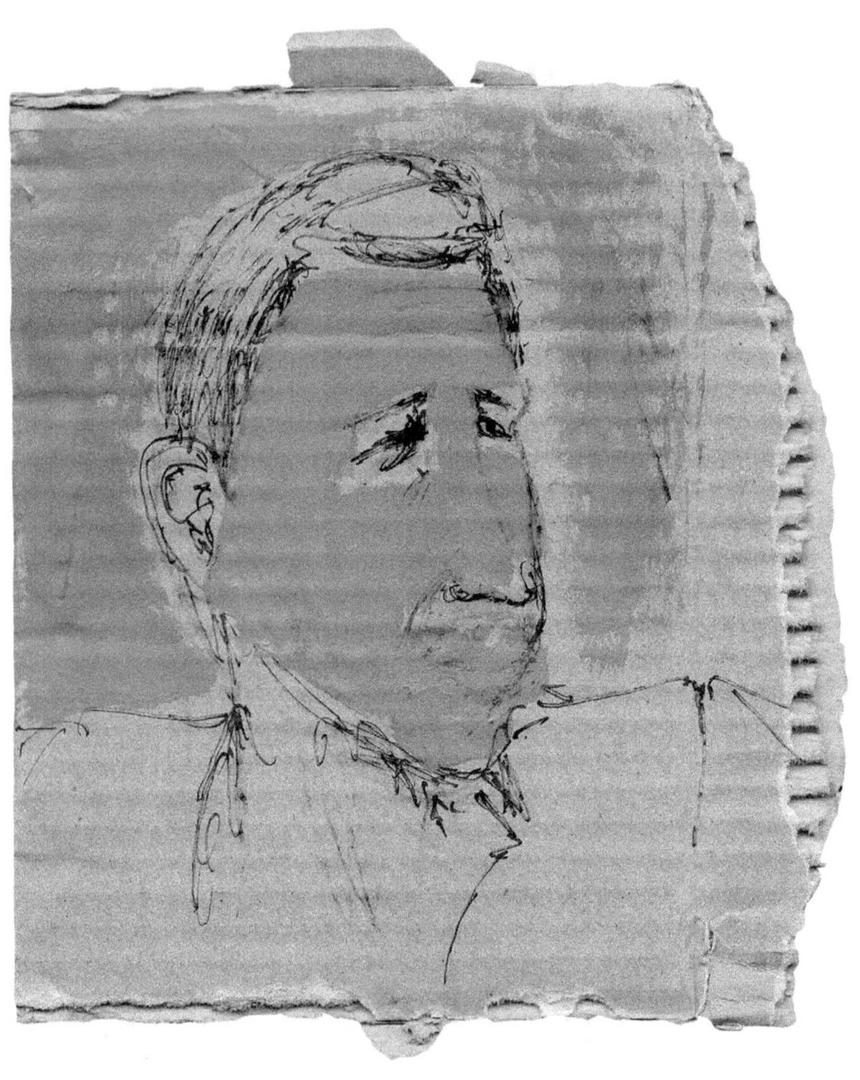

105. Pierrot

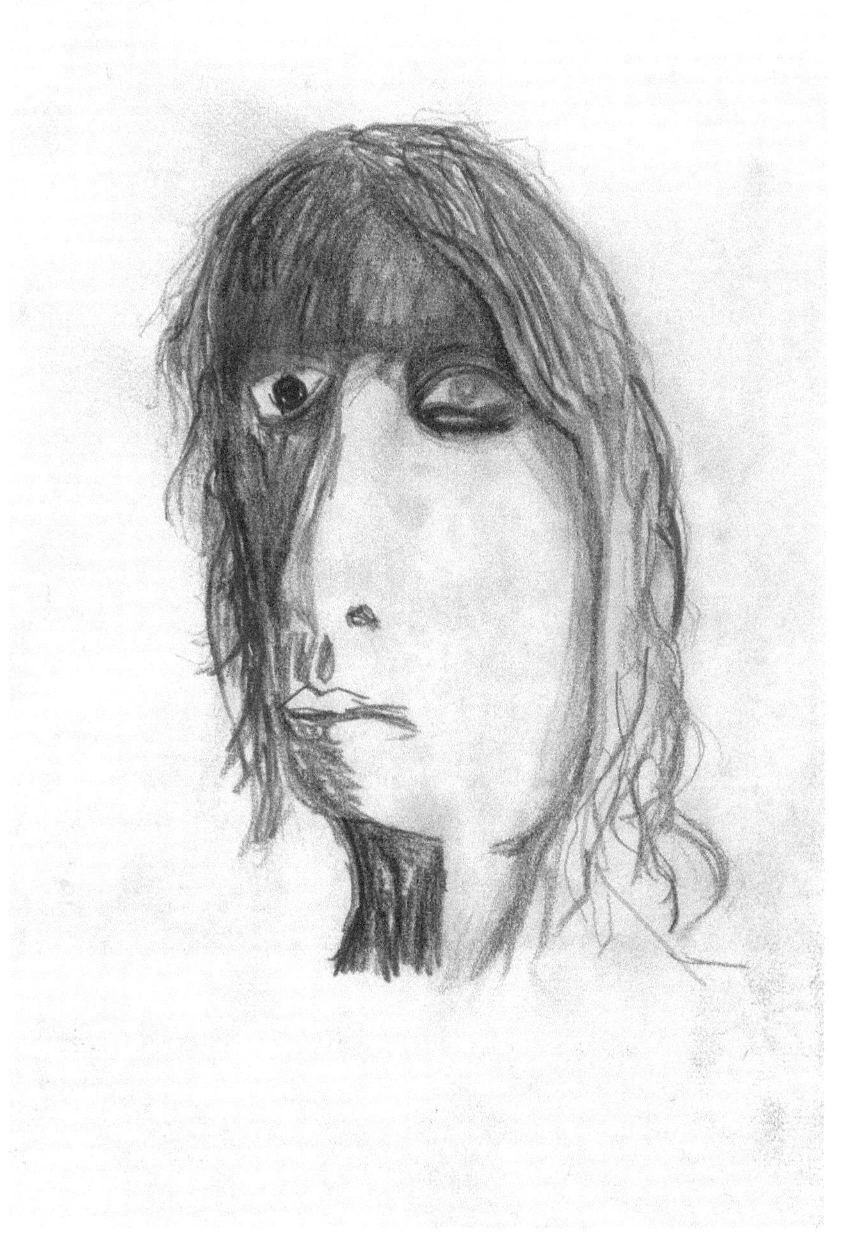

106. After Eleven

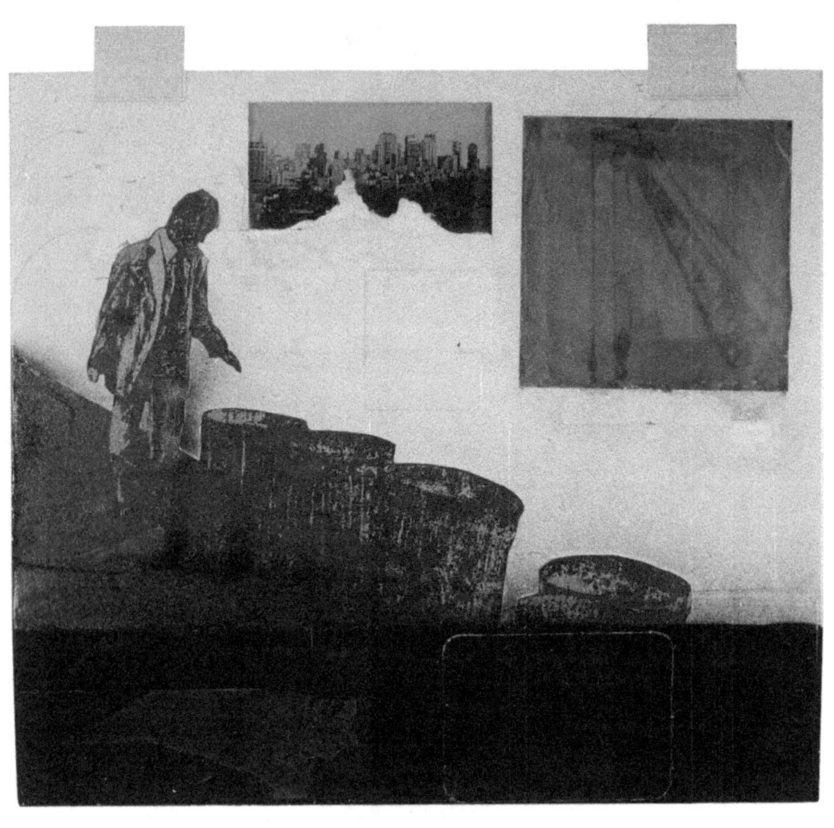

107. Looking For My Lunch

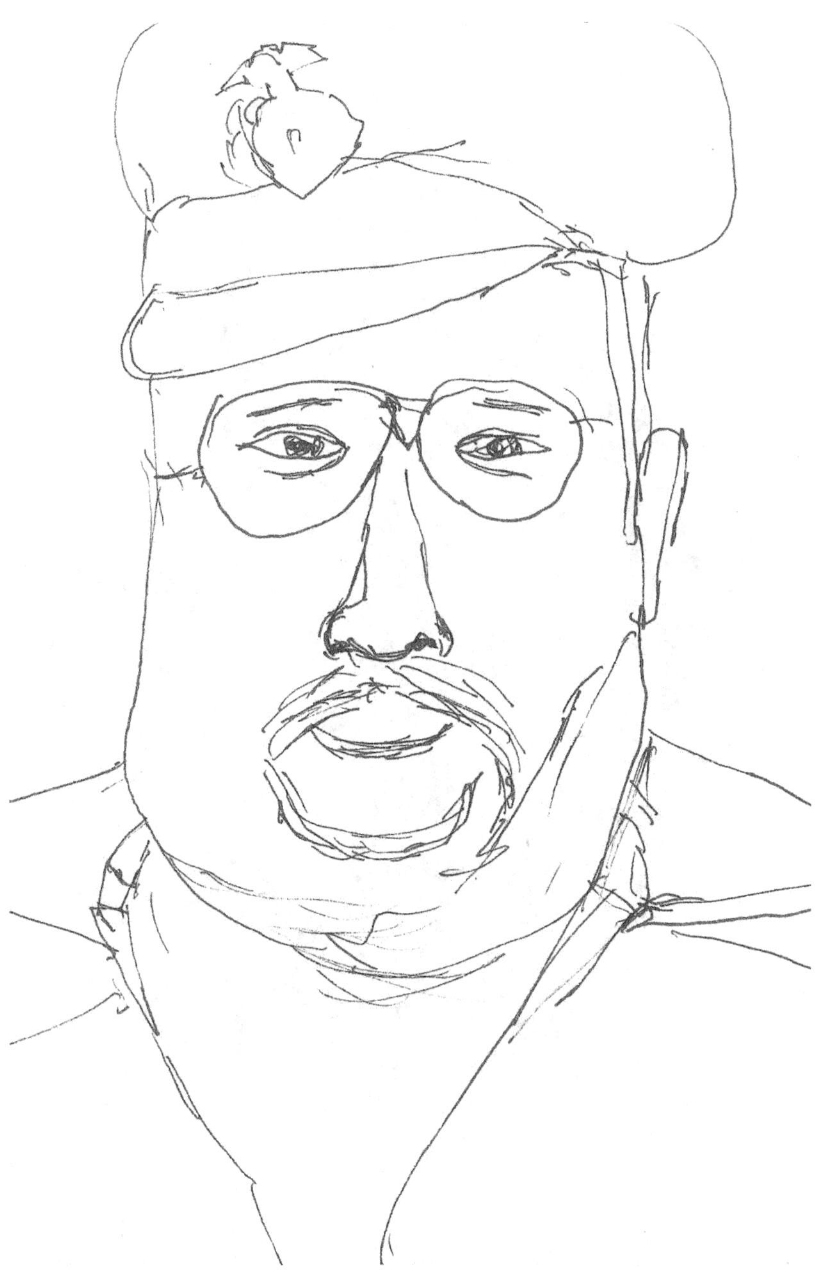

108. Police Story

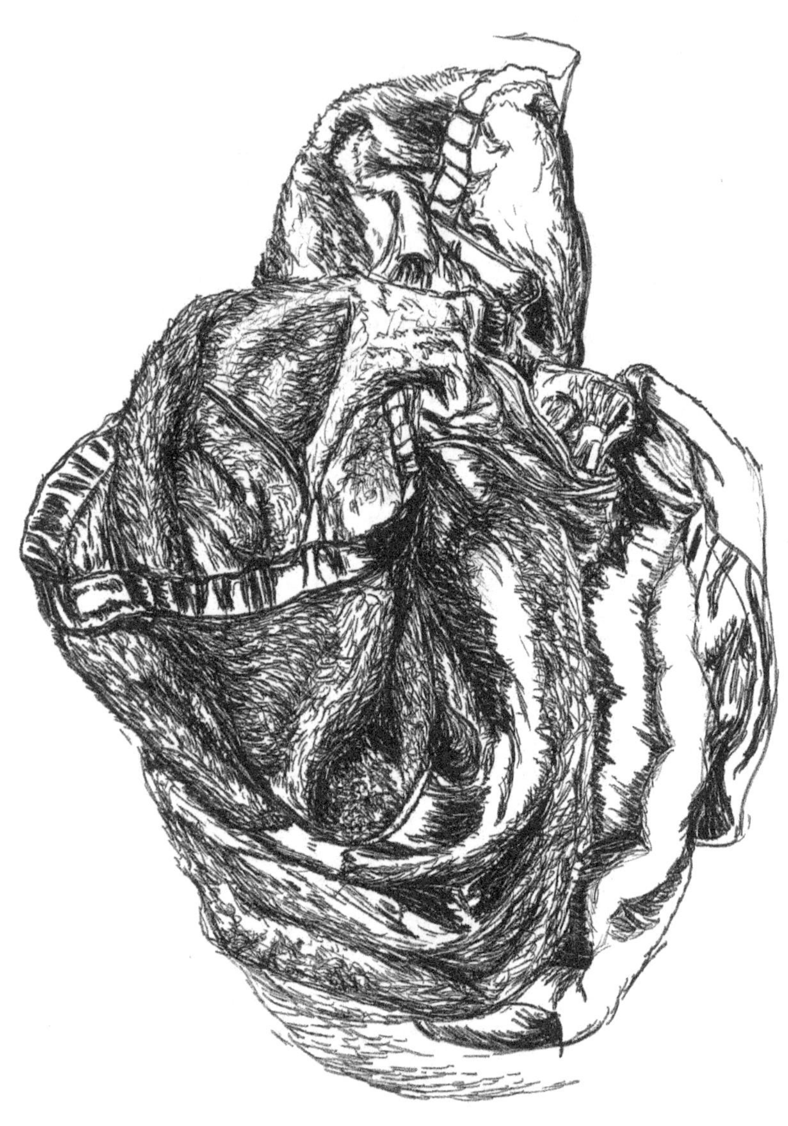

109. Blanket

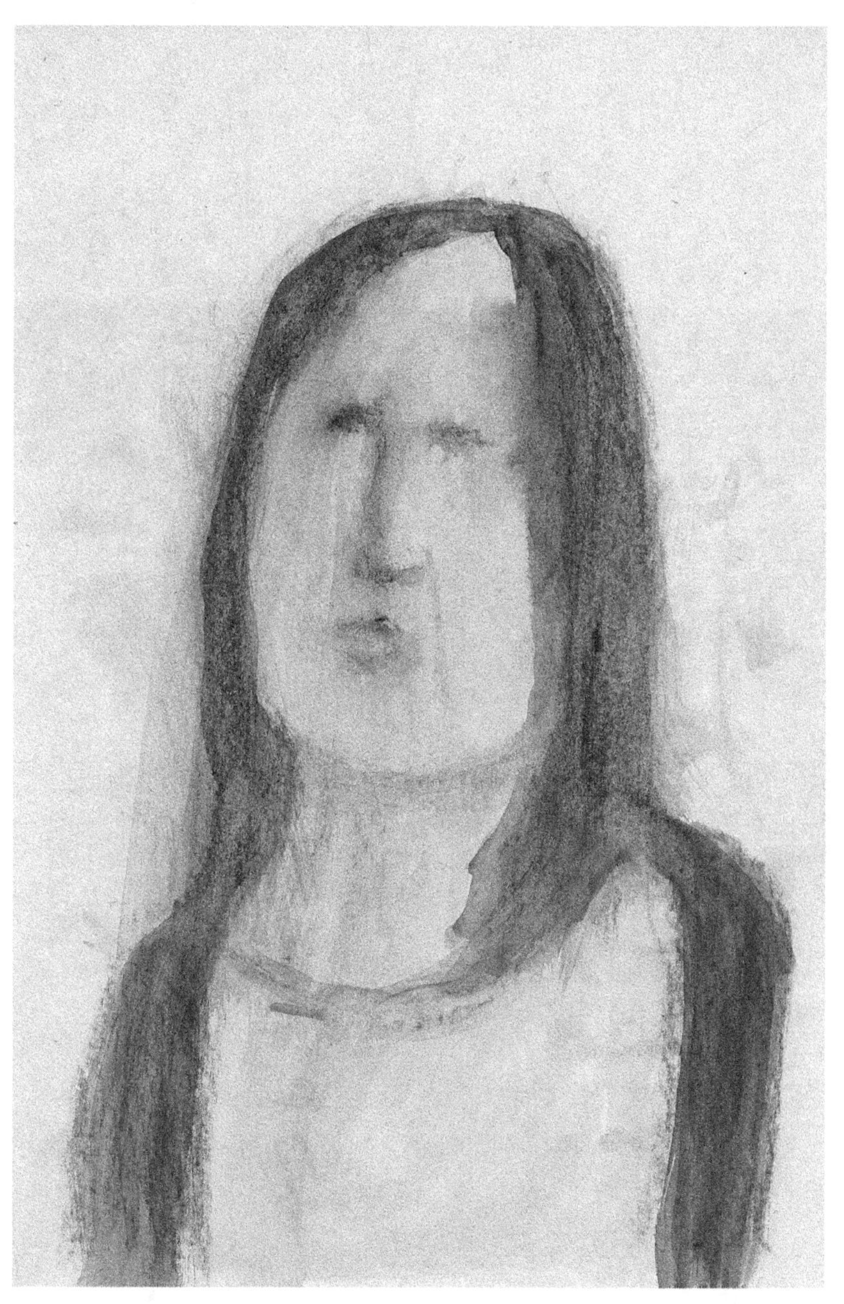

110. Miss Horiuchi

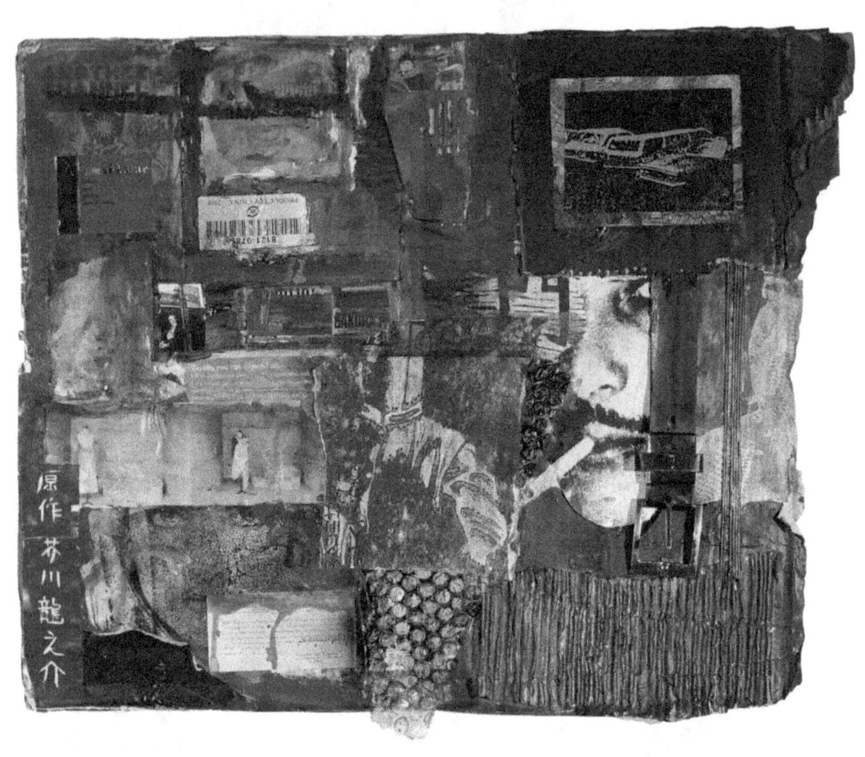

111. A Vague Anxiety

Ryūnosuke Akutagawa is one of my favorite writers. He wrote a lot of great novels until he passed away in 1927. His stories always give me new ideas.

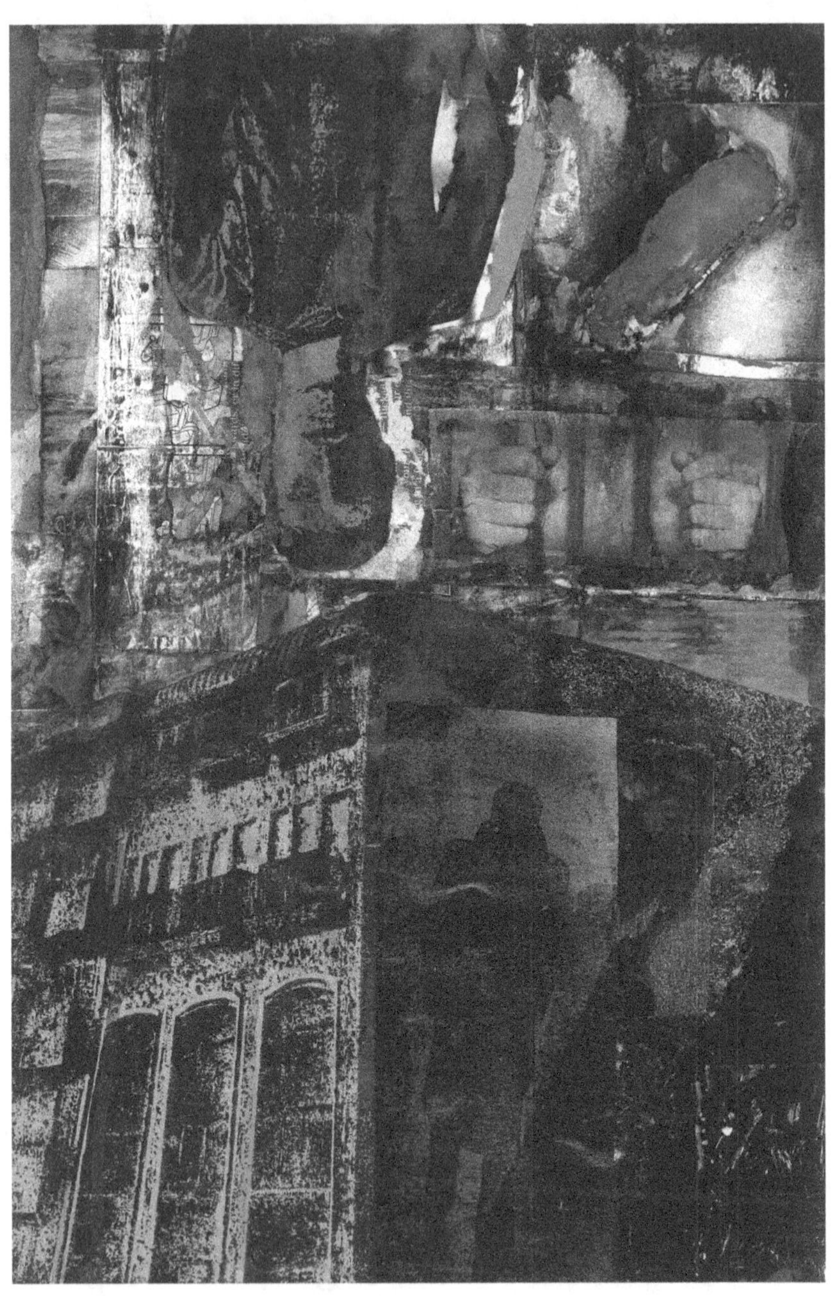

112. He Is Lost

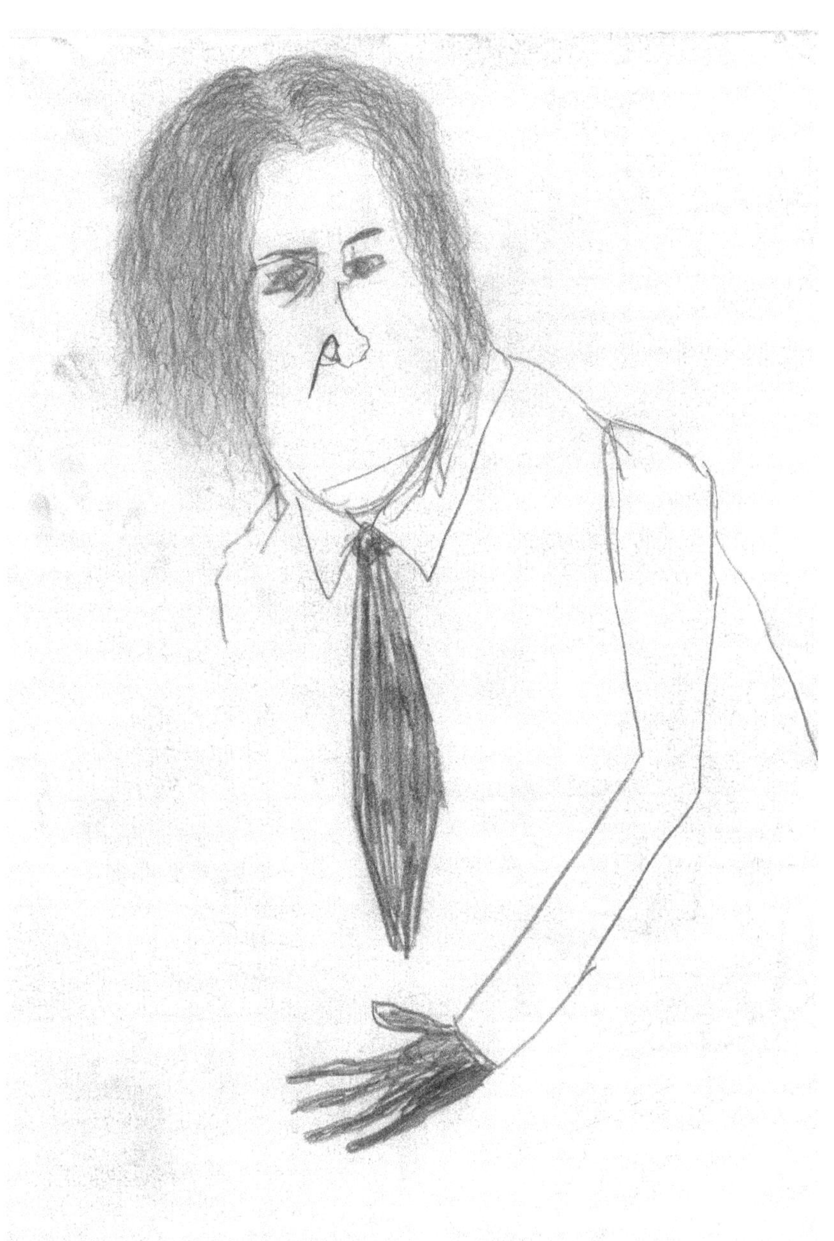

113. Hit Man

Author Biography

Tatsuyuki Kobayashi began making woodblock-prints while studying at Sugino Fashion University. In 2006, he presented his collected works in an international exhibition entitled "Rashoumon" at the Gallery La Mer in Tokyo. He exhibited more of his works in a second exhibition entitled "Self-portrait," a part of "The World of Five Individual Artists," again at Gallery La Mer in Tokyo. Inspired by Daido Moriyama's photography, he is continuing his exploration of the "Interzone" in mixed media - mainly paint and collage - at his studio in Tokyo. Visit Tatsuyuki Kobayashi at

http://kobatatsu.com/

www.ingramcontent.com/pod-product-compliance
Lightning Source LLC
LaVergne TN
LVHW020637100826
845148LV00012B/2220

* 9 7 8 0 9 8 4 1 1 7 5 3 6 *